PRAISE FOR *A CAMPUS ON FIRE*

"Patrick O'Dowd's vigorous debut is a prescient and perceptive tale, a compelling examination of a world in which fact and fiction have become blurred and weaponized. The novel portrays a deeply divided college campus rife with clashing ideologies, power imbalances and misguided passions. Would you lie to see your version of the truth win the day? And how far would you go in the pursuit of a dream? *A Campus on Fire* asks the best kind of uncomfortable questions."

—Christopher J. Yates, author of *Black Chalk* and *Grist Mill Road*

"This vivid debut wrestles with essential questions about the role of personal ambition in the fight for social change. Blending richly drawn characters with timely themes, O'Dowd has written a novel about and for our tumultuous era."

—Wil Medearis, author of *Restoration Heights*

"Patrick O'Dowd's *A Campus on Fire* is timely, urgent, and thrilling. Set at a campus uncomfortably close to all of us, the novel adroitly mixes a quasi-fascist student faction, a cult-like writers' group, a love story, and a student reporter trying to maintain objectivity in the face of crisis. O'Dowd works with complex characters and presents no easy resolutions—like life itself."

—David Galef, author of *How to Cope with Suburban Stress*

"Patrick O'Dowd has gifted readers a phenomenal debut using a university campus setting as a microcosm of our national politics and the epicenter of clashing ideas around consent, class, gender, race, and privilege. The story's journalistic lens through its protagonist Tess cleverly allows for varying angles of storytelling, while the interpersonal connective tissue of the plot is utterly irresistible. At the heart of this novel is the concept of power: who has it, who wants it, and the extremes that people will go to to get it. With *A Campus on Fire*, O'Dowd has cemented himself as a forceful new literary voice."

—Kerri Schlottman, author of *Tell Me One Thing*

A CAMPUS ON FIRE

Patrick O'Dowd

Regal House Publishing

Published by
Regal House Publishing, LLC
Raleigh, NC 27605
All rights reserved

ISBN -13 (paperback): 9781646035298
ISBN -13 (epub): 9781646035304
Library of Congress Control Number: 2024935104

All efforts were made to determine the copyright holders and obtain their
permissions in any circumstance where copyrighted material was used.
The publisher apologizes if any errors were made during this process, or
if any omissions occurred. If noted, please contact the publisher and all
efforts will be made to incorporate permissions in future editions.

Cover images and design by © C. B. Royal

Regal House Publishing, LLC
https://regalhousepublishing.com

The following is a work of fiction created by the author. All names,
individuals, characters, places, items, brands, events, etc. were either the
product of the author or were used fictitiously. Any name, place, event,
person, brand, or item, current or past, is entirely coincidental.

Regal House Publishing supports rights of free expression and the value
of copyright. The purpose of copyright is to encourage the creation of
artistic works that enrich and define culture.

Printed in the United States of America

For Cassie

1

Tess Azar's notes on Rose Dearborn:

Tall. Sharp green eyes. A small, pointed nose. Pale. Red hair, worn down, falls just below her shoulders, framing her compact face. Her posture is pristine, and she appears to be flexing, though that may be her natural state. Her hands are folded, left over right. She sports an unblemished French manicure and light pink lipstick that you'd never notice unless you were looking for it. She has two earrings on her left ear, both in the lobe, and one on her right. They're all diamonds, and I'm sure they're real. She wears a light blue Oxford shirt. It looks like it was designed for her frame—towering and athletic, without succumbing to bulk. Over the shirt, she wears a light jacket, tan and slim fitted, with bronze buttons. It looks like it was born to be a man's jacket but changed its mind when it met her.

She had me from the start. It was her wave. It showed the world she came from, the sophistication, the poise, the casual superiority. It was a wave that had been passed down, refined, choreographed. A stiff hand, a pirouette, a fold. It was elegant in its learned simplicity.

She paired it with a vacant, performative smile. It wasn't for me. It was for the watchers. It told the world that she wasn't, despite appearances, one of those people. She was, in fact, a normal person, perhaps even a kind one.

I nodded my acknowledgment and matched her smile. Mine was professional, a journalist's smile, continuing the performance we were engaged in.

We were meeting at an outdoor café on campus. One of those places where students bring their laptops and pretend to work. It's not a place to work, not true work. It's a place to be seen to be working.

She stood as I sat, a prosaic gesture that nonetheless endeared her to me.

I felt the cool spring breeze and heard birds singing in a tree nearby. A woman shouted in the distance, and I didn't even turn to look. I assumed it was playful. I used to be able to assume that.

"Tess," she said, not a question but a statement of fact.

"And you're Rose?"

"Yes." She smiled and took a sip of her coffee. She placed it down, and I noticed it was uncovered, no lid in sight.

I looked at my own cup, a lipstick-stained plastic lid of shame sitting atop it. I felt her eyes on it, felt the judgment. I shouldn't have had a lid. I should've told them I didn't want one. Lids were plastic, single-use plastic. They were death. They were climate change. They were a stain upon you as a person.

I tore it off, and the steam burned my hand. I didn't flinch, too afraid it would be another strike against me. Rose looked like the type of person who never flinched, who never got sick or hurt. She looked like she went to the cape on the weekends and played tackle football with her brothers and more than held her own.

I pulled out my notebook, almost knocking over my coffee as I did so. The cup rattled, but I grabbed it before it tipped and smiled an apology. I opened to a fresh page, and, as I always did when beginning an interview, I took down a description.

"Are you writing a novel?" Her voice was cold and clipped, formal and challenging.

I blushed, and my skin turned a few shades darker. I'm sure she noticed. Rose looked like she never blushed. Or at least never out of embarrassment. I imagined she did on occasion, but with a purpose.

I hid in my notebook. "No, I, uh, well…"

I hated myself. It was odd for me. I wasn't like that. I wasn't a stammering, stumbling fool. I wasn't often awed. I was the one in a relationship who was distant. I was the one who was unaffected by the end of the affair, the one who needed to be wooed.

But there was something about her, an aura, a magic. Something that changed me, disrupted me. I both hated and loved it. Longed to be free of this pull and to never leave it. One could chalk it up to the difference in age—Rose was twenty-one to my nineteen, but it was more than that. She had something. Something I wanted.

I twirled my pen around a finger and clicked it. It was a nervous habit, one that would take years to tame. Rose watched, a cryptic smile in her eyes. I placed my phone on the table and set it to record. "Do you mind?"

She shook her head, but I could feel her quiet disapproval.

"I just like to get the setting down," I said and motioned to my notebook. I calmed myself by sipping the spring air, a slight scent of grass being cut somewhere in the distance. ""I was taught that if you have the time, you should overwrite, even in journalism. Easier to cut later. 'Never trust your memory' is what my professor says."

This wasn't true. My professors would be appalled by my long, florid notes. They advocated direct, blunt ones. But I wasn't writing for them. Not anymore. I'd already developed my own strategies, my own style, and my notes were part of that.

She met my eyes, an intrigued look cresting across her face. I'll never forget that look and the feeling that accompanied it, tracing up my spine and nesting in my skull. I felt my embarrassment disappear. I remembered who I was. I remembered that I was someone, and she knew it.

"Well." She drank her coffee. I followed her lead. Mine was still too hot, and it scalded my throat. "I guess whatever you're doing, it's working."

And there it was. The reason she'd come. It was a hint, a slight lead, but we both knew where she was taking the conversation. I may have my objective, my questions, my story, but she didn't care. She wanted to discuss it. She met me so she could discuss it.

"I still have a lot to learn —"

"But to have an article receive national attention as a soph-omore." She cut me off with the ease of someone used to doing it. "My guess is it won't be long before the job offers start coming."

They already had, but she didn't need to know that. Not yet. You need to save things. You need to build a relationship with patient precision if you want it to last.

I nodded and went back to my notebook. I should've steered the conversation, transitioned from my success to the work-shop. But I couldn't, I wanted to press on, I wanted to talk more about my article. I wanted to astonish her and luxuriate in that astonishment.

That's all it took. A little acclaim, a little attention, and, as I'm sure she'd planned, I'd forgotten my questions, my story.

"Now." She unstacked her hands and moved one toward mine. "I'm not a journalist, just a fiction writer, but I felt your piece transcended the subject and demonstrated an uncanny ability to be informative, engaging, and unique. I couldn't put it down, and more to the point, I found myself rereading it even after knowing the story, which I feel is a true test of great writing. Your work doesn't read like journalism. It reads like fiction, good fiction."

I felt the familiar warmth of praise pulse through me.

Her assessment was pretentious and vapid, it said nothing. It raised my own work by comparing it to the vaunted heights of fiction and, in doing so, denigrated journalism, but I didn't care.

"Thank you." I tried to temper my grin. "I appreciate that. It was a good article, and I was pleased with the exposure it received. That's an important issue that I think will continue to pervade our society."

I was trying to match her. Her intellectual snobbery, her placid distance, her broad generalities.

"So." She leaned forward, and I found my eye tracing down to the opening of her shirt. I caught a glimpse of lace and looked away, landing on her forearm. It was exposed, and

I could just make out a pale purple bruise. She noticed and dropped her arm beneath the table. "I have to ask. How did you get the interview? How did you get him to agree to that? To say all that?"

I nodded and leaned back. This was what they always asked. This was what made the article. This was why it garnered national attention, why everyone was talking about it, why I was someone.

Hearing her ask the same, tired question settled me.

I ran a finger along the seam of my pants and looked around, debating whether to do it, whether to take the leap. I felt the brief flutter of nervous excitement that we all come to know at some point.

I paused and felt my heart rattle. It felt wrong. She should be the one to ask me out, not the other way. I didn't even know if she was gay. But somehow, I did. I could tell. I could feel an opening. This was my chance. She was curious, everyone was. I had a story, I had cache, I was someone, if only for a moment. So, I leapt. "How about this? You have dinner with me tomorrow night, and I'll tell you how I got the interview. Deal?"

The question hung in the air as it always does, time elongating—heavy and thick with anxiety but exhilarating. All the world is packed into that pause between the question and the answer.

"What, like a date?" She tilted her head, a smile leaking out of the side of her mouth, a slight hue dampening her cheeks.

I nodded.

Someone shouted at a table not far from us, and chairs scraped against the ground.

"All right," she said, her smile spreading. "Deal."

And just like that, the anxiety exploded into a million shards of light. I was ebullient. I was phosphorescent. I was invincible.

After that, I tried to stay present, tried to listen to what she said, to not think about the future that was already being crafted in my mind.

But it was no use, I was gone. My mind was adrift. There

were winters skiing and summers sailing. There were literary arguments and good coffee. There was an initial frigid period with her family. A tense scene with her grandfather where he reverted to his old prejudices, dismissing the whole of me based on the half that was Lebanese, but I won him over by talking history and baseball. I became one of them. And later, there were galas and houses full of antiques and rich wood.

"I guess you're not here to talk about your article, are you?" She shifted back. "You're here to talk about Jack." Her face fell, her hands fidgeted in her lap. The color left her cheeks. The radiance of our previous conversation still lingered, but it was just a residual taste. We'd moved on.

I nodded but said nothing. Being a journalist is a lot like being a therapist. You need to draw them out. You need to make them comfortable and then let them talk.

"Terrible, just horrible." She looked like a different person, like an actor trying to play Rose in a marginal play. "Such a waste."

I let the silence linger, hoping she'd continue. When she didn't, I eased into it. "Did you know him well?"

She nodded, and took her forefinger and thumb and pinched the bridge of her nose as if that could stop the tears and the pain. "Yes, of course. We all... I mean, you know about it, right? About the workshop? Dr. Lobo?"

I did. Everyone knew about the workshop. It was a creative writing group on campus, not an official workshop, whatever that means, just a group of students whom an acclaimed professor had taken an interest in.

Dr. Lobo's workshop. Sylvia's kids. The Creative Writing Cult.

Sylvia Lobo's second novel, *A Wake of Vultures,* was an instant classic. She was teaching here as an associate professor when she wrote it, and after its publication, she became an instant celebrity. Now she teaches creative writing and gives few lectures. I took one during my first semester. Someone had dropped right when I was registering, otherwise, I'd have never gotten in. It was on the erosion of the past in literature. Novels set during times of change with characters who are stuck in the past and grappling with the future. It was an eighty-person class, and I don't think I said more than three words all year.

"Yeah," I said. "I know about Dr. Lobo."

"Have you read any of her work?" The energy that had left us returned.

"I've read *A Wake of Vultures* and *Jezebel.*"

Rose tried to hide her excitement and nodded to herself. I could tell I'd passed a test. "I'll give you *Chariot Races* and *Bubblegum.* If you like those, we can go from there. If not…"

More tests. But that was all right. For her, I would take them.

"You're all very close, right?"

"Yes, Sylvia's big on that. We're all working toward the same goals and have the same interests, and it's essential that we spend time together. She says it makes for better writing. Look at Paris in the twenties. Do you think it was an accident so many great writers were there at the same time?"

I took my time and wrote this down verbatim. It sounded rehearsed.

"Some people even…" She laughed. "…say we're a bit of a cult."

Her laughter stopped, and I made sure not to smile. This wasn't a joke. This was a repudiation of a nasty piece of gossip. I'd have to be careful with that. I'd have to watch that I never hinted at the cultish atmosphere of the workshop.

People had good reason to call them a cult. They took all the same classes, not just Sylvia's, but everything—history, science, even phys ed. They got coffee together at the same time every day. The same table, the same café, the same black coffee, the same far-off look while they drank. They ate lunch together. They ate the same things for lunch. They ate with purpose. Refined but rapid. They walked the same, hurried steps announcing their presence, clearing a path. They talked the same. The same talking points, the same articles referenced, the same political issues discussed, same positions held with fervor. They used the same words. They spoke at the same frantic pace. Their hands moved with their every word, painting a mute portrait of their argument. They used the same pens, same notebooks, read the same books, watched the same movies, chewed the same gum, smoked the same colorful French cigarettes, not because they were addicted, but because it stoked conversation and helped with the writing process.

They were the same.

They were like her.

That was how she drank her coffee, how she ate, how she walked, how she spoke, how she thought.

They idolized her. They forced her works into their conversations. They cited her. Not just her published comments and writing but personal ones from conversations they'd had with her. They attributed immense weight to these citations as if mentioning her name ended all debate. If Sylvia said it, it wasn't to be questioned. It was fact.

The cultish atmosphere of the program was why I decided to write the story. Why I was sitting there, interviewing Rose. Jack's suicide was a part, but not the whole. I hoped to expand it, turn it into a piece on Sylvia and the workshop. Get a glimpse behind the curtain. See what was fact and what was fiction.

Rose stared at me after the cult comment. Judging me, reading my reaction. I met her stare and held it. "Well, these days, I think gossip is the sincerest form of flattery. As for Jack, I'm sorry for your loss."

She nodded and raised a hand to her chest. "Yes, he was, well, very talented. We came in together, same class. We were both in her freshman seminar on literature's obsession with the past."

"I took that class."

"Really? Not the same one though? I'm sure I'd have noticed you."

"No, you wouldn't have. But it must've been a different year, you're what, a senior?"

"She teaches it every other year. You're fortunate you got in."

"I could say the same to you," I said, unable to avoid the opening to flirt.

"Hah." She rolled her head back. She didn't laugh. She said, hah. Spat it. "No, I sent her my writing from high school, two awful short stories about— Oh god, I don't even want to say… one was about my high school friends and a teacher of ours, and the other was about a ski instructor. They were dreadful, but she saw something in them, something in me."

She looked over at the sprouting trees that lined the walk, feigning to hide her satisfied smile. "She reads the work applicants send in, as do her current students, and selections are made. If she picks you, you're assured a spot in her freshman seminar and the creative writing major and some other classes. See, where most creative writing programs don't really get serious until graduate school, she starts right away. Freshmen year. She believes that you need to get to a writer early, before they learn those bad habits and become just a poor imitation of some famous writer. She wants you raw, unadulterated, malleable."

"I thought you said she teaches that seminar every other year?"

She shook her head as if I was a mistaken child. "Oh no, just that one class on literature and the past. She teaches that in even years. She teaches a different one on female writers and the diaspora in odd years."

I nodded and smiled and waited.

She rubbed the bruise on her arm, caught herself, and dropped her hands, resuming her practiced pose of mourning. "Yes, I was close to Jack. We were in all the same classes. I was his shadow, as we called it. Like a peer editor, you read everything they write. He was my shadow too. Sylvia thought our work complemented one another's. He was a genius, and I don't use that word lightly. It's a true tragedy. Not just for him and those of us who knew him but for the world. The world lost a great writer." Another tear, she lifted a napkin to stop it. "I edited his book. The one that we—Sylvia and I—are helping to finish. You know about that, right?"

"Yeah."

"Sylvia worked to get it published, not that it was all that difficult, it's a brilliant novel. But she took it on. She wanted to... She knew it was what he would've wanted. And now, at least, that part of him will live on. A tribute of sorts."

"I hear the money's going to charity?"

"A suicide prevention charity. And some will go to the creative writing program here as well, help to make it official, and I think some is going other places, but I don't have the details on that."

"Any to his family?"

"He didn't have family. An uncle upstate somewhere, whom he grew up with, but they weren't close, and I think he passed away. His parents weren't in the picture."

"Anyone else you think I should talk to?" I was afraid to push too hard too soon. You can always come back with more questions. You can always have a second interview, provided, of course, you remain on good terms.

"People in the workshop. I can give you some names. Introduce you."

"That'd be great." I looked down at my notebook, pretending to scan it, knowing what I needed to ask. "Look, Rose, I'm sorry to ask this, but I have to. Do you have any idea why he would've done this? I heard he didn't leave a note."

A writer not leaving a note. Seemed off.

She shook her head and forced another tear. "He was"— she ran a fingernail around the rim of her now-empty coffee cup—"troubled, like many writers are. It's true what they say, 'genius and madness flow from the same source.' Good work often comes from pain, and I think, not to be unkind, but I think some can court it. Wallow in it. Again, I don't mean to... I loved Jack, and it's a tragedy what happened, but he lived in that pain. It's what his work was about. He'd go into it and be down there and write, and after he finished, he'd come back up. He'd live in joy for a bit. But this time, with the novel, he was down there too long. He couldn't surface."

This, too, felt rehearsed. Maybe not quite scripted but planned. She knew I'd ask about it, and she was ready. There's nothing wrong with that. Meeting with a journalist is stressful, and people like to be prepared.

But still, it felt off.

"Well," I said, "I think that's all I've got for today. I might have some follow-ups, but I'm sure you're busy."

"Yes, I have to decide what I'm wearing for our date."

I blushed and withdrew to my notes.

"I hope we won't have to muddy that up with this?" she said.

"No, I wouldn't think so."

We both stood, and I stared at her, straining my eyes, as she retreated into the falling sun.

2

"Confessions of a Video Rapist"
by Tess Azar (excerpt)

Jason Cooper is a twenty-one-year-old senior. He's a business major with a film minor. He's scheduled to graduate summa cum laude in the spring, and he's the captain of his intramural soccer team.

He also filmed a series of his sexual encounters with fellow students and posted them online.

His partners weren't aware they were being filmed, and they weren't made aware after the fact. For two years, he's filmed thirty-seven different women having sex with him, seventy-one total videos.

In the past three months, he's begun posting these videos online. Again, he did not contact the woman before posting. They weren't aware of the existence of these videos until after they were online.

"I think it's like a compulsion," he said when asked why he had begun to do this. He has a heavy Long Island accent, and I can't tell if it's earned or stolen. "Like an addiction. I just, uh, I get off on it. You wouldn't blame an alcoholic for getting drunk, right?"

I spoke to Jason earlier this week, and he tried to stick to this line about it being an addiction. This appears to be what his lawyers have advised him to say. When I contacted them, they gave me the same coined response.

Jason is tall, handsome, and confident. He slicks his thick brown hair back and wears a heavy gold chain around his broad neck. It's a look that on most men would be ludicrous, passé, but on him conveys an undeniable power.

"Getting laid was just too easy," he said with a lewd smile. "I started when I was fourteen. Older girls too. I hooked up with a college senior when I was still a junior in high school. I tried everything, I did it all, and I guess I got bored."

He fidgets and looks down at his phone. He knows he's gone off script, but he can't stop himself. The need to impress me, to brag about his conquests, overrides his training.

"And look, it's not like I just, you know, put up every video. I only put up forty-two of them. The others I kept. The others were, well, I didn't want to do those girls that way, you know? They were like, uh, nice girls. It wouldn't have been right. The ones I put up were, well, they were, you know."

He pauses, smiles, and leans back in his chair. I tell him I don't know, and he rolls his eyes, sighs, and tells me.

"Sluts. They were sluts. Sorry, I know that's not a, you know, politically correct term or whatever, but that's how it is. They came on to me. They initiated everything. And then, after, they never wanted to like go on a date or anything. It was just about sex. They were using me for one thing, and I figured, well, it's just as much mine as theirs, so why not?"

The women have filed a class-action suit against Jason. The state has also filed criminal charges against him. If found guilty, he could spend up to five years in prison, though as of writing this, the longest term someone has received for this kind of crime was six months.

"It's just ridiculous," one of his victims said when asked about the potential sentence. "That will be online forever. My future boyfriends will see that. Their parents will see that. My kids, if I have any, will see that. Employers, friends, family. Everyone. What if I wanted to be a teacher? What if I wanted to run for office? Those paths are closed to me now. Forever."

She holds a tissue and rips it into tiny pieces. She's crying but doesn't blot away the tears. "And he's going to get what, six months? At most. And he won't even get that. How's that fair? The internet is forever. It's never going to come down. You can't... I tried, I looked into it, and you can't get them taken down. They always come back. It's like a, what'd you call it, a hydra. Internet porn is a hydra."

When I asked her what she thought would be a fair punishment, she responded without hesitating. "Castration."

"I think," Jason said as we neared the end of our interview, "I saw it like, you know, photos on Insta or something. You don't have to ask people before you post them. I know some people do, but I don't. And I guess I saw this like that. They were just so open, aggressive even, I didn't think they'd have an issue with it. I thought…" He lets out a short laugh. "I thought they might like it. I bet some of them did, they just don't want to admit it."

He believes the charges against him are extreme and will destroy his future job prospects. "I didn't know it was illegal. And once I found out, I took them down. It's not my fault that other people have posted them in other places. I can't control that."

Jason is in a twelve-step program for sex addiction and is seeing a therapist. He believes this should suffice for his rehabilitation and that any prison time would be punitive.

3

Tess Azar's notes on Lisa Guerrero:

Short. Full lips. Shaved head. Her skull has a beautiful shape to it. It's petite and round and without a blemish. She's unadorned. No jewelry, minimal makeup, a plain T-shirt, and baggy jeans. She's dressed so as not to distract from the shaved head. It's the focal point. It's defiant. I wonder, just as she planned, if it's a political statement.

"We saw him wandering around without a coat," Lisa said. "Mumbling to himself about his book. We tried to bring him home. Then he hit Tyson and ran off. That's the last we saw of him."

"After France was liberated from the Nazis," she said when she noticed me staring at her naked skull. Instinctively, I ran my fingers along my head. I felt every bump, every imperfection. I was sure I could never pull off the look, even if I dared to attempt it. "The French men took the women who had slept with the Nazis and shaved their heads. They did it in public so everyone could watch and jeer. My novel's protagonist is one of those shaved women."

Was she pointing out the absurdity of shaving the heads of women who were just trying to survive? Or did she feel they should've resisted the Nazi advances? Was she bringing attention to the cowardice of these men? Or of the woman who slept with the Nazis? Was she equating herself to them? Does she feel she's also somehow complicit in a fascist state? Has she slept with a Nazi? Or is it out of solidarity for wronged women of the past?

I pulled my hand from my head and saw that Lisa was smiling. This line of questioning, this confusion, was just what she wanted. If I asked about it, I was sure she'd give a cryptic response meant to evoke more questions than answers. I suspected the truth was that she thought it would be chic and shocking. She thought it would turn heads and focus attention on her. And she was right. Plus, it would look great on the book jacket.

I decided to steer the conversation back to Jack. "What did you do after he ran off?"

"Well." She smiled and then pulled it back. "We'd been out for most of the night. At a party over at Sylvia's, and we'd had more than a few glasses of vino, so it's not super clear."

"You were drunk?"

"No, I wouldn't say that. I'm not some freshman at a frat party. I don't get drunk." She glared at me as she leaned on the word. It was as if I'd called her prose derivative and flat. "We just had some wine. And I'd prefer you not print that. Best to avoid mentioning that we were at Sylvia's at all. It's not that I care, it didn't change anything, but I wouldn't want her to get any questions about it. You know, this ridiculous country with its puritanical laws and mores."

She softened her glare, inviting me in.

I nodded and smiled and made a big fuss about crossing it out on the page. This did the trick, and she leaned back in her chair and relaxed.

"So, you were saying, after Jack hit Tyson."

"Assaulted. It was violent. We talked about filing a report on him in the morning."

"It was that bad?"

"Yes." She took a deep, performative breath. "I suppose it can't hurt to tell you this now. It wasn't the first time. He hit me a few weeks before. And, of course, there was the thing with Henry."

"Thing with Henry?"

"What? Didn't you hear? I thought everyone knew about that." She paused and let me stew in my ignorance. "Well, we were just workshopping one day, and Henry read a story. It was a good one. I think he just got it placed in some magazine or another. He should've held out, it's a *New Yorker*-quality story, but anyway. It's about a female corrections officer, and, well, I won't ruin it, but it's terrific. And we all said so. There were a few notes, like there always are, but nothing major. Even Sylvia was full of praise. Henry had struggled a bit last year, writer's block, I guess. Or maybe just a lack of talent. Everything he'd been writing was the same, the same characters, the same action, the same verbiage. Very dull, very derived. So, this praise clearly meant a lot, and we were all happy for him. Or as happy as writers can be for another's success.

"Then we went outside to have a smoke like we always do on our break, and the second we were in our spot, Jack just lost it. He could get like that. He had a streak in him. A touch of madness. You know what they say, 'Genius and madness flow from the same source.' But this one was bad, even by his standards. He started screaming at Henry, calling him horrible things. Slurs. Words we do not use. I don't even use them in my writing. And he was hurling them at Henry. Tyson tried to calm him down, but Jack wasn't having it. And then Jack just swung and landed a punch right on Henry's nose. Then, before we could separate them, Jack hit him again, this time in the stomach."

My notes were frantic, almost illegible. I glanced at my phone to ensure it was recording, a nervous habit. "Then what?"

"Jack ran off. I think he was crying. We brought Henry to the medical center, and they set his nose, and that was it."

"Did you tell Sylvia?"

"Of course."

"What did she say?"

"She spoke to them. Jack apologized. He said he'd been having a tough time, and Henry forgave him. Not much else we could do."

I'd lost the lines in my notebook, my writing veering off at odd angles.

I looked up and caught Lisa's eye. She was staring at my notes, trying to read them. I pulled the notebook closer.

I took a moment to formulate a question while letting her think. "What did people in the workshop say about it?"

"You could imagine." She let out a dry laugh. "Overall, we let it go. He was deep in his novel, and we'd all read parts of it. It was brilliant. Dark, funny, beautiful, and you could see why he was a bit off. The novel was leaking into his life."

I waited, knowing there was more she wanted to say.

She glanced over her shoulder to make sure the room was clear. "You didn't hear this from me, but he was drinking. Like real drinking. Like Fitzgerald in Hollywood drinking." She leaned back and pulled hard on a vape pen, then let out a massive cloud. "How rude of me." She offered me the pen. "Would you like some? It's a low dosage, just a bit to get the juices flowing. I'm supposed to be writing."

"No, thank you." She wanted me to ask about her writing, but I wouldn't take the bait. "You said you had an altercation with Jack as well?"

She nodded and again glanced around the room.

"Are you expecting someone?"

"No, or, well, yes, I suppose so. Tyson will be here soon."

"Oh, does he live here? I'd love to talk to him as well."

"No, well, sort of. He often sleeps here, but he has his own apartment. We might be moving in together… You know what, now that I think about it, he isn't coming over today. He's working on something, as I should be."

"Of course, I don't want to take up too much of your time, it's just you mentioned a different altercation?"

"Oh, that, yes, no one else saw it. I think I mentioned it at the time to Tyson, but I'm not sure if he remembers. I was helping Jack with his novel. I was critical in the editing process. Jack was frustrated, and I pointed out a passage that didn't work, and he disagreed. It's a classic argument. Writers never want to part with their work. Jack was bad with that. He didn't take criticism well. So, I was explaining the issue, and he just turned and slapped me."

She traced her hand across her cheek and tried to look hurt, but it didn't work.

"What did you do?"

"I turned and slapped him right back," she said with a proud fury and followed it with a laugh.

"And that was it?"

"Yes. That's how we were. All of us. Writing is a tough business. You need a thick skin, so we're a tough bunch. I didn't mind the slap, to tell you the truth, and I loved returning it." Another drag off the pen, her eyes had turned red. "And he removed the passage."

4

I waited outside Lisa's apartment building for a few minutes, hoping to catch Tyson walking in. I'd seen pictures of him on Rose's Instagram and inspected every person who passed, searching for that face. I was sure Lisa had been trying to get me to leave to avoid talking to him. I was sure he would say something I could use, something that contradicted Lisa's story. I was sure there was more to this, something hidden.

But he never came.

As I was leaving, I felt the pull a journalist knows all too well. The confidence that if I'd waited just a few more minutes, I'd have seen him.

But I couldn't wait. I had an event to attend and take notes on. I didn't know if there was a story there yet, but it had potential.

My editor, Samir, had disagreed. "We shouldn't give them a platform. They're just a small group right now, but you give them a microphone, and who knows what happens."

"They're newsworthy," I'd said. "And ignoring them plays right into their hand. Most of what they talk about is the liberal establishment and gatekeeping organizations. 'The liberal media industrial complex,' whatever that means. Ignoring them just gives them fuel."

"Didn't he start as a meme?"

She was right, the man I was interested in writing about had started out as a meme. Maybe you've seen it. It's a tall, long-faced, handsome man looking down with one eyebrow raised, a half-smile, and a thumb pointing off to the side. He's skeptical and confused but above it all.

The meme rose to prominence through right-wing Twitter, Reddit, and some other social media sites. There was speculation that he'd orchestrated it, taken the picture, and, through surrogates, disseminated it, but no one could prove this.

As with all memes, it morphed and became something else. It lost its far-right origins, its edge. It'd become ubiquitous, innocuous even. I'd seen it used to criticize bad pizza and to question someone's exaggerated dating profile. It'd gone mainstream, but it carried that history, that baggage. It promoted him whether the poster meant to or not.

"Well," Samir said, "then let's have someone else do it. Your profile's too high. They'll get a boost just by being covered by you. Let's send someone else. Brando, maybe."

"No. Sending a white man won't be the same."

"They might be more comfortable talking to one of their own, might let something slip."

"I don't think so. They'd respect Brando. They'd be cagier with him. Careful. They'll underestimate me and maybe make a mistake."

"Fine." She didn't like it, but she knew I wouldn't let it go. "Be careful, and I won't promise I'll run it but see what you get."

The event was a meeting for a men's rights group, The Institute for Gender Equality, IGE. They'd formed last year and started with a handful of members, but they'd been growing. They had a new leader, the meme himself, Richard Welch, and, as much as I hated to admit it, he possessed a perverse, brutal charisma.

He was already speaking when I walked into the auditorium. There must've been seventy, eighty people there. All men, all white.

"They're out there," he shouted. "They have a plan. They're organized. We're not. Not yet."

There was vigorous applause and some shouts.

"They've been organizing since the twenties." He tossed his hands and then beat his fist on the lectern. "We're a hundred years behind them. We've let them get a head start. They've been poisoning our children and our educational system with

their Marxist, feminist, anti-men, anti-white, anti-America rhetoric for a hundred years. Is it any wonder what we've become?
Is it any wonder we've lost our freedoms? Is it any wonder this
pussified society is what has been built on the shoulders of
these failed ideologies?"

I moved up the aisle, and heads began to turn toward me.
They lingered and traced me up and down. They met my eyes
and wouldn't break. There was no shame, no embarrassment in
these men. Only hate. Confident, unrelenting hate.

The attention terrified me. It settled in my gut and began to
churn. I was outnumbered, a stranger in a strange land full of
odium and simmering violence.

I scanned the crowd, avoiding the stares and pushing aside
my fear. It was a sea of excited faces. They nodded at everything Richard said. They tapped the person next to them and
pointed and shouted. They were transfixed.

"And look." He'd noticed me. I could tell by the change in
tone. "Just because I know what people say about us, about
our group, we don't hate women. We don't hate anyone based
on their gender, race, or anything like that. We hate bad ideas.
We hate the failures of our society. But we don't hate women.
We want to help women. We're"—he met my stare and smiled,
showing a row of perfect, huge white teeth—"the best advo-
cates of women on this campus. They just don't know it yet."

This drew raucous applause and more than a little laughter.
Richard turned from side to side, sunning himself in the reception.

I felt more eyes on me as the walls closed in. I could've left.
I could've claimed there was nothing there. I could've veiled my
fear in righteous indignation. But there was something there. It
was the beginning of something. It was a story, and my ambition overwhelmed my fear.

He spoke for a few more minutes, all platitudes and rab-
ble-rousing, before exiting the stage, where he walked to a man
that I recognized. It took me a moment to place him, but when
he turned, I saw the heavy gold chain rattle across his neck,

and I knew. It was Jason. It was like seeing a ghost. I thought he'd have fled campus after the article; I thought I'd vanquished him, but there he was, shaking Richard's hand, patting him on the back.

An insatiable rage flooded through me. Was there no shame in these men? Was there nothing you could do to put them down and have them stay down? Was this the world we now lived in?

I headed straight to the stage. Men from the audience hissed and cackled as I passed, but my fear had been replaced by anger and excitement.

"Richard?" I looked up at him from just below the stage. Jason retreated into the shadows, careful to avoid my gaze. "Could I have a word? I'm with th—"

"I know who you're with," he said, without looking at me. He was shaking someone's hand, and the recipient looked like he might collapse with joy. He invited the man up and took a selfie with him. Then he walked to the edge of the stage and stared down at me. "I didn't care for your article."

"Which one?"

"There's a classroom across the hall. We could speak there if you'd like. Give me a few minutes."

And with that, he turned back to his adoring public, shaking hands, smiling, laughing, taking pictures, soaking up the hysterical praise.

5

Tess Azar's notes on Richard Welch:

Richard Welch—tall, at least six feet. White. Thick dark brown hair frozen in place at a perfect right part. He's handsome. Big head, hard chin, focused eyes. He looks like a Ken doll. Like a computer simulation's idea of a handsome man. He wears well-fitted khakis and a blue button-down with rolled-up sleeves and a thick red tie. He looks like he's running for office, which I suppose he is. You can already see his life mapped out for him. Maybe law school first, but then straight to the House of Representatives in some safe district. Then a run for either the Senate or governor. One day he'll try for the big job. The thought terrifies me. Not because of how incompetent and farcical he is but because he's the kind of person who'll do it. A dangerous, capable, charismatic evil.

He kept me waiting for a half-hour. I could picture him standing outside the door, checking his phone, making sure enough time had elapsed. He wanted me to give up, to storm off, to get rattled. But I wasn't interested in giving him what he wanted.

I spent the time researching him. There wasn't much. A short interview where he talked about his grandfather, the founder of the John Birch Society, but little else. I was sure that's how he wanted it. The media, after all, was the enemy.

"Hello." He pushed through the door. "What can I do for you?"

No apology, no reference to the wait.

In his wake followed a man and a woman. The man was short, balding, narrow-faced, and vibrated as he walked. He'd stood next to Jason while Richard spoke, whispering and laughing. I hadn't seen the woman at the meeting, but I assume she was offstage somewhere, watching, studying. She was tall and blond and wore an identical outfit to Richard's minus the tie. She didn't smile. She glared at me with suspicion and hate.

"This is Claire," Richard said, motioning to the blond scowl before turning to the bald convulsion. "And this is Connor. They're going to sit in on this interview to make sure nothing is taken out of context."

"We'll also be recording it." Claire tapped her phone to begin the recording.

Connor pulled over two chairs, and Richard and Claire sat in them. Then he got himself one and put it a few feet behind the other two.

"Works for me." I set my own phone to record. "I'll do the same."

Richard shrugged, and Claire pursed her lips.

"Okay, well, I'm Tess Azar, and I write for the campus paper." I tried to keep it light, but it was no use.

"We know who you are," Claire said.

"Azar, what is that?" Richard asked, squinting at me. "Mexican? Puerto Rican? Something Hispanic, right? Are you an immigrant?"

"I'm an American. I was born in New Jersey."

I waited for a response, some caustic remark, but none came, just a dismissive glance between Richard and Claire.

"Well, I don't want to waste your time," I said. "I'm sure you're very busy, so I'll get right to it. You rose to prominence with a meme, how do you feel about the state of poli—"

"We wouldn't say he rose to prominence from that," Claire said.

"It's a popular meme." I turned to Richard, trying to focus the questions on him. "I'd imagine more people have seen it than have heard you speak. You don't feel that's contributed to your rise?"

"It's reductive to try to strip Richard's wide appeal and messaging to a meme."

"That's all right, Claire," Richard said. "I think it has helped, but not in the way you mean. You're painting it as some trivial matter, that I'm famous because of a picture on the internet, but that's not the case. I'm proud to be associated with that meme because it's about questioning progress for progress's sake. It's about looking at the absurdities of this world and raising an objection to them. I'm happy to be associated with it, but I don't feel it's the sole reason for my appeal or IGE's growth."

"I didn't mean to imply anything," I said. "It's just a fascinating aspect of modern politics. Do you know how it spread? How it became popular? Who started it?"

"No," he said. "We have no idea. I didn't even see it for a long time, and then, suddenly, it was everywhere. We didn't have anything to do with it, if that's what you're asking."

"Interesting. Well, anyway, last year, your organization had maybe a dozen members."

"Seven," Claire corrected. "And it wasn't Richard's then. He wasn't a part of it yet."

"Wow, seven? How many now?"

Richard turned to Claire, and she whispered to him, her lips scraping his ear. Richard smiled. "More."

Connor, whom I'd forgotten was in the room, laughed without looking up from his phone.

"I could see that," I said, conscious of every drop of sweat now forming on my body. The fear that had been driven away was back. "I suppose that's why I'm here. This is a true movement. When you spoke, I could feel the energy in the room. Those men have found something here. I was wondering if maybe we could do an interview—"

"You're doing an interview now," Claire said. "Richard's very busy and doesn't have much time for interviews, not with the likes of you."

"The likes of me? What does that mean?"

They both stared at me and let the silence and my anger fill the room. This is what they wanted. This was their goal. This was how they claimed victory, by throwing you off balance and feasting upon your anger and frustration.

I calmed myself—sipped some air, spun my pen, and moved

on. "What do you think is responsible for your organization's growth?"

"The failure of institutions like this one and the failed ideologies they preach," Richard said. It was rehearsed, worded to be inoffensive on its surface but still hit at the heart of his thesis.

"Would you describe your members and supporters as angry?"

"Angry?" He hesitated and glanced at Claire, who gave him a look I couldn't decipher. "That word can mean many things. It can be manipulated by journalists like yourself. If I say we're angry, you'll make us seem unhinged."

"I don't plan to do that. I'm just asking questions and will report on what you say. I don't have some narrative I'm trying to push."

Claire laughed and shook her head.

Richard looked from her to me. "Not pushing a narrative? Everyone's pushing a narrative. Narrative is all we have. If you thought I'd believe you don't have one, you aren't as smart as I thought."

"You think I'm smart?"

"I think you think you are."

"That's not what you said."

"I suppose not." He let a slim grin slip through his veneer. He loved this, the sparing, the sport of it. He loved it even when he lost a point.

"I doubt your supporters would be thrilled to hear you praising a woman's intelligence."

Claire unfolded and refolded her legs.

"Yes, I think you're smart," Richard said. "I think most of the people who attend this university are smart. But I don't think being smart is the most important thing. I think what you do with your intelligence is far more important."

"And you don't approve of what I do?"

"No."

I waited for him to elaborate. Connor was curled over his

phone, scrolling and smiling, letting out the occasional chuckle. Claire smoothed her shirt, trying to appear indifferent. Richard just stared at me, not angry, not amused, blank.

"You don't approve of journalism at all?" I said.

"It has its uses. But no, by and large, I think it's brainwashing disguised as fact. Same as a university education. Well, any that isn't STEM and even that's being corrupted."

I made sure to get this down and glanced at my phone, thankful for the recording.

"What does your organization believe is the appropriate place for women in society?" I braced, expecting them to storm off. But they didn't. I glanced at Claire. She looked pleased, like this was the question they'd been waiting for.

I felt my stomach rattle, I'd walked into a trap.

"Why do you focus on the role of women in society?" Richard asked with practiced confidence. "What does that say about you that you don't ask about the role of all people in society? Sexism is described as the belief that one gender is superior to another, would you agree?"

"Yeah, bu—"

"Well, then attempting to determine the role of women and being concerned with their advancement and placement above men is a form of sexism, is it not?"

"No, I'm not attempting to favor wom—"

"You didn't ask me about men's roles in our society."

"That's because your group is almost entirely men, I doubted if their role would be in question."

"You didn't ask about minorities or children or the aged. You went right to women."

I could feel my blood pumping through my wrists and hear it in my ears. "Much of your rhetoric is focused on gender, it seemed a logical place to start."

"My rhetoric? You've seen me speak once for all of five minutes. Did I say anything against women? Did I make a single disparaging remark about women?"

"Well." I scanned my notes. "You referenced anti-men

rhetoric and feminism before decrying a 'pussified' society and failed ideologies. I think I'd classify that as anti-women."

"It most certainly is not. It goes without saying that I'm against any ideology that is anti a gender. That's sexism. I'm against sexism and bigotry. It's feminism, not me, that's sexist. As a matter of fact, I'm wary of most -isms. They almost all seem to devolve into the same thing."

"And the pussification of society?"

"That word doesn't have any link to women in my mind. Words are always evolving in meaning. That word means wimp. It means weak."

"And you don't think associating weakness with a vagina is a sexist idea?"

"As I said, words evolve. When I think of pussy, I think of a cat. I try not to keep my mind in the gutter."

Connor spat out another laugh, and even Claire smiled.

Richard didn't give me a chance to respond. He leaned forward, ready to pounce. "But now that we've discussed my rhetoric. What about yours? Your paper's rhetoric. Your individual rhetoric."

I was confused, unsure what his point was.

Connor showed Richard something on his phone. Richard looked down, smiled, and nodded. "Take this article, for instance, it was published just last month in your paper, and the headline reads 'Ban Men from Office.' What about that rhetoric?"

He held the phone in front of me, allowing me to see the headline.

"It was." My mouth had gone dry. "I don't know that article. I didn't write it, but I believe it was an editorial arguing against the overwhelming male dominance in our legislative bodies."

"Hm, well, I don't know about that. I'd have to see the numbers, but that headline is quite sensational. Could you imagine if I wrote an article saying 'Ban Women from Office' or 'Ban Blacks from Office'? Would your paper publish that? Would I still be allowed to attend this university? I doubt it."

He pulled the phone back and switched to another article.

"What about this one?" He again thrust the phone toward me. "'Too Many Men in STEM.' You wrote this one, didn't you?"

"Yeah."

"And you feel that's an appropriate idea to put forth? Not 'Let's Get More Women in STEM,' but 'Too Many Men in STEM.' Again, what if it was reversed? What if it were 'Too Many Women in Teaching'? or 'Too Many Blacks in Basketball'?"

I recoiled every time he used the word *Blacks*. It wasn't the word that was wrong, but it was the way he used it. The hard -ck sound that he leaned on. The tone. The spit that accompanied it.

"In the article," he said. "You advocate rescinding all scholarships to men in STEM majors. How is that not sexism? How is that not discrimination?"

"I didn't…I wasn't… I was quoting a professor who had a theory regarding that. I wasn't advocating for anything, just putting forth a theory."

"And if I wrote an article and quoted a Klansman, would that be acceptable?"

My head was pounding. His points were absurd and off-base, but it sounded like he was winning the argument. It sounded like he was interviewing me. I knew I was right. I knew he was a vicious bigot, but I couldn't show it. He'd rehearsed this too often. He knew the points, knew how to box me in, and I wasn't adept enough in this arena to counter him.

And he knew it.

I flipped through my notebook as if the answer lay in there. "Dr. Chompra is not a Klansman."

"But she expounds sexist beliefs and is protected and encouraged to do so by yourself, your paper, and this university." I hated how fast his answers came, how proficient he was at this. "And you wonder why we're angry."

I heard a shout through an open window. I felt the breeze and smelled spring.

I chose a tactical retreat. "Well, I think that's enough for today. I don't know if there's a story here, but I'll be in touch if there is. I'll let you know if I choose to use any quotes, and I'll let you see anything I write before it's printed. As a courtesy."

Claire shook her head in disbelief.

"Is there a problem?"

"Did you offer Jason the same courtesy?" she said.

"Jason?"

"Yes, you remember him. Jason, whose life you ruined."

"Jason, who filmed and posted illegal, non-consensual sex tapes? Jason, who might soon be in prison? That Jason? I thought I saw him backstage today for Richard's speech, but that couldn't be right, could it?" All three stared at me, stone-faced, immovable in their hate. Refusing to even acknowledge the question. "Jason saw all the quotes before the story ran."

"That's not what he says."

"Not what he says? So, you acknowledge you're in communication with him?"

"I've said too much." Claire smiled and stood, and the other two followed. "Please make sure to run your story by us before you publish. We have an attorney on retainer. If a story is published that's libelous in any way, I assure you we will litigate."

They didn't give me a chance to respond. They just turned and walked out, letting the silence, heavy and suffocating, fall over the room. They'd got what they wanted, shifted the conversation, pushed me to a point of frustration, and I could see how it satiated them. This was what they lived for. This was how they claimed victory.

6

"You have this all recorded?" Rose said. We'd been talking about the interview with Richard since the date began.

The restaurant was quiet and dark. It was in town, away from the college bars. Rose had picked it, and I was thrilled. It was just the kind of place a person like Rose frequents. The food was good, you could hear each other talk, and a small candle in the middle of our table turned her red hair into living fire.

"Yeah," I said. "She insisted that she record, so I did as well. And I always try to record interviews anyway."

"I still can't believe a woman would be associated with them," Rose said for the third time, tossing her hair over her shoulder. "How could you do that to your own kind?"

I heard Richard's voice in my head: *Imagine if she was saying that about white people.*

But no, those weren't the same things. He could make all the false equivalencies he wanted, but I couldn't let that line of thinking infect me.

"I think I know her." She was staring down at her phone, focused, spreading her fingers apart to zoom in. She held it up, and there was a picture of Claire standing over Richard's shoulder. "What's her name?"

"Claire."

"Claire Spencer, right?"

"I didn't get a last name."

"No, that's her. Claire, how could you?"

"You know her?" I found myself offended at her mere connection to that kind of person.

"Oh, we went to high school together." She waved her hand as if swatting a fly.

"Were you friends?"

"Mmmm, I don't think I'd say friends. We knew each other. We were friendly, I guess."

"Friendly? With her?" I was appalled by the ease with which she addressed this. It was like saying you were friends with Eva Braun.

"Well." She grinned and turned to me, using the full power of her stare to throttle my anger. "She wasn't like that in high school. Or if she was, I didn't know it. We just went to some parties together and had a few classes. We weren't braiding each other's hair and having slumber parties if that's what you're thinking." She laughed, and it rolled over me.

People changed. It was hard to remember in a situation like this, but it did happen. Just because Claire had become that kind of person didn't mean she was always that way.

"Did you ask him about the meme?" she said.

"Yeah, I did."

"What did he say?"

"He said he doesn't know who started it, but he's happy with the way it's used. He believes we should be questioning the society we live in, and that the meme is a meditation on that idea. My words, not his."

"Hm." She drummed her fingers across her lips. "Very interesting. He says he didn't start it. Do you think he did?"

"Wel—"

"He must've. How else would someone have that picture? It's so slimy, to manufacture your start like that. But, also, kind of brilliant."

"Would you like to be a meme?" I asked, hoping to return flirtation to our conversation.

"Well." She took a minute, not taking the question as the playful joke I'd intended. "In the right context, yes. I wouldn't want to be his meme, but yes, in general, I think that's a viable way to find success in this day and age. I don't approve of him or his politics, but it was a great strategy. Recognition is key, and he's on thousands of phones every day. People who would never agree with his rhetoric know his face and smile when they see it. It's brilliant. I bet it was Claire, this is just the kind of thing she'd think up."

We sat in silence for a minute, digesting memes and their importance.

It was during that silence that I became aware of the table behind us. A man and a woman. Once our conversation had taken a breath, I noticed that they weren't speaking. They hadn't said a word. They sat out of my sightline, but I could feel their eyes on me. I could hear them listening to us. I craned my neck, pretending to be stretching, and glanced over at them. Their eyes shot to the table, frantic not to be seen watching me.

The man had sunken eyes that disappeared into his head. He pulled out his phone and pretended to study something on it. The woman had large ears or perhaps a tiny head. I couldn't say. Her ears were all that stood out, protruding from her, longing to be free.

Was this in my head? Had they actually been listening? Or was this one of the countless times in life when one imagines the world revolves around them? It didn't feel like that. It felt different, off. It felt like they were watching me. Listening to our conversation. Surveilling.

"Can I listen to it?" Rose leaned her shoulders forward, snapping me out of my spell.

"The recording? I don't know, maybe." I was cautious of what I promised, terrified to have her listen to my failure. "But we don't have to talk about fascists all night. How was your day?"

Rose smiled and took a sip of her wine. She'd ordered a bottle for the table, and I'd been a temporary bundle of nerves, but it was fine. They didn't ask for my ID. Things like that were never a problem for people like Rose.

"My day was good," she said, with a teasing grin.

"Go on."

"Well, let's just say that soon enough, you'll be eating dinner with a published author."

"That's amazing."

"Yes." She pursed her lips. "A collection of short stories. Of course, I've already had quite a bit of my work placed in major publications, but a book is a big step."

"Who's the publisher?"

"Schwartz & Brickland." She paused and added. "Same as Sylvia."

I smiled and took a sip of wine to avoid having to speak. I was happy for her, of course, but it tasted sour, unearned.

"Not that they took that into consideration," Rose said. "I mean, well, they took it into consideration. Having trained with a master is always something to be considered. If someone had been apprenticed to a great chef, they'd put that on their resume. So, I'm sure they considered my time with her, but they were very clear they'd have published my work anyway. I'm sure I would've had other offers, but S&B felt right. Felt like home."

She reached for her glass and almost missed it, just catching it before it fell. She finished it, peering at me as she did.

I looked at her through the soft candlelight and saw her flaws for the first time. I noticed the hint of a pimple forming or receding, her lipstick just a touch off, a slight chip on a nail. There's an intimacy in seeing someone's flaws that one never gets from perfection.

She poured herself another glass and signaled for a fresh bottle. "We're celebrating, right?" Then, for the first but not the last time, she traced her nail across the back of my hand and looked into my eyes. It was a magic trick. It didn't matter how I felt or what I was thinking, I melted when she did that. I always would.

"Absolutely." I raised my glass and threw it back. I tasted the acid in the wine and felt it leave a trail along my throat, but then came the fruit and the warmth.

She described, in meticulous detail, her meeting with the publisher, from the color of the carpet to the musty smell. Then, without warning, she switched to me. "What are you, by the way? I mean, like your parents? They're…"

I was reminded of Richard. *Azar, what is that? Mexican? Puerto*

Rican? Something Hispanic, right? Are you an immigrant? There was no malice in Rose's question, no judgment or disgust, just curiosity, but still, the question was the same. *What brand of other are you?*

"My mother is from New Jersey, that's where I was born. My father immigrated when he was young with his parents."

"From?"

"Lebanon."

I watched her try to pin it. Saw her eyes raise to the ceiling as she tried her best to form a vague mental map of that region of the world. She couldn't place it. People rarely can.

"It's next to Syria and right above Israel. It borders the Mediterranean, not far from Cyprus." I had this answer practiced. My way of helping someone out so they could pretend it clicked and hide their ignorance.

Rose played her part—a smile and a confident nod. "Of course, next to Israel, that's right. But you were born here."

"Yeah, in Jersey."

"Have you been there?"

"Jersey?" We both laughed, but it was short-lived, and she stared at me until I continued. "Lebanon? When I was little; I don't remember it. Things have been difficult over there. I'd like to go back."

"Maybe we can go together." She took a long drink, smiled at me, and any apprehension I had over this line of questioning vanished. A trip. A future. A life together.

"How's Lisa?" she asked, and just like that, Lebanon was gone.

We'd finished our meal. I moved on to coffee while she'd transitioned to whiskey. There was an empty plate in front of us that had held a piece of chocolate cake. I'd taken a single bite. It was too rich for me but just right for Rose.

"She was good," I said. We'd mentioned my article at the beginning of the meal but then avoided it. We wanted a date, not an interview. I didn't want to take notes, and she didn't want to watch what she said.

"What did you talk about?" She waved her frosting-covered fork around to urge me on, conducting me.

I could've stopped it there. I could've changed the subject or mentioned that we didn't want to spend our night on the article. But I didn't. She was listening to me, her eyes locked on mine. I was, right then, the center of her universe, and I loved that feeling.

"She told me some stories." I leaned back to draw her closer to me. "About Jack, troubling stories. Something with Henry?"

Under the table, I pulled out my phone and set it to record, sitting it on my thigh. The recording would be scratchy and hard to make out, but it was better than nothing.

"Hm," Rose said. "Something with Henry?"

I nodded.

"Not a nice story to be telling. Not after everything."

"No, I guess not, but it's good for me to have the whole picture. Helps grant insight into who he was. She said it blew over?"

"I suppose it did. I don't know how Henry feels about it. The rest of us got over it."

"Why do you think that was?"

"Well, not to be too conceited, but this is a top program. I'd argue it's the top program for undergraduate writers in the world. There really isn't another like it. You usually find this kind of thing only at the graduate level. Think about it, of the ten students I'll graduate with, three of us have book deals, and five others have promising leads. The other two have been accepted into top-five graduate programs. If you make it through the workshop, you will be published or secure a future in the field."

"Very impressive."

"You're goddamn right it is." Her words stumbled into each other. "Her past students have won prizes and awards and fellowships. They teach at prestigious universities and write film and television. They're important editors, publishers, and agents. They run the world of publishing."

"So," I said after she'd paused. She was smiling, not at me but at the thought of the workshop. "You were saying with Jack and Henry?"

"Right, it's a top program that draws in the best of the best. And the elite in any field are often dancing on the edge. Some of us aren't. Some of us have it together." She presented herself. "But no one's surprised when someone's a mess. You know what they say, genius and madness flow from the same source and all that."

I registered this phrase that I'd now heard three times. I'd never heard it before and wondered where it came from. "Lisa said there was another incident, one with her?"

"With her? And Jack?"

"Yeah, something about a slap while they were working on his book?"

"Lisa wishes." She laughed. "Her working on Jack's book? No, I doubt that. Jack wouldn't… Lisa's a fine writer, but Jack didn't see her that way. Everyone has…factions form in these settings, and I'd say Lisa and Jack were not in the same faction."

"They disliked each other?" I was slipping further into journalist mode, the date now a pale memory.

"No, I wouldn't say that, just not close. And Jack wouldn't have…as I said, he didn't value her opinion. I know it's cold, but it's how it was. Now everyone wants to be a part of his book. In ten years, saying you worked with him on it will be like saying you went to the bullfights with Hemingway."

"So, you're saying she's making it up?"

"I'm saying I worked on that book with him, I was his shadow, and more than that, I knew him. I knew him better than maybe anyone. And he wouldn't have given a shit what Lisa said about his book." She slammed her glass on the table and stood up in one swift motion.

"Now," she said, leaning down to whisper. "We go to bed."

I stood up, careful to keep my phone concealed as I slid it into my back pocket. Then we walked through the sharp night, our breaths merging and trailing in our wake, to her apartment.

7

I woke with her sheets twisted around my bare leg and a chill seeping in through the open window. I turned to find the bed empty, just a cool indentation where she'd been.

"Rose?"

No answer.

I got up and looked for my clothes. I couldn't find them. They should've been at the foot of the bed, crumbled in a mass, mixed with hers, proof of our hectic scramble to undress each other. But they were gone.

Panic overtook me. I don't know what I thought. I don't know what I feared. But the fear was there.

I sipped some air and felt my mouth—dry and cracked. I hadn't drunk much, but it had been enough to leave a trace. My head pulsed. I turned toward the window, just a trickle of the morning beginning to show itself.

I thought back on the night before, terrified that I'd done something wrong, had turned her off somehow. At one point, she'd taken my hands, placed them around her soft neck, and whispered for me to squeeze. I had, but it wasn't enough. I could tell. Her face was coated in disappointment and longing.

But I'd mentioned it after we'd finished, and she'd dismissed my concerns. She'd apologized for pressuring me. I'd thought it was done, but sitting in her bedroom alone, I wondered if the disappointment lingered.

I decided not to worry about my clothes. Perhaps this was another test. Rose was likely in the other room, waiting, my clothes on the table in front of her.

I saw it as an opportunity. I could be whoever I wanted to be. I could craft a person whom she'd desire. I decided Rose would want a woman who strode around an unfamiliar apartment naked after the first date. It would show I was uninhibited. It would show I was willing to take things wherever she wanted them to go. That next time she wanted something done to her in bed, I'd be open, eager.

I took a deep breath, checked my reflection in the mirror, and strode out into the other room.

But she wasn't there either, she was gone. I searched for a note, I checked my phone for a text, but there was nothing. Just an empty, beautiful apartment.

Rose had a one-bedroom all to herself, an unheard-of privilege for on-campus housing. Her kitchen was white and clean and had a set of copper pots and pans hanging from the ceiling. Next to the kitchen, she had a large, circular table, and in the corners, there were two rolling bars—one for coffee and one for alcohol. Three antique floor-to-ceiling bookcases lined a wall. I inspected the titles. One was dedicated to the classics, but the other two were full of fiction written in the past forty or so years. Naturally, Sylvia had her own shelf. I searched for non-fiction. One shelf. Bottom corner. Hidden from view. A few acclaimed histories. I pulled one out—a famous tome on Lyndon Johnson—it was untouched, the pages still crisp, the massive spine unbent. I put it back and turned.

She didn't have a television. Instead, a painting—modern and striking—hung where the television would be. I knew little about art, but I found myself spellbound. Figures that should've been incidental were placed in the foreground—a man and a boy farming, the boy peering up, drawn to the action. In the background, there was a crowd carrying torches and pitchforks. They were moving along a raised dirt road. You could feel their rage, their violence. In the middle of the mob, there was a woman tied to a stake, and behind ran three small children. I couldn't tell if they were supposed to be the woman's children or just three impressionable souls desperate to be part of the violence. I didn't know which was worse.

The door swung open as I was inside the painting, and I was reminded of my nakedness. I wanted to cover myself but fought against the urge, still determined to play this role.

Rose smiled as she entered and took a long, searching look over my body.

"I didn't think you'd be up before I got back," she said after a minute as a means of an apology. I could already tell that this was the most I could expect from her. She wasn't born to apologize. She didn't have it in her. "I got bagels and coffee."

My eye traced over to the coffee bar but didn't linger. I made it look like I was just inspecting the room, taking in the splendor of her apartment.

"Do you like the painting?" She put the coffee and bagels down. She came behind me and placed one arm across my chest, cupping a breast. It felt like we'd been together for years, and this intimate act was commonplace.

"I think so," I said with a smile, trying to calm my racing heart, knowing she could feel it. "Who do you think the children are?"

"The children?"

I pointed to them.

"Oh, those children. What do you think?"

"Well." I steadied myself. "First, I thought they belonged to the woman tied to the stake, but now I'm not so sure. I think maybe it's just kids who want to be a part of this, join in the violence."

Rose turned my face toward her and kissed me. It was a forceful kiss, our teeth scraping, reminding me that we were not yet one, not yet aware of each other's bodies. Then we separated, and she went to the kitchen to get plates.

"I got everything bagels with cream cheese, is that all right?" This, too, felt intimate. Her ordering for me as if she knew me.

"Perfect," I said, despite it being far from my preferred order.

I sat down at the table, feeling the rich, expensive wood on my bare skin. Then I stood back up, realizing she might not want me sitting there naked.

"Something the matter?" Rose ran a finger along the outside of the bagel, pulling off the excess cream cheese and tossing it into her mouth.

"No." I sat back down. If this was a game of chicken, I wouldn't blink first. "So, do you agree?"

"Agree?"

"The children in the painting?"

"Oh, that, well, yes and no. Like many great works of art, it's a mirror. What you see in it, what speaks to you, says more about you than the work. For example, some people focus on the father and son in the foreground. They focus on the boy being drawn to the mob. Others are fascinated by the mob itself. Some think of the woman and what, if anything, she's done. And still others, like yourself, fixate on the children trailing the mob."

"And what about you? What do you focus on?"

"I focus on it all." She took a bite of her bagel, taking her time before continuing. "But I get to look at it every day. I will give you some background. The painter was raised by Nazis. Her father and mother were both party members, so it may have been her way of showing how the young are corrupted and drawn to the violent crowd."

I chewed, trying to process the information. "Her parents were Nazis?"

"Yes."

"Like active members?"

"Very much so. She even attended rallies as a girl. There's a photo of her when she was three or four on her father's shoulders as Hitler passes. Her face is pure joy. Her arm extended in salute."

The bagel solidified in my mouth. I took a sip of coffee to soften it and swallowed, feeling the hard lump trace down my throat and lodge in my chest.

"She was five when the Soviets took Berlin. Her father was killed in the city's defense, and her mother was raped by various members of the Red Army before she threw herself off a building. The painter lived through the occupation with an aunt and managed to get out through an uncle in England. She learned to paint there, and her work grapples with loving her parents and hating everything they stood for."

I stared down at my plate, frozen. It was too much to process all at once. The scope and trajectory of a life like that. The history and violence and loss that went into her work.

"Do you think I could listen to that recording?" Rose said as if we hadn't been mid-discussion.

I felt my face flush. The recording that jumped to my mind was the one I made last night.

"The interview with the fascists?" she said, and I exhaled.

"Oh, well." I hesitated. It wouldn't be ethical, and beyond that, I was embarrassed by the recording. I didn't want her to see me that way. But when I looked up and took in her shimmering presence, I knew the answer. "I guess, but you can't, you know, it has to stay between us."

"What do you mean?"

"Well, it's just that it's not ethical for me to show it to you."

"Why not? You told me what they said yesterday. You're going to play it for your editor. I'm not sure I see the difference."

She had a point. I'd told her everything they said. But still, it felt wrong, like a violation. It felt dirty.

"I guess, bu—"

"And they're fascists. Do you think they deserve some sort of ethical protection? Do you think they'd give you the same consideration? It's not like I'm going to tell them you played it for me or something."

"No, I know."

"But if it's too much of an imposition for you. If you feel that your loyalty to these fascists is paramount, then of course I understand."

It was a remarkable performance. I can see that now. But in the moment, I was ashamed, horrified by my hesitation. I thought I'd ruined it. I thought I'd destroyed our prenatal relationship. And for what? To keep the mad ramblings of a bunch of fascists private.

"No, no." I'd become hyperconscious of my nudity and

longed to be able to retreat into the familiar safety of clothing. I felt as if I was being watched, judged by a thousand unseen eyes. "Of course, you can listen to it. Sorry, I was just... Habit, I guess. I trust you, and like you said, they're fascists."

She smiled, and I felt the knot in my stomach loosen. I sent her the recording, careful to ensure it was the correct one. She listened to it without a word, her eyes wide and her mouth covered.

She said nothing when it finished, just took my hand and led me back to bed.

8

We lay still after we finished. Our heartbeats returned to normal, falling into a shared rhythm. I couldn't help but stare at her. The long breadth of her figure, the rise and fall of the sheet over her chest, the way her face rested in a contented smile.

She reached over to the table to grab her vape, and the sheet fell, exposing her back. It was covered in bruises. An array of colors—blue and yellow and red and brown. Some were fresh, just forming, others fading, remnants from weeks before. I reached out and felt them, unable to hide my shock. "Oh my god, what happened?"

"With what? Oh, those? It's nothing. Just a masseuse I use who works my back. She really gets at it."

I lowered the sheet. The bruises extended to her waist. I traced my hand across her skin, felt grooves and scabs, pockets where the skin had been broken. "Rose, what happened? This isn't from a massage."

I tore the sheets from her and saw marks on her stomach. How had I not noticed? I'd been caught up in the act, but still, it was an appalling oversight.

"It's a massage." Her eyes were narrow, and her voice flat, formal. I was reminded of our first conversation. The cold, challenging tone she'd felt me out with. "We can get one together if you'd like. It's very refreshing." A weighty pause. "Don't you have to get going soon?" She stood in front of me, defiant, proud of her discolored body. "We could still take a quick shower if you want."

I searched for a retort, a way back into the conversation, but couldn't find it. She'd ended it, and the only way to reopen it was to jeopardize everything.

Instead, like a coward, I stood and followed her to the bathroom.

9

The newspaper's office was in Clinton Hall, an old brick building named after some governor from a well-remembered, forgotten time. We'd been there for over a hundred years. It'd been renovated and shrunk, but still, it was the same place where they wrote about the start of World War I. About the Depression and the Red Scare and 9/11. The same place where all the legends before us had learned their craft. It was an office soaked in history.

When I walked in that day, five people were crowded around Samir's computer, and a voice was echoing from it. A voice I knew but couldn't quite place—smooth and polished but insistent. Then it came to me. Richard.

"About time," Samir said. "Where have you been?"

I checked my phone—11:15. On a typical day, I was in by ten, but there was no assigned time. We weren't punching a clock.

"Sorry," I said. "I was working on a story."

It was a lie. A terrible, transparent lie, but it was all I could think of.

"It's fine," she said. "You should see this. It's your guy."

"My guy? I wouldn't call him my guy. You want to put this up on the TV?"

"Good idea." There was a rare, frantic energy to her. It was condensed and crackling, frightening and exciting.

She cast Richard from her computer to the TV, and we all stood, transfixed, and watched.

The video began with the jerky movements that so often begin cell phone videos. There were mumbles and jostling, and then it focused, and Richard was standing on a bootlegged stage in the quad.

"Let me tell you a story," Richard said in his traditional

cadence, assertive and pointed. He searched the audience, pausing to make eye contact with individuals, to draw them in and secure them to him. "It's a true story. A story people around here don't want you to know. Campuses like this one, high-minded, ivory tower institutions, don't want you to know the real truth. They want you to know their truth. They want you conditioned. They want you doctored. They want you academicized."

"Pussified," someone shouted. Laughter trickled through the audience, and Richard smiled and nodded.

"You said it, not me." He turned his florescent smile toward the camera. He knew it was there. He planned the video.

But there's no way to prove that.

He pushed his already rolled sleeves up further and continued. "They don't want you to know this story, not the true version. They'll tell you their version. They'll tell you about it as long as it fits their narrative."

He leaned on the word and stared into the camera. He was talking to me. I felt a rush of excitement, and I hated myself for it.

"The story is about a man. Now I know people don't like stories about men anymore. They don't want us to talk about them. But they don't get to decide who we talk about. This man was a visionary of sorts. He believed in integration. Truly believed in it. He didn't just tell his white friends about the importance of equality. He didn't sit in his safe space and theorize and pontificate. No. He went out and practiced what he preached. He, along with his wife, became the first white couple in Indiana to adopt a Black child. He even named the boy after himself, Jim Jr. This was in 1959 when adopting a Black baby as a white couple wasn't easy. It wasn't accepted. But he didn't care. He believed in integration, so he adopted a little, abandoned Black boy as well as other children of other races and creeds.

"But was he done there? Of course not. He went further. He worked with the NAACP and the Urban League to integrate churches and restaurants and the police department and universities. The integration of Indianapolis was said to be almost entirely due to this man's work. Next, he founded a church based on integration. On equality. On racial mixing. Because that's what he believed in."

I felt the way I did when I watched a horror movie. I knew something was coming. I knew something horrible was about to happen, but I didn't know what. That's where the fear comes from. The unknown.

Someone shouted a slur from the audience. It's hard to pick out, but once you hear it, you can't unhear it.

Richard paused and smiled out at his audience, at his people, encouraging the hate. "But you know, this man had another belief. One, he felt tied to integration. One founded on the idea of equality. He believed in socialism. Christian Socialism, as he called it. He said, 'If you're born capitalist in America, then you're born in sin. But if you're born in socialism, you're not born in sin.' Think about that. If you're a capitalist, if you're born into America, the real America, you're born with sin. What is that except hate? What is that except bigotry?"

The crowd was nodding, swaying with approval, shouting in agreement.

"That's just what they're like. That's what they believe. Capitalists, Americans, people who believe in freedom, people like you and me, we allow for other ideologies. And why do we do that? Because we know in the end, ours is better."

Laughter, pent up and nervous, broke out. Richard joined in for a moment before continuing.

"We win every time. Every. Single. Time. But they keep going with this. They keep pushing socialism. They keep trying to stop us from having freedom. They keep trying to cage us. Trying to make us feel guilty and evil for who we are. Make us feel guilty for being white. For being men. For being straight. For being Americans. For being capitalists. For being free. But we won't let them make us feel bad for that, will we? No, of course not. We're not weak like them. Not like most of this campus, most of this country."

The crowd shouted back, and the camera scanned over them. Hands flew toward him in violent, pointed gestures. Salutes. You couldn't quite call them Nazi salutes, but they weren't far off. They were, at the very least, reminiscent.

I turned and saw my coworkers, mouths open, hands on faces.

"And I know, I know." He raised a hand to quiet them, and they obeyed without hesitation. "I know what some of you are thinking. You're wondering, What's so bad about this man I was describing? What's so bad about integration and socialism? You're thinking that I'm describing a good man. Maybe even a great man. A model for us all to aspire to."

No one in that crowd thought that, but he wasn't talking to them. He was never talking to them. They didn't care what he said. They were his. He was talking to me, to my coworkers, to liberal America. But even more than that, he was talking to some white man sitting alone in his room, questioning everything. A potential convert, ripe for the picking.

"Later in his life, after he saw the failure of his policies, of his vision, he took his church, cult really, to South America. A country called Guyana, where he planned to institute his vision of a socialist paradise. And while there, after again being met with nothing but failure, he convinced, or forced, 909 people, including 304 children, to drink Kool-Aid mixed with cyanide, killing every one of them. It's now known as the Jonestown massacre, and that's where the term 'drinking the Kool-Aid' comes from. It comes from an event where a deranged socialist murdered nine hundred people."

He paused and looked down in mock solemnity. Snickers seeped out of the crowd. They knew this was a joke. They knew he was mocking those who cry for the dead. But the public didn't know that. The admin didn't know that, and no one could prove it.

"The greatest single loss of American civilian life in a deliberate act until 9/11 was perpetrated by this man in the name of his beliefs. After 9/11, what did we do? We invaded Afghanistan and Iraq and declared a War on Terror. We made the world safe for democracy, for freedom. But after Jonestown, what did we do? Nothing. We let this continue. We let his ideologies further infect our nation. We let it erode and destroy everything that we stood for. We let him win. And now we live in the pile of ashes that men like Jim Jones created."

He shook his head in disgust, and the audience thundered their disapproval. They pulsed back and forth, arms out-stretched, shouting in tongues.

"I say enough is enough." He slammed his hand down, beat his chest, worked the crowd into a frenzy. He was masterful. "I say we take our country back. I say we stop letting them destroy us. I say we find our pride. I say we celebrate who we are. I say we stand up and fight. I say we start right here, right now, by taking back this campus."

Pandemonium. He dropped the mic he was holding, and the crowd swarmed the stage. The phone recording the video zoomed out to show a view of his followers bathing him in their approval. Richard stood, arms outstretched, and wel-comed them.

Then the video ended, and we all stood silent, awed, ap-palled.

10

Brandon, one of our writers whose broad good looks and penchant for leather jackets earned him the nickname Brando, was the one to break our silence. "Fuck this." He'd spent the video pacing in the corner, muttering to himself, and now he grabbed his cracked coat and headed to the door.

"Where are you going?" Samir said, already incensed by his answer. "This was last night, it's over."

"It isn't fucking over. This isn't the end. This is the beginning."

"I know." Samir lowered her head and voice to acknowledge his point. "Don't you think I know that? As an Arabic woman, don't you think I know this isn't the end? It isn't the beginning either, by the way. Maybe it's the beginning for you, for people like you."

"What is that supposed to mean?"

"You know what it means."

"Oh, because I'm a white man, I can't be offended? Is that what you're saying?"

He had donned his jacket but moved away from the door and toward Samir, who was leaning against her desk. His fist was clenched. I knew he wouldn't do anything. I knew he wasn't that kind, but still, a pit opened in my chest.

"Woah," Kim shouted, stepping between the two combatants. Kim was short with these fantastic big brown eyes, speckled and always searching. "Let's not do this. This is what they want."

She was right. I could see Richard smiling from ear to ear at this argument. I could see Claire, cold and remorseless, nod and whisper in his ear. Connor behind them, snickering, staring at his phone.

"There's nothing you can do now," Kim said, putting a hand

on Brando's convulsing chest. "This was yesterday. The damage is done."

He looked down at her, immense in contrast to the two women in front of him.

"Damage?" I said. Somehow, I already knew. I knew it wasn't just the figurative damage. I knew it was something else, something tangible.

The whole room turned in shock and disappointment.

Brando stepped toward me, brushing Kim aside. "You didn't hear?"

"No, I, uh—"

"It was all over the place," Kim said. "Insta, Twitter. How did you not see it?"

"I was, uh, well, I was offline, I guess."

"Not a good thing for a reporter these days," Samir said, not looking at me. Then she sighed and raised her gaze to meet mine. "Some protestors formed as Richard spoke. After the rally was over, there were a series of altercations across campus. There are a few people in the hospital, one in critical condition. The police are still investigating who was involved and who instigated the fights."

"As if they need anything other than this." Brando motioned to the TV.

"They've spoken to Richard, but as of now, no action has been taken."

I nodded, my mind scrambling to keep up. "Was the person who...the one in critical condition, were they—?" There was no good way to put it. I couldn't come out and ask whether they were good or bad, even if I wanted to.

"One of us," Brando said. "Lit student. A sophomore. You might know him, Isaac Lieberman. He got hit by one of the Nazis and tripped and hit his head on the sidewalk. Cracked his skull. He's not responsive right now... I wish I'd been there."

I traced the room and landed on Samir, who was staring back at me.

"How'd the interview with Richard go?" she said after a brief silence. The whole room now focused on me.

"Well…"

"Do you think he'd agree to another?"

"I don't, uh, I mean, maybe." And then it hit me. Rose. I thought of Claire, and I pictured them together at some high school party, laughing and drinking. "I might have an in."

"An in?"

"Yeah, well, I don't know, but I'll see."

Samir, for the first time since I'd walked in, smiled. She nodded and clapped her hands. "All right, good." Then she turned to Brando. "You can write a quick response. Keep it as tame as you can, don't editorialize, but you know, hit him. Focus on the video. Draw the connection that everyone should see."

Brando tensed his arm and nodded with his whole body. Kim smiled and patted him on the back, her hand lingering.

"This might be a two-parter." Samir turned back to me. "So, let's get something going on your first interview. Is there a story there?"

She seemed to already know how it had gone.

"I think so," I said. "I'll have to get creative with the quotations, but I think there's something there."

"Okay, I need it ASAP. We run a special online edition with that, Brando's piece on the video, and a short note from me. Kim, check the archives for anything on fascism. We could link to those for context. Then we run the big interview later in our print edition. You think you can get it, right?"

I nodded and sat down to type out my plea to Rose before getting to work on the article.

11

"RICHARD WELCH: A PROFILE IN HATE"
BY TESS AZAR

Yesterday Richard Welch held a rally on campus for his organization, The Institute for Gender Equality (IGE). Around eighty students, all white men, attended. After the rally ended, these men dispersed across campus and assaulted protestors, leaving one, Isaac Lieberman, in critical condition.

You would recognize Richard without knowing why. His face is familiar yet unplaceable. That's because Richard is a meme. As with all memes, you'd know it if you saw it. It's his face—one eyebrow cocked, a mocking, incredulous smile, a thumb cocked to the side. It's used to express comedic disbelief with a removed air. It's used to point out the absurdity of something without becoming a part of it.

This meme originated in the dark reaches of the far-right internet. It spread, as all memes do, with persistence until it became mainstream. Now you'll see it criticizing bad coffee or outrageous bumper stickers. You'll see it used to insult the right as well as the left, but it began in the hate-filled corners of the internet that we all try to pretend don't exist.

He began there too, and now, just like his meme, he's spreading.

Onstage, you see him in his natural habitat, he's tall and white with the mannerisms of a politician. He'd tell you he wasn't a politician. He'd tell you he was a thought leader or organizer, but you can see his future laid out before him, leading one place—politics.

The crowd breathes as one as he speaks. They contract and

press, swaying back and forth. It's like watching a concert, but the audience is wilder, more devoted.

"They've been poisoning our children," he shouts, slamming his fist on the lectern. "And our educational system with their Marxist, feminist, anti-men, anti-white, anti-America rhetoric for fifty years. Is it any wonder what we've become? Is it any wonder we've lost our freedoms? Is it any wonder this pussified society is what has been built on the shoulders of these failed ideologies?"

The audience erupts, and he smiles, basking in the adulation.

When I asked him about his anti-women rhetoric, pointing to the term 'pussified,' he dismissed it.

"That word doesn't have any link to women in my mind," he said. "Words are always evolving in meaning. That word… means wimp. It means weak."

There's a smirk that lurks beneath his words. A tongue in the side of his cheek. He knows what he's saying, what he's doing. He knows what his words mean and how his audience will read them, but he works to remain palatable for new converts and the establishment. As a result, he's been very successful in his quest for new members. When he joined, IGE had seven members, and they now boast at least five hundred, though he wouldn't verify an exact count. I suspect the actual number is quite a bit higher.

He spends much of the interview evading my questions and drawing false equivalencies between the struggle for minority rights and men's rights. He attacks our paper and journalism in general.

"I think," he said about journalism, "it's brainwashing disguised as fact."

I conducted this interview before he gave the speech that excited violence across campus, but the rally I attended could've caused the same response.

When asked if he felt his supporters—the same ones who would attack protestors less than twenty-four hours later—were angry, he became indignant.

"Angry?" he said. "That word can mean many things. It can be manipulated by journalists like yourself. If I say we're angry, you'll make us seem unhinged."

There's a mischievous, almost wistful, look in his eyes as he discusses anger. You can tell he traffics in it, is comfortable with it. The look frightens me and promises that this is far from the end. This is the beginning.

In the next rally he held, the one that led to the attacks, he ended with a blunt call to arms.

"I say enough is enough," he shouted to his fervent supporters. "I say we take this country back. I say we stop letting them destroy us. I say we find our pride. I say we celebrate who we are. I say we stand up and fight. I say we start right here, right now, by taking back this campus."

You can decide for yourself if this is inflammatory.

12

I left Claire out of the article. I didn't even mention that she was in the room. I don't know why I did that. Maybe because I hoped to use her later. Maybe because she knew Rose. Or maybe just out of some stupid, misplaced allegiance to my gender.

I also left Jason out. I'm even more puzzled by that decision. "Wait to publish it," I said. "Until after I'm out of there."

I was heading straight to a meeting with Richard and Claire, and I didn't want them reading this as I walked over.

Rose had set up the meet. They hadn't answered my messages and clearly weren't predisposed to have another interview with me. I'd thought Rose might take some convincing. I thought she might feel squeamish about trading on her friendship. But I was wrong. She'd been eager.

Samir was standing, reading the article, nodding. "You don't think it'd be better to have this in their head?"

"Not with this kind. They won't respond well to being poked."

"Then make sure you get what you need in this interview. It'll be the last one."

I nodded and walked to the door.

"Hey," Brando said, grabbing me by the arm. "Look, don't let them... Stand your ground." He held up a fist in solidarity.

"I'll do my best."

He'd heard the recording. They all had. They all heard Richard chew me up and spit me out.

I pulled away, grabbing hold of the door, but his grip stayed firm. He leaned into me. "Look, after you're out of there, text me. I'm putting something together for his next rally, something...militant, and I might need you."

I looked up and saw a delighted fury in his eyes. I gave him a half nod, just enough so he'd free me, and then I left, afraid of what he had planned. Afraid but curious.

13

"I just don't know that it's appropriate," I said again. Rose and I were walking across campus to meet Richard and Claire.

Heavy footsteps seemed to follow us. They seemed to turn when we turned, slow when we slowed. At one point, I turned around and saw the sunken-eyed man who'd sat behind us at dinner. He met my eye and looked away, alarmed.

"Look." I could feel Rose's warm breath on my bare neck as she leaned in. It pulled me away from the man and my mounting paranoia. "I heard the other interview, and you sounded so…" I hung on that pause, terrified of what awaited me on the other end. "Unlike yourself. You were timid and unsure, and you let him twist you up. That's not the Tess I know."

It could've been worse. In a way, she was saying I was confident, but it still stung.

"I can help," she said. "Having me there, having me on your side, so to speak, it'll help."

I turned to look at her. She met my eye and shrugged. She didn't want to come right out and say it, but I understood. *These racists will be more amenable if you have a white person with you.*

"Okay, but look," I said. "This has to stay between us. At least until the article's out. I can't… It's my reputation at stake."

"Don't worry, kid. I would never do anything to mess with your reputation. Now that we're together, that reflects on me too."

Together.

With anyone else, I'd have been terrified by that statement. We'd known each other for three days. College romances move fast, but this was a bit much, even by those standards.

But Rose was different. This was different. I glowed. I turned away to hide my joy, played it off like it was nothing when it was everything.

14

The interview was in another abandoned classroom. I didn't know if they had a key or just tried doors until they found an open one. It didn't matter, but I was curious. There was power in it. A feeling that they were both apart from and accepted by the admin.

When we walked in—Rose first, with her sweeping, immaculate posture—Claire beamed. It was the first time I'd seen her like that, the first time she seemed to be a person, someone capable of joy. It was jarring, like watching that video of Hitler playing with his dog.

"It's been too long," Claire said. They embraced without hesitation. This was not their first hug.

A throb of jealousy pulsed through my chest. Rose had undersold their relationship. It wasn't my worst fear, but it was more than she'd claimed. They were close. Maybe not now, but once, and the residue of intimacy lingered.

Richard stood as well, smiling with the same skeptical confusion. I thought we were sharing the same thought. Both wondering what this was. Both trying to assess the threat.

"It *has* been," Rose said as they separated their heads but kept their bodies entwined.

I regretted the whole thing. I worried about what kind of Pandora's box I'd opened.

And I judged Rose. She was so calm and open and amorous with this woman. This monster.

"This is Richard," Claire said, the two of them finally separating. Rose shook his hand, met his eye, and smiled. They looked right together, cut from the same cloth. All of them.

Rose looked from Richard to Claire and back to Richard. "I hear you were a little rough with my girl. Play nice this time."

Richard glowed. She'd turned on her charm, and he was blown away by it. Just as I was. Just as everyone was.

He turned to me and extended his hand more out of reconciliation than a greeting. I took it.

Claire eyed the shake and glanced at Rose. "So, how do you two know each other?"

"Oh, you know, here and there," Rose said, and my heart broke. "She's doing an article on Jack." She dropped her head, and the warmth fled from the room. Richard fixed his sleeve, and Claire sighed, putting a hand on Rose's arm.

"Yes, that was a horrible thing. I'm so sorry for your loss; I sent a text, but I'm sure you were caught up. I was going to call, but…"

"No, I understand. I saw your text. Sorry, I didn't answer. Just a lot, well, you could imagine."

"You knew Jack?" I said to Claire, my reporter's instinct unable to be kept at bay.

Claire shot me a look like the help had dared to speak. "Of course. Not well, but I knew him a bit."

"How?"

"Is this on the record?" Richard may have calmed down, but she hadn't. She never would. "I knew him through Rose. Back when they were, well before."

I couldn't tell what she meant. I assumed it was before he killed himself, but it was hard to say. There was a weight to that pause. A germ that she was planting in my mind.

"But we're not here to talk about Jack, are we?" Claire motioned to two seats. She and Richard moved to the two across from them. It was then that I saw Connor seated behind their chairs. He was in his phone, smirking to himself, scrolling and typing. He didn't look up. He didn't greet us. He just stayed in his phone.

There was silence, and everyone except Connor stared at me. I was confused. I'd momentarily forgotten why I was there, and then I remembered and set my phone to record. Claire did the same.

"Right." I flipped through my notebook, spun my pen and dropped it, my nervous, sweaty hands failing me. Rose picked it up. She raised it to me and met my eyes, and just like that, I was myself again. "Well, I suppose there's no point dancing around it. After your rally yesterday—"

"It wasn't a rally," Claire said. "It was a meeting."

"In a public place. I would argue that makes it a rally."

"We think 'rally' in this instance carries pejorative connotations. We'd prefer meeting."

She was testing me. She wanted to know if I was still rattled from our previous interview.

"I'll keep it under consideration. As I was saying, after your rally yesterday, there were a series of skirmishes on campus between your supporters and protestors. One of those skirmishes led to the hospitalization of a young man—"

"We don't know those were Richard's supporters, and we have no reason to assume they were. Our members don't report being involved in the altercation with that young man in the hospital."

I glanced at Richard. He just smiled and scratched his wrist. It was a deft strategy. Have her make the corrections, have her pick the fights. Don't let him get on the record with anything other than their planned statements.

I turned to Richard. "Do you think any of those—the campus police reported four separate incidents—involved your people?"

"Yes," he said, after looking to Claire for approval. "We know that a few of the incidents were directed at my supporters. They were walking back from the meeting and were assaulted. If we had a better police presence on this campus or student safety volunteers, which we have advocated for in the past, we doubt these incidents would've occurred. As for the accident with the young man, I have no reason to believe those were my supporters. If they were, I'm sure they were defending themselves."

"So, you're saying Isaac, that's the man who's in the hospital, was the instigator?"

"It's possible. I don't know. No one knows. But I won't assume he's the victim because he got hurt. That's a logical fallacy. And assuming that it was my people who hurt him is dangerous."

"Why is it dangerous?" I already knew Richard was careful in his word choice. He used coded words to his supporters. You saw it in his speeches, and I was sure he was trying the same here.

"Well." He paused and looked to Claire. A silent signal passed between them, but I couldn't decipher it. "I worry for the safety of my supporters. This dangerous, violent group of leftists and socialists on campus doesn't need more ammunition against us. We're just out here trying to speak our minds and find like-minded individuals, and we feel that we're in danger. We don't feel the university protects us, we feel they demonize us, and now with this... I'm concerned."

"Do you think you contribute to that danger? Do you think your speech could've excited your followers to violence?"

He smiled and leaned back in the chair, running a hand through his thick hair. "See, that's just what I'm talking about. I give a speech, and you try to turn it into... Look, all I'm doing is giving a voice to a group who have been muzzled on this campus and in this country for years. That isn't dangerous. The muzzling is dangerous. The echo chamber and thought police are dangerous. Not me. And you trying to twist our peaceful gathering into some sort of violent foreplay is dangerous. It'll make those violent groups on campus think they need to seek us out. You should be careful with that. You don't want blood on your hands."

I sipped in a breath and clicked my pen. I needed to stay poised. Not just for the interview but for Rose, whose eyes I could feel on me. "Let's say that the person who struck Isaac was one of your supporters. Just for the sake of argument. Would you feel responsible then?"

"Let's say the person who struck him had just read one of your articles. Would you feel responsible?"

"I don't think there's anything to indicate that was the case."

"And I don't think there's anything to indicate it was one of my supporters."

Talking to him was like being in a different world. The rules that governed reality weren't applicable. They were unimportant, transient. He would use a piece of logic one minute and discard it the next.

I scanned my notes, pretending the answer was there. I tried to form the article in my head. Tried to see how it would read. I needed something firmer, something solid. "What group would you assume was responsible?"

"Well, socialism has been responsible for more historic deaths than any other ideology. They've shown a willingness and aptitude for violence. Socialism is also rampant at this university. I would say that's a good place to start."

"Any others?" I made sure he saw me write down his ramblings.

"Well, they're all interconnected." He donned the manner of a man explaining something simple to a child. "Feminism is a driving force. Not simple feminism, mind you, but what it's become. The combined forces of socialism and feminism and all the other tenets of modern liberalism. This anti-men, anti-white, anti-straight, anti-capitalism, anti-America group that has taken over this university and nation. It's a plague. And it's beyond dangerous. I assume they're responsible. Honestly." He glanced around the room, lingering on Rose this time.

"Honestly?" I said.

Claire leaned over and whispered something in his ear, but he pulled away. "No." He shook his head and waved a finger. "You know what, I'm fine with it. She can print this if she wants. I'm not saying it's definite, but it's possible. I wouldn't be surprised."

Claire shrugged and shook her head. I suppose that's the danger of controlling a man like this. Sometimes he decides he's what you pretend he is.

"Look, I'm a threat, okay. IGE's a threat. We're a threat

to the safe little echo chamber that academia has cultivated. This"—he waved his hand around the classroom—"is built on lies. And they know it. Everyone knows it. Everyone except the students who go here. It's the same with the country. Everyone knows the liberal establishment is lying to them. Everyone knows it's broken, it's failed, doesn't work. Everyone, except the people. Then someone like me comes along and starts telling the truth, exposing these lies. And I gained a following, and my supporters, you saw them, they're the real thing. So, if you're on the other side and you see me coming up, you see my following growing, what do you do? You need to get something against us. Something tangible. Something like violence. Something that makes us look dangerous. And if we won't oblige, if we won't commit some reckless act of violence on our own, maybe you do it. Maybe you pick some fights, hire some guys, put someone in the hospital. Then you blame us, and all of a sudden, my movement, my supporters, look violent, deranged. Then you can call us Nazis all you want. They've done it before, and I think, maybe, that's what happened here."

There it was. Jackpot. Crazy conspiracy theory.

"So." I had to stop my voice from trembling with excitement. "You're saying you think it was protestor on protestor violence?"

"I wouldn't call them protestors, but yes, that's my theory. I don't know that it's true for the record. Don't twist my words and make it seem like I'm presenting this as a certainty. I just think it's possible."

"Do you think it's more likely than, say, your supporters having struck him?"

"Very difficult to put percentages on it until we have more information. If my supporters had anything to do with it, which I doubt, I'm sure it was in self-defense. We're not a violent group, but neither are we cowards. If someone strikes at us, we'll strike back."

I moved to the top of my notes, where I had a quote from

his speech. His closing. I'd been holding on to it, waiting to use it. "You closed your speech by saying, 'Enough is enough. I say we take this country back. I say we stop letting them destroy us. I say we find our pride. I say we celebrate who we are. I say we stand up and fight. I say we start right here, right now, by taking back this campus.'"

I chose not to attach a question. Not just yet. I wanted him to hear the words.

He did. He smiled and looked over at Claire, who was no longer sulking. She was smiling too.

"Is there a question there?" Richard said.

"Do you stand by those statements? After everything that occurred last night?"

"Even more so. Last night was a perfect example of everything I warned against in that speech. We were attacked by the radical elements that control this campus and this nation."

Perfect. Unapologetic doubling down. The article would write itself.

"You said you didn't like the name protestors. What name would you give them? The element on campus and in the country, you're so concerned with."

He pulled his hand to his chin, striking a contemplative pose. It was practiced, but as with so much of him, I didn't know if it was genuine or mocking. "We call them a few names. Socialists, feminists, communists, but I like EOTP. Enemies of the People."

I wrote it down and felt another rush of excitement. Then I waited. I wanted to see if he'd let anything else slip.

"Will this be one article or two?" Claire said.

"Not sure yet."

"So, you don't have one completed?"

Did she know? Had she been contacted for quotes? Had someone at the paper told them? Did the people I now believed were following me find out? Were they Richard's people? Were they even real?

"No, not yet," I said. "I like to see where an article goes instead of rushing to print."

"Okay, but we'll get to see it before it publishes, right?" She shifted forward, and Richard fell back. Connor snorted behind them, but there was no way to tell if it was related to our conversation or his phone.

"I'll do what I can," I said.

"Do what you can? Last time you promised we'd see anything before publication. We wouldn't have agreed to these interviews otherwise. Now you'll do what you can?"

"I don't think I, uh." I pretended not to remember the words I'd used last time. "I don't believe I made any promises. We will, of course, reach out to verify quotes, and, if possible, I'll send you the article before it publishes."

"Unbelievable." She tossed her arms in the air.

I turned to Rose, worried about how this sounded to her, worried Claire was about to lash out at her. She wore a severe face, concerned, but stared between Claire and Richard, past them. She was there but not there.

A tense, violent silence sat with us.

"Well," Claire said, standing. "If you don't have anything else, I'd say it was a pleasure, but it wasn't."

I stood, too, and nodded. There was nothing to say. Nothing would change how she felt about me.

She turned to Rose, and her face went from the cold sheet she'd presented to me to a warm blanket.

"Rose," she said, tilting her head to the side and going in for a hug. Again, jealousy overtook me. It was a short embrace but no less intimate. "Let's get lunch soon, just the two of us."

"I'd love that," Rose said and turned to Richard. "And it was a pleasure meeting you."

"I assure you the pleasure was all mine." He grasped her hand and held it. "You should come tomorrow night. We're having a little meeting out in the quad." Then remembering I was in the room. "You should both come."

Claire nodded to Rose, assuring her she'd be welcome while ignoring me.

"It's not," Richard said, still holding Rose's hand. "You should form your own opinion on us. I think you'd like it, some of it at least."

Rose smiled. "Maybe. I'll have to see what my schedule looks like."

I felt nauseous. It wasn't just the reverence she seemed to be paying these two but the comfort with which I was ignored. I saw all the parties in the past where people like them ignored and disrespected people like me. I wanted to lash out, to grab one of them by the hair and pull them to the ground. I wanted to destroy their perfect polite little conversation.

But then I saw Rose. I saw her naked on the bed. I saw myself climbing over her, drinking her in. I saw the yachting, the skiing, and the future I believed was mine for the taking. I wanted it. I wanted her. I wanted that life. I wanted to be on the inside of those conversations.

Richard shook my hand as he left. There seemed to be no ill will there, no anger. This was just part of the job for him.

It was different with Claire. She brushed past me without acknowledgment, radiating hate. I wondered if maybe it was jealousy. Maybe she saw the spark between Rose and me and hated it. I hoped that was the case. I chose to believe it was.

15

We left the building and went to get coffee. I don't know if I suggested it, Rose did, or if our feet just took us there. My anger built as we walked. I replayed Richard's deranged diatribe. I saw Claire's contemptuous stares. I heard Rose—polite, cordial. I felt it all anew. It was like a cut that kept reopening.

My steps locked in with Rose's, they echoed as we advanced, and people, consciously or otherwise, made a path. There was a power in walking with her. A power, despite my mounting anger, that I enjoyed.

I looked at Rose, she was focused but unmoved. She wasn't angry, she wasn't troubled. She didn't fear what men like Richard did to the world. She was, if anything, excited. She was like a person who'd seen a fatal car crash but escaped without a scratch. She had a story. She was an eyewitness to carnage without being affected.

I watched the faces push by us, smearing together into a blur. I counted how many weren't white. Five. Five of the three dozen faces we passed. I heard Richard's voice echo in my head, *categorizing people based on race is racism*. Another false equivalency, another germ of perverse whataboutism nestling into my brain. Only this time, the thought lingered for a moment longer before I pushed it away.

Behind us, I heard a pair of footsteps, loud, even, in time with ours. Someone following us. I glanced over my shoulder but couldn't make anything out. Just more blurred faces and paranoia. I couldn't focus on that, not just then.

"What was that?" I said after we'd gotten our coffees and sat down.

"I know, right." Rose tracing the rim of her cup. "How do you get to be like that? Do you think it's an act, or does he be—"

"Not them, you. What were you doing?"

"Me?"

"Yeah, 'It was a pleasure meeting you.' 'We should get lunch.' What was all that?"

"Oh, that, well." She blew on her coffee, drawing my eyes to her lips, but my rage wouldn't be put off. "It's just a game."

"A game?"

"Yes, you pretend to be friends with everyone, even the people you loathe. And trust me, I loathe them. But telling them that does nothing. We never would've gotten this interview if I told Claire what I thought of her."

She thought this would push me back, settle me down. She thought she could use the interview and her part in it to excuse her behavior. But she couldn't. My anger was up, and it needed to be heard.

"A game?" The table next to us was listening. I thought it was the big-eared woman from the restaurant, but I couldn't be sure. "You think this is a game? It isn't, not for me, not for people like me. They hate people like me. They want to keep us down, they want to preserve the existing racist order. This isn't a game to us, Rose. This is real."

More tables stopped talking and listened.

Rose smiled. "Calm down. You're making a scene."

"I'm making a scene? Unbelievable. That was a scene. What you just did back there was embarrassing, not this."

Her face broke. The practiced, refined poise that always separated her from the world fell, and I saw shame for the first time stain her face. She dropped her gaze and reached her hands across the table. "You're right, I'm sorry."

She traced her fingernail across the back of my hand, and my spine vibrated. I felt my chest cave in. I still had the anger, the rage, percolating inside of me. I could still feel that sense of righteous indignation. The fury that needed an outlet.

But it felt wrong, unearned. I'd won. She'd conceded defeat. I still had aggression to burn off, but it had become trivial, petty.

"Maybe we should go," I said. "The whole café's listening to us."

Rose stood, confident. She was used to having eyes on her. My knees wobbled as I stood, but then she took my hand and led me out, and I felt her confidence pulse through me.

16

Rose sat up, letting the sheet fall off her chest. "Hey, we never talked about it."

"What?" I was still stuck in the postcoital haze. "Talked about what?"

"The article. You said you'd tell me how you got him to talk."

"Who?" Then it clicked. Jason. "Oh, him."

I took a minute and reached over to her bedside table, where she kept the vape pen. I took a drag and handed it to her.

Everyone always wanted to hear about Jason, to hear how I got him to talk. But no one's impressed by the magic trick after they know how it's done. It becomes ordinary, obvious. Still, I decided if this would last, if this was real, I needed to believe in it. To believe in her.

"Well, it's not as wild of a story as people make it out to be. I contacted his lawyer who said he wouldn't comment and gave me a line about addiction and him getting help and all that. Whatever, that was to be expected. I knew he played intermural soccer, so I asked around and found some of his teammates. I went to a party at their clubhouse and convinced them I wasn't writing a hit piece. I told them that I always thought those Duke lacrosse players got a raw deal."

Rose laughed, and I glowed.

"So, they hooked me up with him, and remember, I was a nobody at that point. I gave him a whole song and dance about how a story about him as the bad guy would be white noise, and I wanted to frame it from his perspective."

She leaned her head against my arm. "And he bought that?"

"Yeah, I convinced him. At first, he—"

"Were you worried about doing that?"

I reached for the pen and took another drag, nodding. "A bit.

It's not, well, I know it's not the cleanest ethics, but I thought it was okay. Cops lie during interrogations."

Neither of us spoke for a minute, both contemplating my horrible rationalization.

"I guess I felt," I said.,"that he lied to them, so I wasn't wrong to do the same. Not if it got the story and helped the victims. In the end, though, I don't think it mattered what I said. He wanted to talk. He wasn't ashamed of what he'd done."

Rose sat up and smiled, and ran her soft hand across my arm. "So, what was he like?"

"Charismatic." She laughed, but I hadn't meant it as a joke. "I mean, he was a monster too. Remorseless, unapologetic. He thought what he did was fine. He thought if he didn't mind having the videos up, they shouldn't. Even so, there's a perverse charisma to him. I guess I understood why he could, you know, with so many women."

"A charismatic sociopath. Seem to be a lot of those around here."

"Yeah, I guess so."

She dragged a fingernail down my exposed thigh, sending a shiver across my body. "How was he after the fact?"

"Well, he's threatening to sue me, so I doubt any party invitations are forthcoming. Aside from that, who knows?"

"In the interview, the other one, the one I listened to, you mentioned him to Claire. You said he was at Richard's speech. Is that true?"

"Yeah."

"Why didn't you…? Seems like it would've been something you'd want to mention in the article."

"I think I… It didn't seem relevant."

"It's all relevant. It makes Richard look bad. It speaks to his character. I'd include it in the next article if I were you."

I nodded, and we fell back into each other.

17

There's a ghost story on campus. It's as old as the university and is told with pride by some and derision by others, but no one gets through their four years without hearing it. There are different versions, and people emphasize different sections, but this is the one I was first told and the one that's stuck with me.

As with so many ghost stories, this one's about a woman. A woman named Louise who believed she'd been wronged by her birth. A woman who wished for nothing more than the possession of knowledge. She didn't want knowledge for any means. She didn't want it so she could change the world. She didn't want it to get rich. She just wanted to possess it.

As a child, this wasn't a problem. She was born wealthy and into a world full of knowledge. There were books in her home, plays to see, conversations to eavesdrop on.

She read everything she could, surpassing her reading level with ease. She finished Shakespeare's complete works when she was nine, Gibbon's seminal volumes on the Roman Empire when she was ten, and was bored by eleven. It was then that she decided to attend school.

She wouldn't accept a girls' school. She wouldn't accept some consolation prize. She wanted the real thing. She wanted to test her knowledge. She wanted to compete and learn with the boys.

Her father was a widower, and Louise was his only child, so he indulged her. He made contributions and got her into a school that met her demands. The school hemmed and hawed but eventually gave in. The financial offer was too much to reject, and they didn't think she'd last a year.

There was a fair bit of teasing and hazing and some things

that bordered on cruel, but she stuck with it. She ignored the taunts. She gritted her teeth, did her work, and graduated two years early at the top of her class.

Her father assumed that was it. He prepared for her debutante season and thought, in an odd way, there might be a man who was drawn to her education. A parlor trick of sorts. A wife who could discuss philosophy and history. Perhaps he'd have to take her to Europe for that kind of man, but he'd find him.

Only, Louise wasn't interested. She told him she wouldn't be debuting. She wouldn't be curtseying and blushing and seeking out a husband. Instead, she'd be going to university, and her decision was final.

So, her father, who knew better than to argue with his headstrong daughter, went from one university to the next, begging and pleading, but none would accept her. Their policies were firm, their answers short. But, as was his way, he offered money, lots of it, and in the end, one small school agreed. Our school.

They had conditions. She could never tell people she attended the university, and her name wouldn't be in any records, but she could take classes and meet all the same requirements as the men. In exchange, her father purchased the land surrounding the university and bequeathed it to the school along with an exorbitant sum of money. Money and land that built the university.

Once the agreement was reached, the dean sat down with Louise. He explained the difficulties she'd face with her fellow students and the professors. He told her she couldn't give in, she had to fight and strive to succeed. She had to show the men what she was made of. He told her he believed she could do this. He told her that she was special.

Upon hearing this, she glowed with approval and believed he was right.

She found lodging in town. A quiet boarding house. Modest but acceptable.

Her fellow students were, of course, outraged at having her on campus. She expected as much. She was ready for the taunts and jeers and hate and simply closed her ears and went about her work. She was used to it. They were the same sort of taunts the boys at her previous school had used.

But these were not boys. These were men.

She was raped the second Saturday she was at school.

The men went out to a tavern in town, not far from where she was staying. She was in her room, studying, surpassing her unspectacular classmates.

It was a dark night, and she didn't see her attacker. She didn't wake when the door opened but did when the man draped a heavy hand over her eyes. She couldn't describe him. Not his appearance, at least, only the smell, liquor and onions, and the feeling of his sweat rolling across her face.

In the morning, she went to the police, but they told her there was nothing to be done. "A single woman living alone above a bar."

"I don't live above a bar," she'd answered.

"Near enough. What did you expect? Place like that, girl like you. Living in a man's world. Asking for it."

She debated going to her father but knew it would destroy him.

Instead, she bought a sharp knife and slept with it in her hand, tucked under the pillow.

And, when the next Saturday came, and the man again broke into her room and held her down, she got the knife loose and slashed his face. She felt the blade pull across his skin, tasted his warm blood, heard his scream recede as he fled into the night.

Monday, she was both terrified and excited to go to campus. She believed he'd be there. She was sure it was one of her classmates.

She got to class early, watched as every man entered, sneered at her, and sat down. She expected each one to be the one and felt her heart lift with anticipation every time the door squeaked open. But none were marred, none carried so much as a scratch.

She couldn't understand it, she tasted the blood, licked it off her lips, felt it run down her hand.

She couldn't focus in class. She was elsewhere, consumed with her thoughts. Could she have imagined it all? No, she had the blade, her sheets were still dark with his blood. Could it have been a townsman? No, they wouldn't dare. They wouldn't risk something like that.

She spent her day replaying the events. She felt it happen anew every time. She felt the penetration, his palm against her eyes, his other hand around her throat, silencing and threatening her. She smelled him, she heard his muffled grunts.

After hours of this torment, she decided it wasn't something she could live with. She couldn't put it out of her head and focus on her studies. She couldn't sit in a classroom with all those hateful men, not after what had happened. She knew they'd won, but that didn't matter anymore. The game was over.

After class, she headed to the dean's office to tell him. She'd prepared herself. She'd return home in shame and tell her father everything. She'd do whatever he asked, find a husband, cloister herself away, become a nun, anything.

The door to the dean's office was open a crack, and when she felt the handle, it was freezing cold. The cold traced up her arm, and her legs went weak. She knew this was an omen, but she'd chosen not to believe in omens. She'd chosen science and reason over superstition, so she moved into the room with confident defiance.

The dean's chair faced the window, and she could only see its back. Slowly, he turned, but somehow, she already knew what she'd see. His face was torn and slashed and covered in bleeding bandages. He smiled at her despite the evident pain it caused him. "Hello, Louise. I hope our meeting today will be nicer than the last."

Louise said nothing and longed for her knife.

"I was just admiring the new building." He gestured toward the rising structure across from his window. "I was thinking perhaps after it's finished, we could give you an office there. A place for you to continue with your studies in safety. Perhaps across from my office, that way, we'll never be far from each other."

A pain shot up her arm and traced itself along her back. She heard a slight, high-pitched ping echo through her head. She left without a word.

That night she returned to campus under cover of darkness and climbed over the planks that surrounded the half-erected building. She'd brought matches, tinder, and a rope with which she secured herself to a sturdy beam. It wasn't long before it was engulfed. She didn't cry out, not at first. Everyone cries in the end, but she stayed silent for longer than most.

The dean created some story for Louise's father regarding her death. No one knows what it was, but it must've worked. Her father changed his will that same week and left his vast fortune to the university.

They say on a cold night, when the wind whips around the buildings, buildings that were built with Louise's inheritance, you can still hear her voice. You can hear her cry out in pain and curse the university. Some people even claim that they've felt her pass through them. Felt the cold consume them, and her frigid hand cradle their heart.

But, of course, that's just a ghost story.

You may be asking yourself how much of that story is true? How much of it is possible?

I don't know the answers to those questions. No one does. It's a story, after all, a ghost story at that, but that doesn't mean it didn't happen.

I can tell you that the second dean of the university, Dean Westcott, did have scars on his face. You can see them in his portrait that hangs in Westcott Hall, among other places. I can also tell you that the money and land that built the university came from one donor. A man named Livingston, a widower who had one child, Louise. She died young.

I don't know how she died. I don't know if it was a fire. I

don't know if she cared for education or ever set foot on campus. But I don't doubt that all those things could've happened. I don't doubt we live in a world where that kind of pain and violence are not uncommon.

Then again, on a campus of storytellers, who knows what's fact and what's fiction.

As for the story, it's told in many ways. It's been the subject of short stories, student films, and contemporary dance numbers. There have been essays written on it. It's been interpreted in countless ways over the years. I won't bore you with my opinions or the various readings I've heard. You can investigate them yourself. You can fall down that rabbit hole all on your own.

All I'll say is that everything worth anything in this world was built with blood.

18

Tess Azar's notes on Henry Putskin:

Tall. Broad. Big bushy beard with short hair. A touch of an accent, southern or western, reminiscent of a cowboy. He wears a tight T-shirt that stretches against his girth. You can tell he'd once been all muscle but was slipping. It would still be a few years before the fat won out, but the process was underway. He sits straight, erect, a soldier at attention. He fidgets a lot with his fingers but is still and constant aside from that. He seems on edge, like he's being watched. Maybe he is. His apartment is spartan, just books in piles, a table, and some chairs. No TV, no couch, nothing comfortable. It feels like the apartment of a man just passing through, but he's been there for two years.

I met with Henry, another of Sylvia's students, that night. He was close to Jack. They entered the program together and shared a love of declarative prose. Rose said that, aside from herself, he was Jack's closest friend, but Henry seemed less sure.

"I mean, maybe at one point." He shuffled his feet. "Can be hard to say at college, you know. Things happen fast here. Even more so when you don't know people. Like neither of us knew anyone when we got here. Then, we're in the same program, we like the same books and movies, and we hang out all the time. It just can happen fast at college."

I turned and caught Rose's eye. We shared a knowing look, and she went back to her phone.

"So, it was a fast friendship?" I said.

"Short, but we were close for a minute. Summer after sophomore year, we bought a car together, a beater, and drove around the country until it kicked, then flew home. Wanted to be like Kerouac, I guess. We never fought. We slept outside or in cheap motels. It was great. We each filled three notebooks. I still go back to them when I'm stuck."

He paused, stood up, and walked to the window. He opened it and breathed in the fresh air, then went to the kitchen, got some water, and returned.

"Anyway," he said. "We were close. Best friends, I guess. Except for Rose." He glanced over at her, apologetic. "It was different, you know. We were, well, together."

"Together?"

"Involved. Nothing like official, I guess. I think I thought… It doesn't matter now. We were friends above everything else. I thought even if the other thing didn't keep, the friendship would. But something changed. I don't know if it was him or me or what, but it all went away. It didn't seem to affect him. He just got distant. That wasn't odd. He was like that. He'd go into his writing for a while. He'd get dark and close himself off. I knew to let him go, give him space. Let him live in it for a while. It's what made him so good. He became his work, lived it, and he always came back, always finished, and was himself again. Until he wasn't."

I waited, but nothing came. "How long ago was that? When he changed?"

"It was almost a year ago. Maybe a little less, ten months? I don't know."

"Around when he, I mean when you…the altercation?"

"Before. That was…it was just a fight. I've been in fights before. He was…he was going through some stuff, and he lashed out. I don't…I didn't hold it against him. It was, in a weird way, kind of a relief."

"A relief?"

"Well, the program's competitive, but people are…they don't come right out and say what they think. It's all passive aggressive, all veiled insults and pettiness."

"Do you have an example?"

"I…" He looked over at Rose as if for permission, she nodded. "One time, we were reading one of Lisa's stories. It was not my kind of thing, political, no subtlety. God, see, I'm doing it right now." He laughed and shook his head. "I didn't like it, okay. I don't like those kinds of stories, and while I love Lisa, I don't like her writing. Anyway, I said something about it, about how it should be more ambiguous, less obvious. I didn't hide my criticism in a series of empty compliments like you're supposed to. And she took it, she took the criticism and smiled and thanked me because you have to, but I could tell she wasn't having it. After that, everything I did, every story I wrote, every opinion I had on a movie, every book I mentioned, even the food I ordered was 'obvious.' She was relentless with it."

"She used that word, obvious? Threw it back at you like that?"

"Either that word or something similar. It's just how it was. People in the workshop hold grudges. They act like they don't, but they do. Jack was…it was a relief for him to come right out with it. To express his anger physically. Something tangible."

"I heard he used some language tha—"

"Nothing I hadn't heard before. And he didn't mean it. I don't…I knew where his heart was, so it didn't bother me. And he apologized, and that was it. Nothing else needed to be said."

"So, you noticed the change before that?"

"Yes."

"Do you have a sense of what changed? What caused it?"

He pinched his nose the same way Rose had done to stop herself from crying. "I think about that all the time. Maybe I could've…you know… I know you're not supposed to think like that, but it's hard not to."

Rose stood up and walked over to him. She put a hand on his shoulder and whispered something in his ear. He grabbed her hand, smiled, and kissed her cheek.

"Some of it was the novel," he said. "It was the longest thing he'd ever written. He was just down there with it for so long. We tried, you know, me and Rose and Tyson, we did what we could. Tried to get him to go out, get drunk, watch a movie. But he was just down there, wallowing. We didn't realize…if we'd have known…"

I felt dirty being there, asking those questions, like a voyeur watching someone else's intimacy. Not sex, something more. The intimate moments that make up a life.

I put down my pen and closed my notebook. I leaned forward and put a hand on his knee. "There was nothing you could've done. You were there for him whenever he needed you, and that's all anyone can do."

He nodded and patted my hand.

"Look," I said. "I don't want to take any more of your time. If you have anything else, please let me know. It doesn't have to be about the end, it can be about before. A story from the road trip or something. Or if you just want to talk. Off the record."

He smiled, and as I stood, he met me in an embrace. I felt tiny in his arms, swallowed up in his grief. Then he let me go, and I longed to return.

Rose walked over to him, and they hugged as well. She finished by kissing him on the cheek.

"Oh, I read your article," Henry said as we reached the door. "It was good, but I hope there's more. Felt like you just skimmed the surface."

"More? With Jason?"

"No, not that one. The one about Richard and the fascists. I hope there's more. That's an important story."

I said nothing, just stood holding the door, frozen in shock.

"It posted while we were walking over," Rose said. "Is your phone not on?"

It was on airplane mode. I tried to avoid potential distractions while conducting an interview, seeing as I used my phone to record. I flipped it back into its normal state and got a flood of messages. The first few from Samir telling me it was going up. Then a series of spiteful ones from Claire.

Unbelievable, I thought we were going to see this first.

I thought this wasn't a hit piece.

You'll never get another interview with us.

Lawyer up.

They were to be expected. I texted Samir to ask what the traffic was like. I got a one-word reply. *HEAVY.*

"Sorry, Henry, I've got to—" My phone buzzed again. Samir. *Get down here, we've got a problem.*

"Of course," he said. "I might take you two up on that chat, maybe a beer sometime."

I nodded but couldn't verbalize a response. I was already gone, already out the door.

19

"They released the recordings," Samir said before I was through the door. She eyed Rose as she entered behind me. "I think they edited them first, but they're out there. Who's this?"

"She's a friend," I said, catching my breath. "She's the one who got me the second interview, and she's helping me on the Jack thing."

"Should she be here for this?"

Brando and Kim also gave her a long, hard stare.

"Yes," I said. "She's fine."

"Okay, well, they posted it. That woman sent it to us a few minutes before it went up. I think they're getting a ton of traffic. We are too, but I don't know, this isn't good."

"You've listened to it?"

All three of them looked away and nodded.

"Bad?"

Samir was the only one who dared to raise her head. She nodded.

20

The room was silent for a long time after the recording stopped playing.

They'd changed it. Not much, but enough. Some clever editing, some omissions, some cutting and pasting. That was all it took. They fit it to their narrative, to make me look worse. To make me look deranged and reactionary. They cut out Claire completely. They made Richard seem calm, composed, rational.

Even so, I had to admit the cuts were minimal. They didn't need to do much. Richard got under my skin, and it came through. There was nothing in there I hadn't said. Yes, they'd cut it up. Yes, they'd made it seem like I responded to things in ways I didn't. But hadn't I done the same with my article? Hadn't I selected what worked best for me?

The post had text accompanying it.

This is an unedited recording of the two interviews I had with a reporter for the student paper, Tess Azar. She has misrepresented one of those interviews in a recent article to make me appear as I am not. I can only assume she is planning to do the same with the second interview. Instead of sinking to her level, I have chosen to post the unaltered recordings of these interviews. I ask that you listen to these recordings with an open mind. Compare what Ms. Azar wrote in her slanderous article to the recordings. Then make up your mind on me, her, and her paper.

And following the release of the recording and a transcript, another post.

That concludes the full, unaltered recording of our two interviews. I don't know why Ms. Azar chose to manipulate my words as she did. I don't know why she decided to twist them to make me out to be something I'm not. But this is what they do, and I cannot say I am surprised.

I would like to note that, despite Ms. Azar's assurance, I wasn't informed of the piece's content before it was published. When I was approached to confirm quotations, I pushed back but was told they would run the piece as is. I must wonder what this means for the veracity of her other work. She isn't concerned with the truth, and I find myself thinking of the other lives she's ruined, and I wonder, what lies did she tell then? What was the truth in those stories?

I felt sick. My hand shook, bile rose in my throat, the room swam. I felt my knees buckle, and just as I was about to collapse, Rose rested her hand on my shoulder. "I'll get a lawyer. I know some good ones. Some specialize in this kind of thing. And you should print a comment on this. Say that the recording was edited, manipulated. Say this is a lie."

"We have lawyers too," Samir said, all action. "I'll get on the phone with them now."

"It won't matter," I said. "It's out there. It's online. It'll never go away. People are listening to it, people are reading it. I'm a public figure, this will spread. This is a stain that won't wash out."

"Yeah, but we'll fight back just as hard. We won't let this stand. We won't let them win."

"It doesn't matter. We'll have to release the full recordings. They aren't that, but they aren't what I wrote either."

"Your piece is a fair representation of the interview and events. I know because I checked it myself. I'll stand by that piece—"

"Can't you see? Don't you see this is over? So, what if we're right and they're wrong? That doesn't matter. Not anymore. He has this. They planned this whole thing. They crafted every answer. They baited me. They set me up, and I fell into their trap. Now they're going to coast off my status. They'll destroy me and catapult themselves into fame. And it's all my fault. I was too stupid to see it."

Silence returned to the room. A chair squeaked as someone leaned back. Gum was chewed. Phones were checked.

It was Kim who broke the tension. "She can't even write the second article now."

She was right. They'd published that transcript almost unaltered. He was proud of all the madness I thought he'd want to avoid, the conspiracies and crazed ramblings. He wanted his supporters to hear that. He'd planned on that getting released.

I collapsed into a chair and dropped my head between my legs, trying to catch my breath. I felt the air fill my lungs, focused on the rise and fall of my chest.

After a minute, I scanned the room. They all looked away when I came to them. They found the ground or the window, afraid their eyes would reveal them. I hesitated before moving to Rose, knowing I couldn't accept her rejection. But she didn't break. She met my stare, welcomed it.

She crossed the room and knelt between my legs, placing her hands on my thighs. "There's a way out of this. You can't see it right now, but it's there. We can spin this. We post a statement saying this is contested. Then we get a lawyer and force them to pull the altered recording."

"It won't matter. It's like porn. It's a hydra. You can't remove anything from the internet."

"That's true, but that won't be what this is about. This is about two sides. Both will claim victory. Sure, their people will hate you, but they already do. They always will. But the rest of us, the sane world, will see them for what they are."

"He'll still become famous off this. I bet he's already booked on—"

"I'm sure he is, but he was always going to get there. We both know that. There's always someone like him. They're out there. And yes, this will help him, but in the end, it'll help you too. Write the other article. Tear him to pieces. If there isn't enough left in this interview for an article, go to that rally. Hound him. Make sure your quotes are bulletproof and bury him with his own words."

She lifted my chin and forced me to meet her eyes. She leaned in, and I felt her warm breath on my ear. "This will be okay."

And just like that, it was.

21

We went to a bar that night. It wasn't one of the neon college bars that populated the town adjacent to campus. It wasn't even the dive bar on the edge of town where the students who were too cool for the college bars congregated. It was a different bar. A bar a world apart.

It was the next town over. It was clean and well lit.

Or at least I think it was.

I can't say I remember much of the night. What little I do remember are fragments scattered about with no discernable thread. There's a flash where I knock over a drink. Another where I breathe in urine but can't see where I am or what I'm doing. I share a cigarette with a stranger. I yell with all my might at someone but have no recollection of what they'd done or who they were.

I think the couple from the restaurant was there. I think they sat near me and listened to everything I said. But I'd begun to see them everywhere. They invaded my dreams, occupied my fantasies. They were skiing with Rose and me in the glorious future I'd planned for us. They asked me questions at the presser for the book I'd publish. They lived in me now. I'd grown accustomed to them, to their ongoing, unrelenting surveillance.

I have only one clear, unbroken memory from that night. It's brief but vivid, seared into me.

There was a woman at the bar, a student. Short, with dark brown hair let down. She swayed and danced. Drinks were poured but not paid for. She wore a low-cut shirt and a tight skirt.

She was loud, and people noticed. Conversations around her stopped. People gave her dirty looks. She knew but refused to acknowledge the jeers. She was in it. She was forcing out everything in her life, focusing on that night, that drink, that moment.

I recognized her. The small dark eyes, the way she combed her hair straight back and froze it in place with product. Even the way her hips rotated. The way she moved not with but against the music. I'd seen her before. I couldn't place her, but I knew her.

And I knew I didn't like her.

I couldn't say what it was I didn't like. Maybe her outfit, maybe her volume, maybe her general sense. It didn't matter what the reason was. I was drunk, and I knew, without considering why, I didn't like this woman.

But I couldn't look away from her. No one could. The whole bar had stopped to observe, to take in the spectacle. Everyone was whispering and pointing. Everyone was happy to pause their lives and judge this woman.

At a table nearby sat three men, maybe students, maybe locals. They were dressed like teenagers, but that doesn't mean anything. Not anymore. As a society, we're a few generations into men refusing to grow up. Men in their fifties in baseball caps and graphic tees and sneakers. Adults parading as children.

Where most of the bar whispered their judgments of this woman, this table was loud. They were shouting at her. Gesticulating, waving her toward them. For reasons that would soon become clear, they believed they had a chance with her.

She ignored them. Ignored their taunts, their lewd gestures, their brazen invitations. But that didn't deter the men in the slightest.

The table next to them stood up, abandoning prime real estate to extricate themselves from the situation. No one in the bar moved to take the table. We all just watched and allowed this to happen, complicit in our fascinated indifference.

The woman continued to sway and drink. She allowed a few men and the bartender to flirt with her. She didn't flirt back. She stayed in the moment and tried to ignore the table.

But they wouldn't be ignored.

"Come on over here, hon," one of them said. "I've got something hard you can sit on. I know you like that." He cackled and knocked into one of his friends.

I wondered what they'd have done if she'd gone to their table. If she walked over to them and offered herself up. I imagined they'd self-destruct.

"That's right," another said. "We all know what you like."

"Let's get out of here," the third said. "We can go make another video."

And just like that, I knew. I knew why I recognized her. I knew where I'd seen her. I knew why her hips, of all things, were familiar.

And I knew why I judged her.

She hadn't agreed to an interview, but I'd watched her video. I hadn't wanted to. I'd struggled with it. Gone back and forth. In the end, though, I decided it was news, and I'd be remiss in writing about it without having watched at least one. At random, I'd picked hers.

I couldn't finish the video. It made me nauseous, and it was clear there was no journalistic merit to watching it. I closed out of it and cleared my history, but it didn't go away. The images were there. Inescapable. Permanent.

"I feel kind of bad for her," a woman at the table next to us said to her friend.

"Don't," her friend answered. "That's what she gets. Don't go around making sex tapes if you don't want that kind of attention."

"You're right," the other agreed.

I should've said something. I should've corrected them, pointed out that she hadn't "made a sex tape." One had been made of her without her consent. I should've asked if they'd ever made a video, sent a picture, put something personal out into the world they could never get back. I should've asked if they'd ever trusted the wrong person.

But I didn't say anything. Instead, I turned and watched the woman storm off, saw the men laugh and order another round, saw the bar return to normal.

Then I finished my drink, and another appeared before me. That's the last thing I remember.

22

The next day, I woke up in Rose's bathtub, naked aside from my socks and a hat I'd never seen before. There was dried vomit streaked across the tile wall and in the drain. I was sure I'd peed myself.

Next to me, on the floor, was a vape pen, a glass of water, a bottle of Gatorade, Tylenol, and a note.

> *Hey Tess, I had to go out. Stay as long as you want. Feel free to move to the bed once you're sure you're settled.*
>
>

Rose

>
>

P.S. In case you were worried, you didn't do anything too bad, we're good.

I was mortified and still drunk, but I managed to get to the bed. That's where she found me when she got home, asleep in her bed, trying to hide from the world. She woke me up by pulling on my toes, and even in my hungover state, I fell just a bit further in love with her.

I had her tell me everything, every humiliating detail. Most aren't worth noting. Just your basics—not knowing how to use a toilet, shouting at a bartender, things like that. It would've been just a standard, shame-filled blackout if not for one thing. Apparently, in my drunken state, I'd told Rose that I loved her.

I recoiled into her pillow and pulled the sheets over my head when she told me. I wished I could go further. I wanted to dive into the mattress and burrow my way out of the room.

Or a part of me did.

The rest of me, perhaps the larger part, wanted to stay there. Wanted to hear her response. Believed, somewhere deep down, that she felt the same. That I shouldn't be humiliated by this rushed proclamation. That it was, in fact, the truth.

I didn't feel embarrassed about expressing the emotion. I

didn't feel that it was too strong a statement. I can't say I know for sure what love is, but I know what I felt for her approximated it. I know that I'd never felt that way before. And in the end, isn't that what love is? Isn't it a sliding scale? A new height you've never reached before that you ascribe the clichéd yet perfect term "love" to.

I clutched the sheets tight above my head and held my breath, bracing for her response. She pulled on the sheets and laughed. It wasn't a mocking laugh, it was playful, intoxicating.

"Come out, Tess." She punched me on the shoulder.

But I didn't surface. I held fast. I wouldn't emerge for air until I knew. Until it was settled.

I felt the sheets twist and pull but just held tighter. Then, at my feet, she appeared. She crawled up close, her warm breath tapping against my face.

"What's the matter?" She pulled out the last word till it stretched around me. I said nothing and buried my face in the pillow to hide my smile. "What?" she said. "You don't feel that way? Just the booze talking?"

I both hated and loved this. It was just the right amount of torment. It was nothing I didn't deserve. I was sure I'd given her hell the night before, and some retaliatory teasing was warranted. And she wouldn't be doing it if she was going to end things. She wouldn't be there, under the covers with me, if she was about to destroy me.

"All right, fine," she said. "I'll say it, but you have to look at me." I lowered the pillow to reveal one eye and half of my smile. My arms and legs were numb, my chest pounded. "I love you," she said and kissed my sweaty forehead.

My world exploded into color, shattering it into shards and fragments and reforming around her.

"I love you too," I said, just above a whisper.

I know what you're thinking.

I know it's fast.

I know you're saying that we were kids who didn't know anything about love. But that's wrong; love doesn't work that way. You can't time it. There's no age restriction. It just comes on you in a flash and changes everything.

After we made love, we lay in bed, my head resting against her firm, bruised stomach, feeling her breath rise and fall.

She sat up after an eternity of comfortable, content silence. "You know it's not fair."

"What's not?"

"The way you did that. You got to blurt it out drunk, no nerves, no terrified anticipation. Then I had to walk around all day, trying to write, talking to Sylvia, editing Jack's novel, knowing I needed to say it. Not knowing how you'd respond. A bundle of nerves. It was a complete reversal."

"Excuse me? I had to live with the horror of having an embarrassing drunken night where I blurted out that I loved you."

"But you didn't know you said it. I had to tell you. You lived with that embarrassment for like a minute."

I opened my mouth to counter but then closed it. I had nothing to say. She was right. Telling someone you love them takes courage. You leap into the great unknown, hoping to catch a breeze and fly but knowing you might not. You might fall and hit the ground. I'd avoided that. I leapt while drunk and awoke to find myself flying.

"You're right," I said and burst out laughing.

At first, she feigned offense but couldn't keep it up. She caught the laugh, and we both lay there, two fools in love, forgetting the world outside us.

"I'm sorry," I said after catching my breath. "You're right. It wasn't fair."

"No, it wasn't." She lunged at me and bit my shoulder, hard, almost breaking the skin. "But you're going to make it up to me."

"Oh, I am?" I fought back, pinning her to the bed and staring down into those peerless eyes.

"You are."

"And how am I going to do that?"

"Sylvia wants to meet you."

23

Sylvia Lobo. Pulitzer Prize–winning novelist, voice of a generation, thought leader, literal god on campus, wanted to meet me. She wanted to meet me. It wasn't that Rose wanted her to meet me. It wasn't that I wanted to meet her. Sylvia Lobo wanted to meet me.

A ball formed in my esophagus. "She wants to meet me?" Rose was up, half-dressed, searching for something, though even she didn't know what it was. "Sylvia wants to meet me?"

"Yes." Rose half turned to me, ready to burst.

"What for?" Fear crept into my thoughts. This, too, was a test. The biggest one yet. And unlike the painting or my reading list, I wasn't sure I could pass this one.

"She's interested in you." She walked out of the room, taking my breath with her. She returned a minute later with glasses of water and a bottle of whiskey. "In case you need a pick me up."

"I think I'm all right with the water." She shrugged and put the bottle down. "Interested in me?"

"Yes, interested." I was on her string, and she liked it that way. She liked giving it a tug and watching me squirm.

"Rose, come on, what's this about?"

"Okay, okay, well, she's read your articles. Not all of them, but the one on Jason and the one on Richard. She likes your writing. She compared you to Joan Didion."

This was meant to be high praise but did little for me, my mind too occupied to process the compliment.

She sat on the edge of the bed. It caved in toward her, and I was pulled down. "She wanted to meet you before this whole thing but thought she should hold off given the article about Jack. By the way, is that still on?"

"Yeah, or I don't know, maybe."

"Either way, after everything that went down with Richard

and the audio release, she decided there was no point in waiting. She wants to help if she can but also wants to meet you. She thinks you have a future."

There it was. She wanted to add me to her stable. I'd heard of this. She was a collector. She'd hear about an interesting prospect on campus and summon them. She'd have them to dinner and decide if they were worthy. Aside from her writers, who littered award shortlists and university staffs, she had two senators, one governor, five acclaimed film directors, and three Fortune 500 CEOs. I'm sure there were more, but these were the ones I knew of. And now she was adding me. Or, at the very least, entertaining the idea of adding me.

"Even after." I pulled my knees to my chest and held myself. I was fishing. I wanted her to assure me, to cast away my fears.

She obliged, reaching out to hold her warm palm against my cheek. "How many times do I have to tell you? This isn't the end for you. This isn't even bad. This is good."

"I just don't see—"

"No one will care in the long run. It'll increase your exposure. It'll make you more famous and, in the end, all people will remember is that you went toe to toe with him and didn't blink. That'll help you."

I was starting to think she was right. It didn't feel like it was a good thing, it felt like my world had collapsed. But she was so confident, so assured. And she was Rose, so I believed her.

24

We took a shower and ordered lunch. She gave me clothes to wear while we ate. Then we both did a bit of work, but we couldn't concentrate, and before long, we were discussing the dinner.

"I don't know." We had less than an hour before we had to leave, and I was pacing. "Etiquette, I guess. Like which fork to use or how to eat my soup. I don't know."

"She's not the queen."

"Isn't she, though?"

"Okay, okay, maybe I've built her up a bit. She's just a person. We'll sit down and eat and talk and then maybe have a few drinks and talk some more. Nothing crazy. She just wants to get to know you and see if she can help."

She walked to the window and opened it a crack, letting the cold air in and the stress out.

"There is one thing." She breathed in and looked me over. "I don't think you can wear anything you have here."

She was right. Of course, she was right. All I had with me were jeans and a T-shirt that I'd destroyed the night before.

I tried to think of what I had at my dorm that would suffice. Some dresses I hated, some business casual tops that would be all wrong. I had nothing. I didn't own a single item that would allow me to walk into Sylvia's home and feel anything other than shame.

And, from the look on Rose's face, she knew it. "I don't want to…you don't have to wear it, but I have an idea."

She walked to the bedroom and returned with a dress in dry-cleaner's plastic. She uncovered it and hung it in front of me. It was a dark red, almost black, with subtle lace dancing along it. I crossed the room and paused, scared to touch it.

"Who?" I stopped, afraid of the answer. "Where did you…"

"It was mine. It doesn't fit me, but I think it's about right for you."

I was four inches shorter than her and fuller. There was no way a dress she bought for herself would fit me. But I decided not to question it. It was better to accept it—wear the dress and live the life that was unfurling before me. Focus on the future and ignore the past.

I put the dress on. It couldn't have fit better if it'd been tailored.

I turned away from the mirror and looked at Rose, she was dressed in a pale blue button-down and gray pants. She still looked a vision, but a subtle one. I could tell that tonight I would be the one to stand out. Just this once, if heads turned, they would be doing so for me.

25

Sylvia's house was just off campus. It had once belonged to the university and, legend has it, was gifted to her during a tense contract negotiation. It's said it'll revert to university after she dies. But this, like so much of Sylvia, is shrouded in mystery.

The house is old, turn of the century, with ivy growing up to the iron-crossed second-floor windows. It looks like a castle, a small one but a castle, nonetheless. There's even a tower stretching out from the southwest corner. The door is heavy, a cherry wood that closes out the world when it shuts behind you.

Inside, a transformation takes place. The historic exterior disappears into a cold, modern interior. Gray paint, gray couch, an exposed brick accent wall, plants, sharp angles, recessed lighting, floating shelves, the only things missing were the large glass windows, which of course, she could not create.

There was a single remnant of the former interior, a staircase set off to the left of the door. It was untouched by Sylvia's renovations, the last survivor. It was dark wood, the spokes hand-carved spirals, each baluster a miniature globe, the continents etched into them with painstaking precision.

A short, handsome man helped me out of my coat. He was young, a student, and his eyes shone full of enthusiastic rapture. He wore pressed black pants, shined shoes, a black tie, and a black vest over a crisp white shirt. He said nothing.

Another student, it was clear even then that they were from her workshop, appeared out of the ether. She was dressed the same. She was tall where he was short, and her teeth glowed in a fixed, troubling smile. It didn't feel forced like the one all service people give off. It was deeper than that, a smile sowed into her brain. She, too, was silent.

I took the champagne she offered, unable to process what was happening.

Without looking at either of the students, Rose tossed her coat and a tote bag she'd brought with her to the young man and took a glass of champagne, moving past them without breaking stride.

"Thank you," I said, apologizing for being there. "Thank you both."

They both smiled, nodded, and disappeared before returning a few minutes later with trays of exquisite hors d'oeuvres, the contents of which I couldn't even guess at.

Rose strolled around the living room, inspecting books and selecting one, which she brought over to the couch.

I eyed the book. "Are we going to be a while?"

"Oh no…or maybe. Hard to say. If she's writing, it could be a bit."

I felt where my pockets would typically have been, hoping to take refuge in my phone, but it was in my coat. Well, not my coat, Rose's coat that she'd lent me. A coat that was worth more than anything I owned. "Should I go get my phone? If we're going to be a while."

"No. Get a book. No phones."

No phones? I looked around. No television, no charging cables, no cords of any kind. I felt my wrist start to tremble.

I walked to the wall of bookcases and reached for a book I'd read. Short stories. Something I could drift in and out of. Something I already knew.

I turned to head back to the seating area, but Rose was staring at me, horrified. She shook her head.

"What?"

"No, not that one." She looked around in a panic, trying to ensure no one had noticed. "Pick something else."

I didn't know if I wanted to laugh or cry, but this wasn't the time or place for either. This was a strange land, and I didn't know the rules, but they were strict and needed to be obeyed.

I could feel Rose's panic enter me, and all the confidence the dress had given me evaporated. I returned the book, ensuring its spine matched the others, hoping it wouldn't be noticed. I picked another at random, showed her the cover, and hoped it would suffice. She nodded and again glanced around the room.

I went to sit next to her but was met by another vigorous head shake. She pointed to a chair on the other side of the room.

Was she embarrassed by me? Who did Sylvia think I was? Did she know about our relationship? Or was Rose's rejection about something deeper?

I didn't have time to spiral any further. The two students entered and cleared their throats before announcing in unison. "May we introduce the lady of the manor, Ms. Sylvia Lobo."

She swept in behind them, smiled, pretended to be embarrassed, and waved at them. "I told you not to do that," she lied. They hadn't come up with that on their own. Maybe she'd presented it as a joke, maybe it'd been passed down from student to student, but that entrance was what she wanted. It was required.

I longed for a pen and paper to take down my customary description of Sylvia. Her voice was even and refined, a bit deeper than I'd expected. She had vibrant hair. It was gray, not white, not graying, but a shock of beautiful, defiant gray hair. Her face was still young and made to look younger by the hair. It was the opposite of what you'd think, the gray brought into sharp relief how young the rest of her features were. She was tall, towering a few inches above the world, inspecting and critiquing it. She carried her stature well. It was all in her limbs—long, taut legs and arms. Her eyes were small, blue, almost transparent. They hunted across the room. She wore tight, florescent blue pants and a white T-shirt with a flowing black cape that glided behind her. The outfit hung somewhere between formal and casual but didn't belong to either classification.

She greeted Rose first, pulling her up from the couch. They

kissed on both cheeks and then pulled back to inspect each other. It was as if they hadn't seen each other in months though I knew they'd been together earlier that day.

I had stood as she entered and now regretted it. Rose seemed so calm, so comfortable sitting down, waiting for Sylvia to come to her. I became hyperconscious of how formal my dress seemed in comparison to their outfits. I wanted to leave. I wanted to throw the book on the chair and rush for the door. This was all too much. I couldn't handle it. I wasn't prepared. I wasn't worthy.

And then their hands separated, and Sylvia turned to me. She stood back for a minute, taking me in. I felt naked. I felt like a child. I felt my cheeks grow red and a cold sweat break out on my lower back. I shifted my weight from one leg to the other and back. I held the book in front of me and then behind me. I looked foolish and knew it.

"My, my." She smiled, and it unsettled me, it seemed to quit halfway up her face, never quite reaching her eyes. "Aren't you an absolute dream? Rose, this one's a keeper."

So, she knew. At least there was that. At least my position in Rose's life was real. For now.

Sylvia reached out, the bracelets that engulfed her forearms singing as she did. She held my hands and kissed my cheeks. The gesture reminded me of home, of my dad's mom and the smell of kibbeh and tabbouleh, and the warmth of her hugs. "Are you hungry? We can eat right away or have a drink first?"

"A drink," Rose said.

Her voice startled me. I hadn't realized till now, but it had changed the more time we'd spent together. It had grown softer and stretched itself out. But now her clipped, polished voice was back. A clear echo of Sylvia.

Sylvia turned and raised her hand, summoning the two students. A stiff hand, a pirouette, a fold. Elegant, practiced simplicity. It was the same way Rose had summoned me at our first meeting. A carbon copy down to the same compact pressed smile.

I looked over at Rose, but she was gone, staring at Sylvia, noting her every movement. Storing it away for later use.

"Martinis?" Sylvia said. "We do Gibsons here."

There was no expected response. This was the way to drink a martini, and a martini was the way to drink alcohol. They were already being mixed and poured, and one was in my hand before I had time to think. I didn't even notice which of the students brought it.

"Aren't they doing a wonderful job?" Sylvia said. "Two of my freshmen. Excellent talents. They both have stories under serious consideration at important publications."

I looked around, wanting to congratulate them, but they'd already vanished.

Sylvia was next to me now, she leaned in but didn't lower her voice. "I don't make them do this. I know how it looks, but they volunteer. They fight over it. Life experience, I suppose. This could become a story or poem, or chapter in a novel. You never know where inspiration might strike, isn't that right, Rose?"

"Quite right."

"I think you worked one of my parties once, didn't you?"

"Yes, more than one. My first was your birthday party, it was a wonderful time. For us servers too. I worked a few others that year. I remember I wanted to work one my sophomore year, a book launch, but you said no. Had to give the freshmen a chance."

Sylvia laughed with staged remembrance. She reached out a hand and touched Rose on the arm. "For something like this, just a dinner between friends, I don't even need them, but it's become a whole thing. A rite of passage."

"Quite right." Rose leaned on the consonants like she was hammering in a stake. "I remember being so excited at the prospect. You must keep it going. I don't care what anyone says. We all did it, and we all loved it."

I saw an opening. I needed to remind them I was there. Needed to shift the conversation to a footing where I would be comfortable. "Did Jack ever work one?"

"Is this on the record?" Sylvia took a step away from me and donned a severe face before laughing. "You should see your face. We must be able to take a joke, even as a journalist."

I caught Rose's disapproving gaze out of the corner of my eye.

"Though I can't blame you for being serious after the past few days you've had," Sylvia said. "Poor thing. But you know what they say, 'Nolite te bastardes carborundorum.' Don't let the bastards grind you down. There will always be those kinds of people. It comes with the territory, even more so as a woman. It's just how the world is."

She patted my arm and then sat in one of the chairs before motioning us to return to our seats. No one spoke for a minute, and we all took a sip of our drink. I remember it tasting sweet for some reason, though I doubt that's right.

I wanted to ask about Jack. I felt rejuvenated at having just broached the topic. I remembered who I was, remembered how I'd gotten there, remembered that I belonged. But something held me back. Maybe the look Rose had given me. Maybe Sylvia's perceived sympathy. Maybe just the house and the setting and the woman.

Sylvia took a long drink from her martini and then held the empty glass. The female student scampered out from some invisible hiding place to refill it. I saw the desperation and fear in her eyes. Sylvia didn't so much as turn her head.

They ignored me and discussed a scandal on campus surrounding a professor whose heroin habit had become a problem.

"He's done it for years," Sylvia said. "I assumed he had it under control. It was just a quirk."

"I know, everyone knew," Rose said.

"But I suppose that's the way of the world. You have control until you don't…pathetic, though. Men." She rolled her eyes and let out a caustic laugh. "But we have more pressing issues to discuss." Then, to the invisible students. "Take these to the table. We'll eat now."

26

We walked from the living room down a long, narrow hallway, a coiled ball of anxiety and desire building inside of me with every step.

The hallway walls were covered with photos—Sylvia with famous people and their fake, practiced smiles. Rose stalked behind me, taking them in, pausing to admire specific ones. It was as if she were picking out the place where her photo would eventually reside. I caught myself wondering if I, too, might one day make it.

The dining room was more in line with the house than Sylvia's interior design choices. It was all dark wood, old world. You could still smell the smoke from days long gone, you could taste the history.

The room was lined with glass-cased cabinets containing finery that I doubted had ever been used. One cabinet didn't house any dishes or crystal, it was full of books on stands, her books.

Sylvia swept her arm along the massive table. "Please, sit."

We obeyed. Rose, sitting to her right, me to her left. I noticed then that Rose's posture was another imitation of Sylvia—stiff and erect, chest raised to the ceiling. It was odd to me as I'd attributed it to Rose, a defining characteristic that I now saw was stolen. I wondered what else she'd stolen. I wondered how much of each of us was truly original.

I looked down and realized I was hunched and corrected myself, not quite able to reach their level of practiced rigor but trying.

Rose and Sylvia took on most of the conversation during dinner. I would nod or add a quick agreement, but no one was interested in my opinions on the topics they were discussing—the writers in the workshop, Sylvia's past pupils, trends in contemporary literature. At one point, they drifted toward a film I'd seen, but when I tried to interject, I was met with confused stares.

I focused on the food. It was easy to get lost in that meal.

First, a winter salad with kale, endive, and spinach dressed with orange and lemon that cut through the bitter greens. Second, an odd choice given the still crisp spring weather, a chilled tomato gazpacho filled with cucumbers and peppers and tasting, for some reason, of the sea. Then the main course, honey-glazed duck with a beetroot and mint sauce, served with potatoes fried in duck fat and salted cucumbers. Finally, there was a light key lime pie with fresh whipped cream and strong black coffee to finish. It's one of the best meals of my life. Simple and to the point, everything was prepared to perfection by a chef we never saw and never heard mention of. The credit for the meal belonged to Sylvia and Sylvia alone.

It wasn't until the dessert dishes had been cleared that I was brought back into the conversation. Sylvia nodded to Rose and turned her long, elegant frame to me. "So, what are you going to do?"

I opened my mouth, but it felt coated in sand. I swallowed hard but got only dry air. I took a drink, and it evaporated before it touched my throat. I took another and another, only managing to form words after finishing my glass. "About what?"

She smiled and glanced toward Rose. It was an unambiguous look. A look asking, *Are you sure about this one?*

"About the fascists." She studied her nails at a distance.

"Well, I, uh." I felt like a kid at the grown-ups' table who was asked a question they'd never be able to answer for the amusement of the adults.

"The paper has put up a letter on their site. I helped them craft it," Rose said, both rescuing me and showing off. "It says that Richard's version of the recording was doctored."

"Was it doctored?" Sylvia said. At first, she directed the question to Rose, but as it hung in the air, she turned back to me, carrying it with her. "How doctored was it?"

"Parts were," I said. "Parts weren't. The first interview didn't go well, but it wasn't what they posted. The second one is… more accurate."

"Hmmmm." Sylvia drummed her long fingers against her lips. "Not good. Not good. Very clever of them."

"Yeah."

"They've got you in a bind."

"Yeah."

"Because if you release the full recording, much of what they say will be confirmed, including the entire second interview, which is, in theory, the more damning for them. Though I doubt they see it that way. Did he say other crazy stuff in the first interview that they cut?"

"There's some crazy in it, but nothing worse than what he said in the second one. They didn't clean those things out. Like you said, they're not embarrassed by the crazy."

"Very clever. Ingenious even. Anything you say now just takes attention off the outlandish things he said, dilutes them. And his supporters, current and future, still get to hear those things and revel in them. Very well played by them, and Rose said you didn't…sorry, but Rose was worried about you after the first interview, and she asked for my advice."

I felt anger and jealousy course through me, but I kept my face even. "That's fine. I assumed she was consulting with you. I was hoping she was."

"Good, that's good. Well, what was I saying? Oh yes, Rose mentioned your first interview, the more doctored of the two, wasn't ideal? You were caught off guard, ambushed."

"Yeah, I'd say that's accurate."

"So, as for releasing the full version of that interview, I guess you'd prefer not to?"

"That's correct."

"Hmmmm." Again, her fingers rumbled against her lips, turning her humming staccato. "Well, what options are left to you?"

And, in that moment, as she uttered that sentence, I saw

it. It unfurled before me as if she'd planted it there or as if merely being in her presence had allowed me to see clearly. I hadn't even glimpsed it before, but sitting at that table, her stare clawing its way under my skin, I saw it all. "Well, there is something."

"Go on." She was a professor now leading her pupil forward.

"Use a—what's it called?—an arbitrator. An independent one. External to the university, so they can't claim any liberal education bias. Maybe someone from the business sector. A corporate lawyer."

"They'll claim liberal bias either way, so no need to go overboard." She wasn't condemning my idea, just adding texture.

"That's true." I felt the warmth of this brilliant woman. I understood why Rose was like she was around her. I had drunk from the well and wanted more. "Still, it's best if it's outside the university."

"Yes, but—" Rose said.

"Keep going, Tess." Sylvia reached out her long, thin arm to pat my hand.

"I'll insist the arbitrator release a simple statement after they come to a conclusion." My posture now forward and erect, my chest pointed toward the ceiling. The words poured forth from somewhere deep inside of me. Confident, assured. "Richard will have to agree because he won't want some lawyer editorializing. The risk is too high for him. His views are too fringe. He'll want to reject the whole arbitration, but that would make it look like he had something to hide. And we'd just go ahead with it anyway."

"Very clever, go on."

"So, we have them review the recordings and release a simple statement, which will confirm that they were doctored. And per our agreement, they won't be able to say how doctored. Then, even if Richard decides to release the originals, it won't matter because he'll have lost credibility with the mainstream media."

"Which he won't care about."

"No, but so what? His people will back him, but I regain my reputation."

"Then do you release the recording?" Rose said, trying to catch up.

Sylvia waved her hand without turning. "No, of course not. How would that help us?"

And there it was. Not the dismissal, which I'll admit felt good, but the "us." She was with me now. I was in her stable, I was protected, I was one of them. It felt like a warm, heavy blanket had been draped across my shoulders. "I'll say I want to move on to other things."

"Well." Sylvia pulled out the word, making me doubt myself. "You'll write another article. A big one. A national publication, I'd think. With quotes from the interviews, verifiable quotes, and with the violence, and a first-hand account of his rally. The one tonight. The one you're going to go to."

I swallowed hard and began to sweat, just picturing myself walking through that crowd, a sea of furious men staring hate at me. It was a terrifying thought.

"And then," she said, "all anyone will talk about will be your article and the violence and the fascism. And yes, his side will claim he was railroaded, and he'll yell fake news and assert he didn't lie. But who cares? That's their narrative, and you have yours."

"Which is the truth." Rose took a long drink. She'd switched from coffee to whiskey.

"Yes and no. It'll be our truth. They can have theirs." Sylvia clapped her hands together, smiled, and rolled back in her chair. "Now drink up, Tess, I think you might need something stronger for what's coming."

She snapped her fingers, and the male student appeared to pour me a glass. No one looked at him. No one acknowledged him. Not even me.

"Now, while you drink that," Sylvia said, "I'll tell you a story."

27

I wasn't much of a drinker and had always found whiskey painful, but that one wasn't. It was smooth and smoky and breathed life into me.

"Have you ever taken ancient epics with Dr. Weidel?" Sylvia said as I drank in that smoky life.

"No, should I?"

"One of the top experts on *The Iliad* in the world. Most would say he's the best, which is quite the distinction with a work like that."

"Yeah, that's amazing."

She took a deep breath. "I've taken a real shine to you, and I'd never do this otherwise, but…well, the word *amazing*, you might want to eliminate it from your vocabulary. It's nothing against you, and I don't judge you for using it, but the world might."

"Thank you, I will." I blushed, and my appreciation was genuine. "Please let me know if there are any other words or phrases I should eliminate."

She smiled and patted my hand.

Rose finished another drink. I'd lost count. She snapped her fingers for Paul to refill her glass. Sylvia noticed but said nothing.

"Where was I? Oh, right, Dr. Weidel. Dr. Weidel studies *The Iliad* and the Trojan War. He's read, analyzed, and written about every ancient text that touches that war. He can tell you the similarities and differences between accounts. He can theorize when the things were written and how far back the oral telling stretched before that. When a new piece is uncovered that people think might have a connection to the Trojan War, their first call is Dr. Weidel. He's both a historian and a literary scholar. At times an archeologist. At times, a cartographer. A detective and an explorer. He's been to Greece, Turkey, Macedonia, Bulgaria, Cyprus, Syria." She paused and turned to me. "Where are you from, by the way? Your people, that is."

"I, uh." That question again. How many times have I heard that question in my life? But I chose not to linger on it. I was immersed, completely engulfed in the charm and spectacle of a woman like Sylvia. "My father's from Lebanon."

"Lebanon, good. That's very good. I'm always happy to help a person of, well, someone from a diverse background." She paused to let her liberality sink in. "I believe Weidel's been to Lebanon. He's been all over, searching for evidence and potential locations. He's hunted for remains and burial sites. He's been to the ends of the Earth investigating alleged relics—the shield of Achilles, Odysseus's dagger, Agamemnon's crown, Hector's sword, Paris's bow. All were found to be forgeries. All left him disheartened, but none could sap his spirit, his belief that out there, somewhere, evidence exists confirming the tale."

She lingered and took a delicate sip. Then dabbed the sides of her mouth with her napkin and stared straight ahead, waiting for some imperceptible cue to continue. "Now, if he heard me call it a tale just then, he'd explode. Not that he believes all of it. He understands that parts are a stretch. How could he not? Gods interfering in the battles and all that. But he believes, without a shadow of a doubt, that the Trojan War occurred and that most of the key actors and events detailed in *The Iliad* happened. He believes there was a man named Achilles. He believes there was a Trojan Horse. He believes the story was passed down from one keeper to the next in an unbroken line for centuries before Homer transcribed it. He believes this more than he believes anything."

In the next room, metal bowls fell and cried out. Sylvia looked to the ceiling, breathing in her exasperation. There were frantic whispers from the kitchen and then silence.

"About ten years ago, I was at a party with Dr. Weidel. It was the first party he'd attended since his divorce. See, he'd been married twenty-three years. His wife was a beautiful woman.

Short and alluring with these magnificent blond curls that danced on her shoulders with her every movement. She was the type of woman who stuck to you. You'd be in the grocery store or staring off into the distance, and she'd pop into your head and stay there, haunting your unfocused moments for days.

"Dr. Weidel wasn't the type of man who could possess a woman like this. There are people capable of holding on to that kind of beauty, that kind of magic, but he wasn't one of them. He was handsome enough but lacked the magnetism, the drive to pull her in and secure her to him. I can't blame either of them for what happened. She fell for him, but it wasn't enough. That's not her fault. She tried, it just wouldn't hold. The world called to her, and she couldn't ignore it forever. As for him, what was he to do? He loved her. She was all he'd ever wanted, more even. He was out of his depth, and everyone knew it.

"So, instead of monogamy or divorce, they came to an unspoken arrangement. She took lovers, and he never asked and refused to see. It was obvious. We all knew. We all saw. There were students, his students often, researchers, professors, administrators, gardeners, and once, for a few months, even a certain novelist.

"Mrs. Weidel didn't work to hide these affairs. They were in the open. And Dr. Weidel accepted them. He never spoke of them, never acknowledged them. He'd chosen to ignore and preserve the marriage. He'd chosen to believe the myth."

I looked down and saw that the plates were gone though I hadn't even noticed when the students entered to take them away.

"This went on for years until one night, they attended a party. She was there with her new lover, and they were all over each other. She'd grown more brazen as the years had gone by, and this was a particularly visceral display. The rest of us were doing our best to ignore them. We were talking about campus politics or books or whatever we could. And Dr. Weidel was stoic, talking about this burial site in Amyclae that he thought might house the remains of Agamemnon. And as he was going on about this, his wife walked in and heard. She began to cackle. She was loud and drunk and swayed with her laughter. She proclaimed to everyone at the party that he wouldn't find anything there. That this quest, like all the others, was futile. That he'd never discover anything, and he'd go to his grave grasping at the past, never sure what was fact and what was fiction."

Rose finished her drink, and as a student came to fill it, Sylvia raised her hand and shook a finger. "No, she needs to accompany Tess to the rally. We can't have her unable to walk. Not again."

Rose opened her mouth to protest but stopped.

"So." Sylvia never so much as glanced at Rose. "Mrs. Weidel was mocking his quest. She started telling stories, private ones, of times when he was sure he'd found something. When he'd left full of hope and confidence and returned broken, crying to her about his failure. And we all sat in wrapped, tense, horrified silence. Listening. Unable to look away.

"And Dr. Weidel said nothing. He just stared at his hands. And, when she finished and let out another hateful cackle, he stood up and left. He didn't speak to her. He didn't speak to the room. He just left. He went to his office and slept there. In the morning, Mrs. Weidel woke up with a hangover, a sense of regret, and a lawyer at her door with divorce papers. As legend has it, Dr. Weidel never spoke to her again. He saw her once, in the lobby of his attorney's building, and walked right past her in silence as if she were a stranger."

She took a long pause here. The longest of the night. I breathed the story in, tasted it, desperate for more.

"Sorry, long way of getting to my point," Sylvia said. "But as Homer taught us, sometimes a story needs a story. Anyway, we were at this party, the first he'd attended since the disastrous one that ended his marriage. I had just re-read *The Iliad* because I was writing a novel, *Chariot Races*."

She looked at me, trying to gauge if I'd read it. I hadn't, but I smiled and nodded. I decided I'd read it that weekend. I'd drop everything and make sure I finished it before seeing her again.

"The novel deals with the Homeric epics, and there wasn't a better person to discuss those with than my colleague, Dr. Weidel. I asked him for his interpretation of a passage, the one where Priam comes to Achilles and begs for Hector's body. I was working on a section where a character attends a funeral, and I wanted to draw some connections. He was quiet after I asked about it. He didn't look at me for a long time. I almost left, thinking he either hadn't heard or had chosen to ignore me.

"Then he turned and said, 'Did you know that Cassandra was Priam's daughter? Most people seem to forget that. They know of her but don't always associate the two. Cassandra, of course, was cursed with, what I feel, is one of the worst punishments. She could see the future, but no one would believe her. Isn't that sad? To know with complete certainty what would come and still be unable to change it. To be ignored by those you love when you try to save them.'"

Rose's posture had collapsed, and her head had begun to fall.

"Now, of course, we were no longer talking about Priam or Cassandra. We were talking about Dr. Weidel and his ex-wife. I felt quite honored because no one had gotten him to speak so much as a word about her. People would express their condolences, and he would assume they were talking about his latest failure in the Mediterranean. He never acknowledged that they'd divorced. He never even acknowledged that they were married. He never spoke of her. But now, through the shadow of Cassandra, he was talking about her.

"My mind began to race. I traced what I remembered of Cassandra. I knew she was raped by the lesser Ajax during the fall of Troy. I knew it was a brutal, horrible rape in the temple, and it offended the gods. I knew she was then taken as a concubine by Agamemnon and brought back to Greece, where they were both slain by Clytemnestra, who had taken a new lover in Agamemnon's absence. I tried to piece this together. Was Mrs. Weidel Cassandra? Was she Clytemnestra? Was she

Agamemnon? Was he Cassandra? Was he Agamemnon? Was someone else Cassandra? Could he predict the future—and the future for him was, of course, the past—or could his now ex-wife? What did this story mean?

"I had no way of knowing. I still don't. I couldn't ask him. He'd never answer me. So, I chose not to even broach it. Instead, I asked him how he was so sure it had all happened. How was he so confident that the people and events in those texts had occurred?

"He paused before he answered, taking a deep breath in, as if he was preparing for a feat of enormous strength. Then he spoke, 'Life is about faith, not fact.' And with that, he stood up and walked away and found someone else to talk to about his latest theory on the resting place of Menelaus and Helen."

Sylvia leaned back in her chair and smiled as she stared at my awed face. She crossed her arms and nodded, urging me to think and process.

"Have you ever spoken to him about it?" I asked.

"About what?"

"Mrs. Weidel or Cassandra or his conviction?"

"No."

"Never?"

"There wouldn't be a point. This is what he believes. This is what he's decided on. He won't change. He can't. His world would collapse if he ever entertained the mildest doubt."

She was right. This was his defining trait. If someone built a time machine and proved to him that the Trojan War never occurred, he'd deny it. He'd choose to believe the lie even in the face of fact.

"Do you think he's…all there?" I said after a moment of contemplation.

"He's a genius," she said without hesitation. "A singular mind on this topic. But it's true, and I've said this many times, that genius and madness flow from the same source."

I felt a chill run down my back. There it was. The origin of the phrase that so often had been used to describe Jack. It was hers. Of course, it was hers.

"Well." Sylvia clapped her hands together. "That's enough story time for tonight. You will come back, right?"

"Yes, of course," I said. "As soon as possible."

"Great, next weekend then." She checked her watch and turned to Rose, whose head was now resting on the table. Sylvia rapped her fist hard, close to Rose's ear. "Up, up, come on now, Rose. We can't send Tess out there on her own. The rally starts soon, you two must be off. Would you like to take the students with you? For protection?"

She hadn't asked them, but that didn't matter.

"No, I, uh—"

"Right, right. Not a good idea with that bunch. Just you and Rose, then."

"I don't think I can." I'd forgotten about the rally, and now my fear was overwhelming my excitement. My confidence evaporated. "I can't, not in this dress. I look ridiculous."

"Not to worry," Sylvia said with a wry smile. "We planned for this."

One of the students appeared, Rose's tote draped over their shoulder, my clothes from the night before cleaned, pressed, and folded in their hands.

"When did—?" I turned to Rose, but she was gone.

Sylvia kept smiling. "We had them cleaned for you after last night. Thought you might need them for the rally. Now, there are plenty of rooms upstairs, take your pick. I'll get some coffee in Rose in the meantime."

I searched for another excuse, but there were none to be found. They'd planned for everything. They'd known the whole time where this night would lead.

I should've been hurt, offended that Rose had kept this from me. But I wasn't. I was excited. It was comforting to know that someone else was looking out for you. Someone had a plan.

When I came back downstairs, Rose was up, swaying a bit

but stable. At the door, I paused for a moment, allowing my hand to linger on the globed staircase before we left.

Once outside, Rose regained her posture, the cold night sobering her. I felt it too, but where it righted her, it startled me. I wasn't ready for that transition. I was still in Sylvia's dining room, still thinking about Dr. Weidel, absorbed in his past and awed by his conviction.

28

I could taste ash in the air as we started toward the rally. Ash and smoke and destruction.

Of course, there was no fire. Not yet. It was in my head. A premonition of things to come.

Once we turned a corner and the last window of Sylvia's castle was out of sight, Rose drew a flask from her jacket pocket. It was silver and solid, and you could tell it was old. It looked expensive, like the type of thing families like hers used and families like mine displayed.

She took a deep pull, and I watched her smooth neck rise and fall as the liquor cascaded down. I took in her posture, the long, straight line that stretched the length of her body. A body I believed I knew. I possessed. Belonged at least as much to me as to her.

Richard appeared in my mind, grinning, *And what if a man said that about a woman?*

I heard the cold, stiff grass crunch behind us. Someone was watching, hidden in the darkness, just out of sight. The sunken-eyed man? The big-eared woman? I paused and listened, trying to hear them breathe. Then Rose grabbed my hand and pulled me along, and the watcher was lost to the dark, possibly imagined past.

I focused on the ground, the cracks in the cement, the root that had forced the path up, the smell of lilac. I tried to push out Richard's voice and the paranoia, but they wouldn't leave. They lingered. They'd taken residence and weren't going anywhere, squatters in the dark recesses of my mind.

And then, out of nowhere, I felt it.

My stomach turned over, and I had to stop as a stitch tore across my abdomen. I crouched down and dropped my head between my knees. Cold filled my lungs, my chest tightened, and a frigid hand seemed to grasp my heart.

"Tess." Rose's voice, faint and distant, drowned out by a piercing wind. "Tess."

I felt myself sinking, falling away into the cold darkness, but just as I was about to be swallowed up, the hot light of Rose's hand touched my shoulder, and the chill retreated.

She straightened me up, passed me the flask, and I took it and felt the warmth of the liquor fold over my heart.

Rose pulled me by the elbow. Her hand was soft and firm, ushering me to safety. I don't know how long we walked. I don't know what we passed or what path we took. It was all a blur, a dense fog shrouding my vision.

"Here." Rose handed me a magenta cigarette. She lit hers and motioned for me to put mine in my mouth. I obeyed, and she lit it. "Breath in so it catches."

I did, and the smoke poured into my lungs. I coughed and couldn't stop.

She placed a hand on my back. "It's okay, let it out. Then take another drag. It gets better."

I looked up and met Rose's eyes. They were curious, inquiring, excited. They ran over my body and returned to my face to linger there and flutter across it, searching for something. "Did you see her? Or just feel her?"

"What? Who are you talking about?" I said, knowing full well.

"It's okay. It's okay, I don't...you're not crazy. Same thing happened to me last year. I was coming back from Sylvia's, almost the same spot, and I felt it. Felt her. It was like a shower of cold water, but worse. It penetrated me. I felt it in my chest, and I couldn't breathe and thought it was, I don't know, consuming my heart or something."

I said nothing, silence serving as my answer.

"When you're a kid," she said and handed me the flask, "you believe in them. You think, why not? There are all these stories about them, and you do feel, I don't know, things. Things that seem off. So, why not ghosts? And monsters and demons and fairies and all that? Why couldn't the world be full of those things? But then you get older, and the magic goes out of the world. Reality takes hold and squeezes it out of you, leaving behind a brutal, cynical husk."

She paused, and I looked around. We were behind a building on campus somewhere. There were tall red brick walls speckled with ivy on two sides of us, hugging us, protecting us. The ground was caked over, stained with petrified ash. This must be where they all smoked. Not just Sylvia's people but everyone.

The campus had gone smoke-free a few years before. First, they'd quarantined them into smokers' areas, tiny corners of campus where the degenerates could be watched and judged by all. But then, they took those too. Smoking banned, smokers cast out into the wilderness.

But, of course, that's not how it works. People always find a way. No matter how much you believe you've eradicated something, it always survives. Festers somewhere to return with a vengeance.

Just then, we heard the loud murmur of a group of men. It grew in volume as they neared us until we saw them crest the side of the building and appear. We both turned and stared.

"Oh, my bad," one of them said. He had flat, careless brown eyes that rolled across me and lingered on Rose. He opened his mouth and smiled. "Didn't mean to disturb. We'll head over to Dickinson, no worries. Carry on."

They were all dressed the same. White sneakers, gleaming in the moonlight, and khakis with polos tucked into them stretched across their chests and stomachs. They grinned and looked us up and down, taking their time, before leaving. As their voices trailed off into the distance, we could hear their laughter and appraisals.

"The redhead was fucking fire."

"Hell, yeah, I think I know her."

"You don't know her."

"Yes, I fucking do, I almost hit that at a party. She wanted it but was sloppy as fuck."

"Bullshit…" The cold wind and thick walls blocked out their voices.

"Where was I?" Rose said. "Right, you come to take this cynical, a-magical world for granted. You reject those things as the stuff of children and the uneducated. You become reasoned, enlightened, above all that superstitious nonsense. And then something like that happens. You experience it. You find out it's real, and you're not prepared."

She finished her cigarette and dragged it across the brick wall, the burned paper scraping and leaving a trail of ash, joining all the others that had come before it. The cherry fell and landed on the ground. Rose, in a careful, practiced motion, snuffed it out. Then she walked over to the garbage and tossed the filter.

I followed her example, but I was sloppier, more chaotic. The cherry burned my hand on the way down, and unburned tobacco fell to the ground.

"You good?" Rose said. Something in the words, the tone, the casualness of it all made me sure she was back. She was mine again. The person who had reappeared at Sylvia's had vanished, and I no longer felt cold or afraid.

"Yes." I pulled her to me and kissed her. "I'm good."

Rose smiled, and we walked off into the night, completely unprepared for what was to come.

29

We saw people the second we emerged from the smokers' haven. It was surprising. Campus should've been dead. The parties, the real ones, wouldn't get going until midnight.

I looked around at the dorms. They'd be full. People pregaming, downing shots, listening to bad techno, gossiping, trying to finish that last assignment before the night could truly begin. They'd emerge at twelve or one and stumble off to some frat house or bar, nothing on their minds aside from making it home with a story.

So, who were these people?

They were all the same. White men, eager, dressed in identical uniforms—khakis, polos, conservative haircuts. They spoke in excited voices. They jumped and bounced as they walked, pushing each other, brimming with energy.

Often a lone man would emerge from a dorm, hesitant, skeptical. Their eyes would trace the horizon, and then a group would appear, and they'd call out to the loner, welcome him. He would rush over, joy in his gait. They would shout and prod him, and laughter would echo through the dark, empty campus.

Later, people would misremember that night. They would claim that the men arrived with torches. That they chanted on their way to the quad, and that they were met by a line of protestors. Countless students I've spoken to about that night have assured me, without a shadow of a doubt, that they were one of the protestors.

But they weren't. This is just a story they tell. Maybe even one they believe.

We saw some protestors, Brando among them, as we neared the quad. But it wasn't more than a dozen people.

The torches came later. They were passed out by men who claimed no association with Richard or IGE. They'd swear they just had the idea and chose to arrive with hundreds of torches. They'd say they had no way of knowing what would happen, no way to predict the violence and hate.

No one believes this.

No one except the courts.

The chanting and people leaving their dorms to protest did happen. It happened after the rally. It happened once Richard sent this furious mob out into the moon-soaked campus.

But we're not there just yet. First, we need to hear his speech.

30

As we neared the quad, I could see the energy pouring off the crowd. The ground rumbled, and the air was charged. My hand trembled. With fear or excitement?

We found out later they came from all over. Community colleges, high schools, other universities. And not just students. Cashiers, construction workers, cops, lawyers, businessmen. Some traveled over states traversing as much as a hundred miles just to be there. Just to be part of it.

But even with them, our university was well represented in the crowd. Young men who were fed up. Outsiders longing to be accepted. People who felt they'd been passed over, left behind, desperate to be accepted.

And Richard was perfect for them.

There had been some discussion about canceling the rally. The university would later admit that it erred in not doing so.

Richard had booked the quad and publicized the rally for months. He'd made a point of discussing it in his recent television appearances, goading the university into canceling it.

Of course, it would've been great for him if they had. He could've ranted about the injustice of the liberal establishment. Argued that they were silencing him and conservatives across the nation. He would've smeared the university for being against free speech and pointed out a litany of times they'd allowed far-leaning liberal groups to assemble on campus.

Maybe that was it. Maybe that had scared the university.

They released a statement. *While they were concerned with the previous violence, they were still conducting their investigation and didn't want to limit free speech on campus.*

They told themselves that it wouldn't happen again. That more damage would be done by canceling it than by allowing it. They bet on civility and lost.

I wonder if maybe there was more to it, someone on the board or a donor got to them. Some supporter of Richard's in a powerful place.

Or maybe they were concerned that they couldn't stop it even if they wanted to. There had been murmurings about Richard going on with it regardless of the university's stance. He'd likened it to the Civil Rights movement and even compared himself to Dr. King. Said he'd go to jail for the cause.

In retrospect, it's impossible to know why they let it happen. Why they didn't push to stop it. What they were afraid of. History is like that sometimes. The truth is lost in a sea of theory and guesswork.

When we arrived, Richard was hidden away somewhere. Some adjacent building where he could sit and watch his followers flood to him. Watch them fidget and talk. Watch the anticipation grow to a crescendo that he could then ride.

I wondered if he was waiting for me to arrive to witness his coronation.

But of course, he wasn't. It wasn't, as I had come to see it, a struggle between the two of us for the soul of the campus. He didn't think of me like that. I was a tool. A tool he had harnessed to catapult himself to greater fame. He'd use me again if he needed me, but otherwise, I was in the past. And people like him don't trouble themselves with the past.

I didn't see him emerge. I heard it. A trickle of excited voices and pointing spread through the crowd and culminated in a deafening roar when he arrived onstage. Despite the spring cold, he wore no jacket, no hat, no scarf. Just a pressed white button-down, no tie, sleeves rolled about halfway up his forearms. His shirt was tucked into khakis matching at least part of the uniform.

The crowd couldn't agree upon a chant as he ascended the steps and waved.

"USA, USA," broke out in one corner, but the other side had already begun. "You will not replace us. You will not replace us." Another group added to the chorus. "Fuck the EOTP. Fuck the EOTP."

There must have been others, pockets of chants that were abandoned before they reached critical mass. But these were enough. These made me want to leave. Turn away and never look back.

I felt Rose's hand on my shoulder. She could sense my fear. I turned and looked into her eyes. They were calm, steady, unmoved. She nodded and clenched her fist. "It's fine. We'll stay over here. They won't come after us."

We were standing off to the side of the crowd on the steps that led into the quad. About ten yards or so from Richard and his stage but above and away from the horde.

I guessed there were three hundred people in the crowd, but it's just that, a guess. I know some people on both sides have claimed outrageous numbers. Thousands. I don't think the quad could've held that, but I can't be sure. I don't feel the numbers matter as much as some do. I know there were a lot, and I know there are more out there.

When I think about it, I focus on the energy, the passion. That's what sticks in my mind. Those images of men screaming and crying as he spoke. Of them clutching each other's arms and cheering Richard's every word. Of the devotion and adoration that pulsed through the crowd. Those are things that will stick with me. Not the numbers.

"What a turnout," Richard said.

They returned a roar.

"Not that I can say I'm surprised. We are the future. This is the beginning of a movement that will conquer this country. Reconquer it. And you, every single one of you, are in the vanguard. When you're old men, sitting in your houses, comfortable, secure, watching your nation prosper, you'll be able to tell your children and grandchildren that you were there at the beginning. You saw what was happening to your country, and you did something about it. You changed it."

The crowd had become a solitary mass, pushing in and out,

beating as one. The sound pouring from it wasn't clear, it didn't seem to be words, just the joint garbled tongues of a possessed throng.

"That's right." He pulled the cord that trailed the microphone behind him like a tail. They had six speakers lining the quad, and his voice echoed through them, filling the cold night with life. "Great turnout. Fantastic. Historic. It really is. You know they tried to stop us. They didn't want this to happen. The admin came to me and begged me to cancel it, to postpone it."

Boos rattled out from the crowd.

"I know, I know. Can you believe that? They thought I'd buckle. They offered me bribes—references, connections, establishment prizes. They thought they could buy me off. They thought I was that weak. They clearly don't know me. Not yet, but they will."

An eruption.

"And here we are. They couldn't stop us. They were too afraid to stop us. And let this be a lesson to all of us. Moving forward, let us learn from this and from the past. Learn from successful movements, those we agree with and those we don't. The Nazi movement, the Civil Rights movement, we have to learn from both."

Neither for the first nor last time, I was astonished by Richard. I hated everything he stood for, but you couldn't help but marvel at his deft touch. He'd managed to let his supporters hear what they wanted. If they liked the Nazis and agreed with what they'd done and tried to do, you could say he was with you. If not, if you despised and detested the Nazis, you could claim he was likening himself to the Civil Rights movement and condemning the Nazi message while admiring their success. It was beautiful. Elegant in its doublespeak.

It also subtly linked those two movements. It tethered them to each other, implying, if not outright stating, that they were equal. That they were both complicated movements that had good and bad elements.

"History," he lowered his voice and looked at the ground. "History. I've been thinking a lot about history. I think we all have. A part of this country wants you to be ashamed of your history. They think you should apologize for it. I don't like that. I don't agree with that. I think we have a great history, and we should embrace it. I think it's all right to be proud of your history. It's all right to tell people that you're proud of your country. I'll say it. I'm proud to be an American."

Garbled approval.

"No, come on, say it with me. I'm proud to be an American."

They repeated with militaristic precision.

"I'm proud to be a man."

Again, they repeated.

"I'm proud to be white."

Again, they shouted the words back at him in unison.

"Now the liberal media is going to play that clip and make us look like a bunch of racists." He shook his head in disgust. "So just for their sake, I will say, even though I shouldn't have to, that I don't hate any other races. I don't hate immigrants. I don't hate minorities. Saying I'm proud to be white doesn't mean I hate non-whites."

There was a spattering of laughter in the crowd but little shouting. This was lip service, and they all knew it.

"White, straight men are the only group in this country who can't be proud. It's a sad state of affairs when you can't be proud to be yourself. It destroys. Destroys your strength, your power. Destroys your nation."

Here the cheer returned. Defiant in its rage.

Rose squeezed my elbow and pointed to the left of the stage. Claire was hidden by a tree, wearing an earpiece, whispering to someone while staring at us. She smiled when she caught my eye and gave a vicious wave.

Not many, but a few people turned and glared at me. Maybe they recognized me. Maybe their minds clicked, and they put two and two together. But maybe not. Maybe they just hated me as the off-white woman I was.

The fear was up, I could see the danger, feel it. I understood the myriad ways this could go wrong for me. But with the fear came more excitement. An understanding that this was significant. This was newsworthy. Things like this made a career.

Connor walked, hunched and hidden, to the edge of the stage. He, too, wore an earpiece, and it wasn't too much to assume who was speaking to him through it. He brought forward a note. Richard paused and leaned down to take it from him. He kept smiling and motioned Connor away, shooing him like a pest. Connor obliged and scurried off into the darkness.

I couldn't help but follow him. I watched as he traced the outside of the crowd, avoiding the pit, living on the fringe. He disappeared between two buildings, and my eye returned to Richard, who was standing, reading the note, scanning the crowd.

He found me and smiled and waved. "We have one of them with us. An EOTP. One of those who believes you should be ashamed of who you are. And not just any EOTP. We have the one who smeared me with hate and lies in our university paper."

Boos and hisses cascaded down on me. I could feel the hate, feel its heat. The crowd surged forward, pulsing toward us. It stopped at the steps and exhaled back, but I knew they'd come again. I felt my legs buckle, my body pull me away, but underneath that surface, something simmered. Exhilaration. Elation even.

"Don't," Richard said, holding up a hand. Later, I'd think of this moment when he'd claim he had no control over the crowd. "That's what they want. Nothing would make her happier than to become a martyr. I get it, I'm with you. Her and her like… what they've done to journalism in this nation…it's deplorable. But we won't sink to that. Not against her. She's not worth it. She's just a person. It's the institution we're going to tear down. It's the liberal media complex that we're out to destroy. And she'll have to watch us do it and live in the ashes."

Live in the ashes. Another phrase that stuck with me. Another phrase that's unavoidable when looking back.

I realized I wasn't recording this. I had no evidence of what he was saying. I reached for my phone but turned and saw that Rose already had hers out. It'd been out the whole time, I just hadn't noticed.

I scanned the crowd and saw the phones, a sea of them recording Richard's every word, eager to post it for the world to see. I saw professional cameras at the edges with men operating them. I saw the recording devices at the foot of the stage. Even if Rose hadn't been recording, it wouldn't have mattered. This wasn't meant to be hidden. I didn't need to record this, they would put this out. They were proud of this.

"So let her be. I don't want to give them any fuel. And this way, if she, as I'm sure she's thought of, decides to beat herself up and claim it was us who did it, we'll know she's lying."

Another masterstroke. If I left unharmed, it was a demonstration of their restraint, of his power. If I was assaulted, they'd claim it was manufactured.

"Because they do that. That's what they do. They claim things that never happened. They stage violence and blame us. Psychological warfare, PSYOPS. That's what they did with that kid in the hospital."

Here a cheer rushed out, and I thought I saw Richard flinch his displeasure, not for the sentiment but for the optics.

"That's right. That's what they do. They've painted us as violent, crazed fascists for decades, and we've never been that. We're not crazed, they're the ones who are crazed. They're the ones who are forcing their ideologies on this nation. Their failed ideologies. And we're not violent. They're violent. We will, of course, defend ourselves, but we don't seek violence. That's their game. So, what do you do when you've painted your enemy a certain way for decades, and they've not acted that way? When you've claimed that they're violent, crazed fascists when they aren't? Well, you commit acts of violence, and you blame them. And don't think they aren't capable of it. Don't think it isn't in their playbook. It is. They've done it for years."

I could sense what was coming. Not the exact details, but I

could sense how this would end. Violence. Rage. Destruction. Ash. I should've left. The fear should've won out completely, and I should've fled to safety. But I didn't. The more frantic the atmosphere got, the more I wanted to stay. The excitement was winning out, and I found myself hoping for the most extreme outcome.

"So, what do we do? What can we do? We look to history. That same history that they've rejected and co-opted and distorted. That same history they want you to be ashamed of." He paused and took a deep breath, pulling in the cold air and the manic energy. "History. We look to history.

"Have any of you heard of Romaine Tenney? No, I hadn't either. They don't teach us about people like him. He was a farmer. Just your run-of-the-mill farmer in Vermont. He was born in 1900 on a family farm. His father died when he was fourteen, and Romaine and his siblings and his mother worked that farm from that day on. And he was still working that farm, his farm, sixty years later when the government came for it. When the government, a liberal governor of Vermont, told him that his farm, his family farm, his property, should be a highway instead."

The crowd hissed and jeered.

"I know, I know. That's what they do. They won't let you live. Progress for progress's sake. Disgusting. Now, Romaine tried to fight it. He tried to stop them, but what's one man against the liberal establishment? What can one man do in the face of that type of evil? Well, he knew what he could do.

"The night the liberals came to take away his land, his family implored him to leave. They begged and pleaded. They told him it was just a farm. But he didn't see it that way. He wasn't going to leave. Instead, he set it on fire. The farm, the shed, the house. They say the blaze climbed sixty feet in the air, and it was so hot that even the next day, the smoldering ashes couldn't be approached."

The crowd roared.

"They found a shotgun in there, melted and destroyed, with

expended shells and bone fragments nearby. Romaine had shot himself after setting the fire. He decided he'd rather burn it down than let them take it. He'd rather kill himself than let them destroy his life."

There was a momentary silence where the audience attempted to wrap their heads around this complex story before they shouted back praise.

I, too, found myself moved, pulled in a thousand different directions. I felt for this man. I thought it was wrong to take his farm to build a highway. I thought his act tragic and beautiful, poetic. I saw the resignation and defeat at the hands of indifferent bureaucrats.

Then I saw Richard standing there, nodding and pulsing with the crowd. I heard their shouts and watched them throb. And I felt nauseous. I wondered what Romaine Tenney would think seeing this. I wondered how he would view these crazed neo-fascists using his memory for their own cause. I wondered what his politics were and if it mattered.

"Now, I'm not advocating suicide." Richard's face grew grave, and he took a moment to scan the crowd, landing on faces and holding them. "We aren't like him. Not now. We have a movement. We have strength in our numbers and in the righteousness of our cause. We'll succeed where he failed. We'll take down the liberal establishment that's ruining this nation. We'll start here, at this very university. We'll show them that we won't go quietly. We'll show them that we're here, and we're angry, and we're united, and we won't be silenced."

An eruption.

"We'll learn from Romaine. We'll take his message of anti-liberalism with us, and, in his memory, we'll go out and change this campus, and then we'll change this nation. We'll stand up for ourselves. We'll be proud of who we are. Proud to be white, proud to be men, proud to be straight, proud to be conservative, proud of our history, proud of our nation."

He thrust a pointed finger forward toward the crowd with

each proclamation. They surged with every thrust and retreated with every recoil, puppets on his string.

"Now go forth and show them who we are. Show them we're here. Show them what we believe in. Let our voices ring out through the night. Let this campus and this nation know that we're awake and we're just getting started. This is our time. Our era. We'll take this night and then take this country."

Pandemonium.

Shouts and squalls and cries. Men with tears streaming down their faces hugging each other, punching each other, getting ready to do…something. Something manifest.

It was then that I saw Connor returning through the gap in the buildings he'd disappeared into. He was followed by a dozen men, all dressed in the uniform, all holding armfuls of tiki torches. Each man must've carried twenty. Maybe more.

I recognized one of them following a half-step behind Connor. Tall and firm, a head above the rest, a gold chain dangling from his neck.

Connor motioned to his men, and they took up posts on the steps, vibrating with anxious anticipation. Laughing and talking and basking in the attention of the crowd who had turned to face them.

Richard had already left the stage, disappeared back into some building.

But he'd lit the spark, and the campus was all tinder.

31

They handed out the torches. The air smelled of kerosene and rage. The men skipped and shouted, they beat their chests and howled at the moon. Then they stood and waited, pacing and throbbing, tight balls of energy longing to explode.

Once they were all equipped, they marched across campus, chanting.

"You will not replace us."

"Take the night. Take the country."

"Proud. Straight. White. Men."

Rose and I hid behind a building once the torches began to be handed out.

"We have to follow them," Rose said.

A few men were moving around in the spot where we'd watched the rally. They stared at the ground and searched the surrounding area. They were looking for us.

"What? No way." But my words carried no conviction. I wanted her to convince me. I wanted a push. I could already feel the gravity of the mob pulling me toward them. The fear was there, but it was just an aftertaste, the excitement having vanquished it to the recesses of my mind.

"This is a huge story." Her eyes were enormous, pupils dilated. She pulsated with nervous anticipation. "We need to see it through."

She reached out and held my hand still, then she ran a fingernail along the back of it, tracing the bones. Even in that moment, with the world collapsing around us, I still trembled at that touch, still felt my heart race and my mouth grow dry. I still felt the world slow down when she looked into my eyes.

I nodded, and we took off into that fire-soaked night, moving from building to building, chasing the sound, remaining hidden. We rushed past people trickling out of their dorm rooms, half-drunk, unsure what was happening. People shouted questions at us that we didn't hear. They giggled and murmured and speculated.

"Proud. Straight. White. Men."

The mob was on the other side of the building. We could feel their vibrations, hear their chants, but we couldn't see them. We had to get around the building, get eyes on them.

People were pouring out now, bleary-eyed and dazed. Rose pulled me through a closing door, fighting through the stream of departures. "There's got to be an exit on the other side."

"Hey, what's going on?" someone asked, their voice trailing off behind us.

We rushed down a hallway, our cold bodies pierced by the sudden heat. We passed a common room and saw the glow of torches through the window.

"Proud. Straight. White. Men."

People were staring out the window, phones pointed toward the mob.

"What's happening?" someone shouted. "What's going on?"

No one answered. There was no answer.

We kept moving. Rose holding my hand, our feet skimming across the ground. Her strides were long and effortless, elegant even. She darted in and out of groups having animated, pointless conversations.

We turned a corner and found a stairwell. A man was sitting on one of the steps, alone, frightened, tears streaming down his face.

"How?" he said, his head pointed toward the ceiling in despair. "How?"

Rose didn't even pause to take him in. She stepped over him, dragging me along. Our heels bounced off the steps. Above us, we could hear concerned voices and loud footsteps.

We reached the basement and jumped over a metal chain telling us not to enter. Then we ran right down the long hallway that traced the building. I looked up at the exposed piping and then down at the slick, cheap floor. It smelled of cleaning supplies, tasted damp. It felt like a different world from the campus I'd come to know.

I needed to catch my breath, but Rose was moving faster. Driven on with purpose. As I slowed, she gripped my hand tighter and pulled.

"Where are we going?" I said.

Rose was unfazed by the exertion. "There has to be an exit, we need to beat them to the turn."

She seemed to have a mental map of the campus, something I lacked. Smartphones have destroyed my capacity for those kinds of things. You could drop me a block away from my childhood home, and I'd pull out my phone. But not Rose. She knew. She led.

"There," she said. At the end of the corridor was a door with a red handle and a series of signs warning not to open it. She didn't even pause, just hit the door at full speed and burst back out into the cold.

I braced myself for an alarm that never came. Then I felt the cold hit me, and my sweat froze to my skin. I dropped my head and panted, trying to catch my breath.

"Good, good," Rose said, standing up straight, unfazed, not a hair out of place. "Deep breaths. In and out. We need you calm for the video."

The video? My heart, which had just slowed, sped up again. Rumbling.

"You will not replace us. You will not replace us," echoed in the distance, drawing closer. I saw the incoming glow on the building across from us and swore I could feel the heat from the torches.

"Video?"

"We'll record you talking, with them in the background."

"But I don't—"

"Tess, you have to. This is gold. This is going to be viral. You need to catch the wave. You need to be the face of this."

She was right. This was my moment.

We did what we could to wipe the sweat from my face and control my hair. I didn't look good, but it was dark, and, given the circumstances, focusing on my appearance felt trivial. We moved into the light, testing a few angles before finding one that showed my face and framed the incoming mob.

"Take the night. Take the country. Take the night. Take the country."

They came into view, pouring around the corner.

Students had begun to line the walkway. Some shouted back at them, but most just stood and watched, mouths agape, terror in their eyes. Some held each other. Some cried. Some clenched their fists and held their breath in repressed rage. Everyone had their phone out, pointed at the mob, trying to capture the uncapturable.

"Behind me," I said, Rose recording, "we have the aftermath of Richard Welch's latest rally. A few hundred men, almost all white, have picked up torches and are now marching across campus chanting white nationalist slogans."

I paused and let their voices fill the video, on cue, they switched back to a previous chant. "Proud. Straight. White. Men."

"Richard Welch is not among them. I watched as he ran off after finishing his speech. But he set this loose. He revved them up and encouraged them to 'take the night and take the country.' As you can see from this terrifying display behind me, they've taken his advice to heart."

I thought of Richard, his rhetoric, his ability to pull a crowd toward him. To enliven them. I tried to channel him the best I could.

"This happens when we allow them, the far-right, to go unchecked. This is what happens when our university takes the path of cowardice. When they allow Richard, after he incited violence just a few days ago, to again rile up a crowd of his most devout followers. If the university doesn't act this time, it'll happen again. They embolden them by ignoring them."

I turned and motioned to the crowd.

"This is who they are. This is what they stand for. This is where we're headed."

Rose's camera zoomed past me, scanning the mob, capturing their faces of joy and anger and determination. She caught an exchange between a protestor and a marcher. You can't make out the words. It seems "fascist" and "faggot" are tossed back and forth, but you can't be sure. It could've been anything.

After the video finished, we watched it back.

"This is perfect," Rose said, unrestrained awe in her voice. "How did you...that was just off the top of your head?"

I smiled a knowing, confident smile. It was perfect. I'd pulled it off.

We sat back and smoked and watched as the orange blaze moved through the corridor and off into the distance.

Onlookers continued to cry. They paced and shouted at the mob after they were gone, courage appearing once it no longer mattered. We watched a crowd form and a woman in the center of it rally them to action. She shouted about organizing, about fighting back, about how they'd win in the end because "only light can drive out the darkness." Empty words after what they'd just witnessed. Empty words and emptier promises.

It was while this woman was finishing that I felt my phone buzz. I pulled it out and saw that I had a dozen messages and half as many missed calls. Most were from friends asking if I was seeing this, asking if I was all right.

I had five messages and three calls from the same number. Brando.

> *Hey, what are you doing?*
> *We're headed down to protest Richard's rally.*
> *Can you make it?*

>> *Hey, change of plans.*
>> *I'm going to call you.*

> *Can't get into it over text,*
> *but I have a plan.*
> *I could use your help.*

Need people who can keep their mouths shut.

> *Where are you at?*
> *We're moving on this thing soon.*
> *Pick up your phone.*
> *This is going to be huge.*
> *This could change everything.*

Delete my messages.
Plan went off.
We took it to them this time.

I dialed his number. No answer. I dialed it again. Still nothing. I felt a lump form in my throat and sweat trickle down my back.

What happened? What had I missed? What had he done?

Rose was on her phone too. She turned to me, grabbing me by the elbow. "Tess, look." She thrust her phone in front of me and played a video from someone's Insta.

It was a building on fire. The flames poured out of the shattered windows, licking up the side of the building, charring the brick. I watched as the fire danced and swayed in the moonlight. It took me a minute. Even though it was a building I'd been in a thousand times, it didn't register at first. It looked different engulfed in flames. But then it hit me, and we broke out into a silent sprint.

32

Clinton Hall was a conflagration by the time we arrived. The area was swarming. Firefighters and police, some from campus, some from the surrounding towns. We heard shouting and arguing and saw people being led away in handcuffs. We heard performed cries of anguish from desperate people trying to own the tragedy. And we smelled the ash and fire. It smelled like fall, like roasted marshmallows and camping. Like childhood.

We felt the smoke fill our lungs. It got trapped in our hair, and we'd smell it there for days and weeks to come. It was impossible to wash out, as if that night had soaked into our follicles.

The once quiet night was now deafening. Sirens blared and whirled. The moonlight was drowned out by flashing red and blue, turning the darkness purple. We heard screaming students, and the building buckling and cracking, crying out in pain.

And then we heard laughter coming from behind us. I turned to locate it, but the smoke and purple and chaos clouded my vision. I saw men in Richard's uniform walking by—unmolested, unchained—but I couldn't be sure it was them who laughed. It could've been anyone. It could've been out of joy or fear. It was impossible to say.

"They're letting them go?" Rose said, pulling me close and speaking into my ear to cut through the noise.

I just nodded.

"Unfucking believable." She pulled out her cigarettes, putting one in her mouth, and spoke with it dangling from her lip. "You know there were fights again? All over campus."

She lit the cigarette and breathed it in before passing it to me. I took it and felt it fill my lungs, replacing the smoke from the fire. Even in the chaos, I was moved by the intimacy of this gesture.

"Excuse me, miss." A campus officer who seemed to materialize out of nowhere said to me. "This is a non-smoking campus. You'll have to put that out."

Rose reached out and took the cigarette back. Then she turned and motioned to the enflamed building, threw up her arms, and took another drag. The officer shrugged and walked away.

I thought I saw the big-eared woman milling around behind us. I looked down, blinking away tears from my smoke-filled eyes, and when I looked back up, she was gone. Vanished into the haze of uncertainty.

We watched until they got the fire under control. They used their hoses to create a boundary and then worked toward its heart, a practiced method that sacrificed the part for the whole.

While we watched this choreographed dance of water and flame, I saw it. A figure floating across the fire. I wasn't alone in seeing it. People posted about it online. They recorded terrible videos that showed nothing, but it was enough. The idea spread across campus, and before long, people who weren't there were swearing they saw it. Saw her.

If I'd never heard the ghost story about Louise and felt her cold grip on my heart earlier that night, I don't know what I would've thought. But I knew the story and knew what I'd experienced, and that's where my mind went. That's where everyone's mind went.

You can say what you want about memory and the unreliability of eyewitness accounts. I'm sure I'd say the same if I were you. And maybe you're right. Maybe it was in my head, in all our heads. Maybe it was from the stress and excitement and fatigue, a collective madness. Maybe someone mentioned it, and it spread, and all our minds have retroactively altered our memories.

But maybe not.

She wasn't there for long. She'd floated in and out of focus, living on the edges of my vision. She'd disappear and return in another spot, captivating and terrifying her audience.

Rose saw her too. We didn't need to speak about it. She grabbed my hand, and we stood and watched until we were sure she was gone. Then we turned and left.

An unreal miasma blanketed our walk back to Rose's apartment, and more than once, I thought I might wake up and it would all have been a dream. But, of course, it wasn't.

That night was the first night we slept together and only slept. There's an intimacy to that which transcends sex. I didn't know about it until that night. We didn't shower or undress, we just laid down in her bed, held each other, and drifted off. I don't think I dreamt. Nothing coherent, at least. Just flashes of fire and yelling and marching and rage.

33

Last night, a fire broke out at Clinton Hall. We're still determining the cause. We do not know if it was an act of arson or a malfunction.

At the same time, unrelated, a march took place. It began as a simple gathering, which was peaceful and sanctioned by the university, but turned into an impromptu march. We spoke to the organizers who were unaware and did not participate in or organize the march.

The march was, by and large, peaceful. The university will investigate the allegations of hate speech, but as of this moment, we have no definitive evidence, and no action is being taken on this front.

A few arrests were made across campus. Some were related to the march. Five marchers and eleven protestors were arrested for disorderly conduct. These arrests came from three different incidents of violence. The incidents were quickly and efficiently brought under control. We have a zero-tolerance policy for violence on campus, and all those arrested will be prosecuted.

At this time, no other arrests have been made. The university is investigating the various incidents and will act once that investigation is complete.

University statement about the night of the Clinton Hall fire:

> An investigation is ongoing into the cause of the fire. We do not know if it was related to the other events on campus that night. It is essential to let the investigation run its course.
>
> The incidents of violence, be they by the marchers or protestors, are uniformly denounced by this university. Violence is never the answer, and we will take swift and decisive action against any persons who commit acts of violence.
>
> We have spoken to the organizers of the gathering and are confident they played no part in the march or any of the other actions that took place that night. After conducting their sanctioned gathering, the organizers left and did not participate in the march. They are not under investigation at this time.

TWEETS FROM THE NIGHT OF THE
CLINTON HALL FIRE:

Yooooo the campus is in smoke!

> *I heard some Nazis are burning down the campus?!?!?!
> What year is it?!?!?!?*

> > *BURNING DOWN THE HOUSE!!*

> > > *Do you really think this is an appropriate
> > > time to joke around?*

> > > > *I'm not joking, but yes.*

> *Someone grab some hot dogs and marshmallows!!*

> > *Do you think classes will be canceled tomorrow? Dead-
> > lines extended? Asking for a friend??*

Tess Azar is BAE! YASS QUEEN!

> > *This was a lib. I'm calling it now.*

> > > *Your people are LITERALLY marching through
> > > campus with torches.*

> > *Shut up lib.*

I think I left a lit cigarette somewhere, hope it doesn't cause any problems.

> *This isn't funny.*

> *Yes it is.*

> > > *Richard Welch 4 President! BURN BABY
> > > BURN*

> *Actual Nazis on campus. Wild. Stay safe out there.*
> > *You call everyone a Nazi. You should look them up. They
> > were liberals. Maybe if you liberals read a book once in a
> > while we wouldn't be here.*

> > > *Tell me you're a Nazi without telling me you're a Nazi.*
> > > *RIP ROMAINE TENNEY*

34

Brando was one of those arrested. He'd shouted at some marchers and then stood, with another person, blocking their path. The marchers pushed past him, and when they touched him, he swung and landed a punch. The man fought back. Brando's friend joined in, throwing punches at another marcher. There was blood and screaming and the ecstatic release of pent-up rage.

Brando and his friend were arrested. So was the marcher who had fought back. The other marchers, who attempted to break up the fight, weren't arrested. None of them threw a punch. They only chanted hate and marched.

We know none of them threw a punch because it was all on video. The video was provided and posted online by Brando himself. He was proud of it. He thought it was a defining moment in his life.

"I don't care if I go to jail for ten years," he said. His parents had posted bail, and we'd all gotten together at Samir's to discuss the fallout. "I know I did the right thing. Admin can say whatever they want about violence never being the answer, but they're wrong. And they know they're wrong. Violence is the only thing fascists understand. Peaceful protest to a Nazi is a joke. You got to draw blood. You got to show them you're not afraid. Fight fire with fire."

He glanced at me as he said this, and his eyes grinned.

He was on his fourth cup of strong black coffee, and his fingers rattled against the table. He bounced and rocked with every word, unable to keep his energy internal, bursting at the seams. He needed to keep it going, needed to bound from one thing to the next. If he stopped, he'd have to consider, he'd have to realize what he'd done and contemplate his future.

"Are they going to press charges?" Kim said, mist coating

her eyes. I don't think I'd seen it till that day. I knew they were close, but I hadn't seen that look. "Are they going to expel you?"

"I don't know, maybe." Brando waved his hand around, not even turning to look at Kim. "My lawyers are talking to them. If they want to expel me or press charges because I punched a fascist, let them. Let them pick a side."

He stood up and began to pace.

Kim stared at the carpet and composed herself. I could feel her pain. She saw him leaving and never returning, their future together vanishing before it had begun. She'd been waiting, biding her time, planning a move, but it was too late. He'd go off somewhere, and someone else would claim him. She'd lose him forever.

"Well," Samir said, "we all have our part to play. I hope this…I mean, I don't want to…I don't know if we can publish anything from you right now. We'd love for you to write something that we can put to the side, but I don't know the lo—"

"Really, Sam?" Brando said. "I have something ready. An editorial. You have to run it. You have to show that we…show where you stand. Pick a side."

"I don't think it's in the best interest of the paper to do that righ—"

"Fuck." He threw himself on the couch next to Kim. Her face lit up, and she put a hand on his shoulder. He dropped his head, and the life drained from his face. The room seemed to grow colder. "They got to you, didn't they?"

Everyone turned to Samir. She hesitated just a second too long. It was enough. We all could see it on her face.

"Look," she said, "after this all dies down, we might be able to run it, but right now, we have to think of the paper as a whole and not just one person."

Brando's head hung between his legs, his energy gone. Kim ran a hand along his back in a clockwise motion and tried to hide her smile.

A silence fell over the room. I was torn. I understood Samir's need to keep the paper going, to keep her leadership in place, but it felt wrong. It felt like a betrayal. I was sure Brando's editorial was nothing short of a manifesto, but still, he was one of us.

"Post it online," Rose said. There had been fewer murmurings when she arrived with me this time, but it still felt out of place for her to be the one to break the silence. "On your Insta or something. It'll still carry weight. And everyone here can like and share it. That way, you have the endorsement of the paper's staff without having to endanger the paper itself."

Excitement began to leak back into the room. Brando's head was still hung low, but his foot began to tap. Kim let her dormant smile surface.

It was a good idea. It would work. Of course, it tied each of us to his manifesto and restricted our editorial input. Who knew what he'd post? And now we were all committed to sharing it, condoning it.

"Would you all do that?" Brando said, his back still bowed but his head peeking up.

There was a murmuring of agreement, but I remained noncommittal.

"Tess?" he said. "Would you share it?"

I swallowed hard and turned to Rose. She nodded. "Yes, I could… I'd want to talk to you first about it, but yes, of course."

And just like that, Brando was up and pacing again. Kim was bouncing in her seat. The whole room seemed lighter once there was a plan. It didn't fix everything. He still faced expulsion and legal consequences, we still had Nazis marching on campus, and our office was still a pile of ashes, but at least we'd solved one issue.

35

"Okay, but what was the plan?" I said. "What did you do?" I couldn't get a clear answer out of him.

"We did what we did." Brando loved this.

He'd asked to talk more after we all left Samir's, so we went to Rose's. Kim came with him.

"And that was?" I hated this. Twisting around in circles, being led. "Brando, look, I need to know. We can only help you if you tell us what you did." I wanted the words back as soon as I said them. I sounded like a cop, a bad cop trying to coerce a confession.

"Only way you can help? If you wanted to help, if you wanted to know, you'd have been there. I called. I texted. I wanted you in on it. But you were off filming Insta videos and upping your circulation."

He looked at Rose. She was sitting off to the side in a timeless leather chair. She had a drink in her hand and sarcastically toasted him when he looked at her.

"I was reporting on the event," I said. "I was at the rally. The rally full of people who want me dead. We were there, we filmed it, and then, yes, I had to film them marching. That's what journalists do. They follow and report on the story. I don't know what you did, but it doesn't seem journalistic."

"What I did will make waves. What I did took the fight to them. It doesn't matter how many think pieces and editorials we write on the dangers of fascism. It hasn't done shit. It's here, it's growing. The time for words is past. The time for action is now."

He sounded like a politician. A violent, fringe politician, but a politician, nonetheless. His words were rehearsed. They reminded me of Richard.

I looked up and met his eyes, they were flat and even, with a fire lurking beneath the surface. Again, I thought of Richard. I saw Kim at Brando's shoulder, nodding, sitting by for support and guidance. His own Claire.

"We don't mean any offense by this," Kim said. "But we're taking a different approach, and we don't think talking to a journalist about it is the best plan."

"We?" I said.

She reached her hand out and took Brando's. He looked down and squeezed it.

I'd been wrong. It wasn't unconsummated. It wasn't a crush. It was ongoing.

"Oh, I, uh, I didn't know."

"Yeah, well, we didn't take out a press release," Brando said. "Anyway, it's not the point. The point is we're going in a different direction. More, and don't quote me on this, more militant. Take it to them. We, you know, respect what you're doing, and I didn't mean to, well, sorry, Rose." He looked over at her and shrugged. "Just heat of the moment, you know. You're doing great with everything, but we have a different road to take."

"We hope you understand," Kim said.

"Can you?" I looked over at Rose, who took another drink and lowered her eyes, pushing me on. "Can you just tell me if you had, and I know this sounds ridiculous, but you didn—"

"I think we'll stop you there," Kim said, her brown eyes carving into me. "We don't want to go any further down this path. If you ask us something we can't answer, you'll get offended. If you ask us something outlandish, we might get offended. No one here wants to get offended. We're all friends. How about we just have a drink to Richard's downfall and be done with it?"

I didn't want that. I didn't want to leave it there. I wanted them to answer, to assure me that what I was thinking was insane. I'd have taken their anger, it'd have been a soothing balm. This was worse, far worse.

But Rose decided for me. She stood, walked to the kitchen, and pulled down glasses. It was a silent toast, full of tension and punctuating the end of something. The vodka burned on the way down but left behind a smooth, clean taste. After they left, we had another and watched the sunlight fade through her window. We had another and then another, and before long, I don't remember what was said or done.

36

When I woke, the sun was up, and it was almost noon, a soft murmur of activity filtering in from outside. A reminder that the world goes on, it continues no matter how much you think it's ended.

I woke thirsty with a headache and a pain in my neck. I woke longing for my dorm, feeling like a nomad who hadn't been home in a long time. But then I saw Rose, the coils of her incandescent hair spilling onto the bed, framing her head, and the sensation receded.

I looked over at the nightstand and saw the almost empty bottle of vodka sitting there. The night throbbed in my head. It wasn't clear, but there were pieces.

The sheet was pulled to the side, revealing Rose's long, discolored back, rising and falling with her breath. I ran a hand along it and felt a slight abrasion. I picked up the sheet, it was stained pink, subtle but undeniable. There were new bruises, too, light, still forming. I sat up and felt my heart quicken. A rolling pin and a wire hanger were on the floor by the bed. What had we done? What had I done?

I went to wake her but stopped. She'd asked for this our first time. I hadn't initiated it. She had. And she was still there, content, sleeping, peaceful. I didn't want to make it a thing if it didn't need to be. I didn't want to seem closed off, traditional. A tremble ran up my leg. I'd liked it. I hadn't been forced. Once it had started, I'd been a willing, eager participant. And if it was what she wanted, I'd have to accept it. After all, a relationship is about compromise.

I picked up my phone, hoping to distract myself. My Insta had exploded. My Twitter and email too. I had offers to go on news shows and podcasts. Rose would handle it. She'd volunteered to take care of those things, and I'd agreed. I'd given her my passwords, and she would use my computer to handle the surge we both knew was coming.

I closed out those apps and saw I had two messages from an unknown number.

This is Tyson. Do you still want to talk?

Don't tell Rose.

Tyson. I'd forgotten about him. I'd forgotten about Jack and the story. It'd taken place years ago in some faraway land. It'd happened to a different person.

Still, I didn't hesitate. I felt the rush that overcomes you when a story reveals itself. I didn't even pause to wonder why I felt I shouldn't tell Rose. I just answered.

Yes, I would still like to talk. When can you meet?

The three dots appeared to let me know he was typing.

Now. The Sprague Public Library. The one just off campus.

Come alone.

Come alone? What did he think this was? It was so dramatic, learned from some movie. But it excited me, nonetheless.

Everything seemed to be exciting to me. The fear that had once competed with it, a faint aftertaste.

Ok leaving now.

I turned over and went to wake Rose but stopped. She'd want to come. She'd want to know where I was going. She'd ask questions. She'd see right through my weak lies.

So, I just left. I looked over at my bruised and battered lover and walked out the door.

As I crossed campus, I saw the windows full of protest signs.

No Room for Hate

Light Will Drive Out the Darkness

We Shall Overcome

I felt nothing positive looking at them, just a subtle, simmering rage. They seemed so futile, so empty. I wanted to go door to door and tear them down and shake the people who had put them up. I wanted to yell at them that signs don't do anything.

When they're marching through your campus carrying torches and chanting hate, it's too late for signs. It's too late for empty words and think pieces.

But who was I to lecture them? What was I doing? Chasing down an unrelated story. Recording videos so I could go viral. Upping my circulation.

I passed Clinton Hall and saw the carnage. It was like some giant had taken her hand and scooped out a chunk of the building. The chunk where the paper had been. The chunk where I'd spent so many hours writing, editing, laughing. The chunk where I found myself, my purpose, my people.

You could see its insides now, the steel reinforcements that hide beneath the brick façade. There were wires and tubes and crumbling brick. There was ash and the metal bones of desks. A few dozen people were standing out in front of it. They were posing. Looking severe and contemplative while their friends took pictures of them. Then they'd switch, and the picture taker would become the subject. Some were recording videos, speaking in platitudes, decrying what had been done.

Again, I felt a rage consume me. I wanted to slap the phones out of their hands. I wanted to scream at them. I wanted to tell them that it wasn't their tragedy. It was mine and mine alone.

I left. I felt the cold and smelled the smoke and ash that still clung to my hair and clothes. I reveled in that smell. I wanted to never wash it off, to hold on to it forever, a badge of honor, proof of having been there.

I heard footsteps follow me. Felt someone's eyes on me. I shook it off. It wasn't the time to allow my paranoia to consume me.

I'd never been to that library before. Had never even seen it. Aside from bars and restaurants, I hadn't seen any of the town. It was a different world. One we pretended didn't exist.

The library was just off campus, hidden between a grove of trees and a staff parking lot. It was small, and unlike all the buildings on campus, which were covered in red brick and ivy, it was plain, unadorned. It looked like a middle school from any town in suburbia, brutal in its utility.

I walked in and was struck by the familiar smell of old books and temperature control. I stood and closed my eyes and sucked it in, letting it fill my chest, remembering my childhood. I felt safe, insulated from the world, from the fascism and the fires and the frenzy.

"Can I help you?" said an older woman sitting at the front desk. "Do you need help finding something?"

"Yes, I, uh." I was a kid again, wanting to find a book in the library, daunted by its vastness but too afraid to ask for help. "I'm sure I'll find them."

"If you're meeting someone, there's the café in the back. Just down that hall and up the flight of stairs at the end. I would try there."

She didn't smile. There was no kindness in her voice, no faked sincerity. She wasn't mean either, just unwilling to adhere to the false joviality that we've all become so accustomed to. She went back to her book, and I headed down the hall.

37

Tess Azar's notes on Tyson Groff:

Pale. Worn out. Beaten down blue eyes. His hands, smooth and plump, chatter against the table, buzzing, never still. He looks old. His face is drawn and thin, but you can tell it'd once been full. He looks like a man more comfortable with some fat on him who's lost weight. Lost it in an unhealthy, nervous way. He wears a large hoodie that falls off his shoulders and swallows him up. His hair is covered with a baseball cap, but I can just make out wisps of light blond hair that seem to be turning gray. His face is speckled with growth, not a beard, just neglect. It looks like it hasn't been washed in a week. I want to pick him up and hug him. I want to bring him somewhere to get a meal, a shower, and a shave. I want to tell him it'll be all right, but I can't, and I doubt it will be.

Calling it a café would be a stretch. Six tables with twice as many chairs shoved into the far corner of a room from 1982. Two large windows that overlooked the woods leaked in some natural light, but they couldn't drown out the septic yellow of the ancient bulbs.

Tyson sat at the farthest table in the corner, wearing a baseball cap pulled down. It was the most conspicuous way he could have tried to hide. Anyone could see he didn't want to be seen. But it didn't matter, there wasn't another person in the building, and I doubted there would be.

"Tyson?" I said as I approached. He faced the window and didn't look up.

"Did you come alone?" He strained his voice to sound gruff and mangled.

I motioned around, indicating that it was apparent I'd come alone. Still, his head remained down, and I decided to play along. "Yes, of course, and I don't think I was followed. Can I sit?"

He nodded, looked up, and glanced around. Then he pulled on his hat to ensure it covered his face and shifted his chair so his back was turned to the room.

"I'm surprised you came," he said and took a sip of his coffee. He pursed his lips and shook his head. "Don't get the coffee."

I thought I saw a smile creep across his shoulders but couldn't be sure as his face was still covered. "Of course, I came. This is very important to me."

It was then that he looked up, and I saw his face.

"Where have you been keeping yourself? You're a hard person to find," I said. I'd been trying to get ahold of him since I started on the article, but no one seemed to know where he was.

"I've been hiding out, taken a leave of absence for the rest of the semester. I've been living off campus in a room above a pizzeria. I had to lay low, get off the grid for a bit."

He watched, concerned, as my hand fluttered across the page, taking down his words. Then he glanced around the room, his tired eyes always searching.

"Can you…" He shifted in his seat. "Can you not write down the thing about the pizzeria? I don't…I can't have them finding out where I am. They'll, you know, look for me. They'll find me."

"Of course." I made a show of crossing it out. I turned the notebook to him, careful to hide my description of his appearance. "See, all gone."

"Thanks."

"I'm going to record this, though, if that's all right with you." I showed him my phone. "I just want to make sure I'm not misquoting you. No one will hear it but me."

"I guess that's all right. Just don't go showing it to anyone."

"I won't, I'm not trying to…you know… I'm on your side. I'm just trying to get the story. Now when you say they'll find you, who are 'they'?"

"They?" he echoed with more than a trace of disgust. "Are you serious? You don't even…what do you know?"

"About?"

"What are we doing here? About Jack. About the workshop. What do you know?" His voice rose, and the texture he'd been forcing into it fell away. "Do you know anything?"

"Well, I, uh." I didn't know anything. It was obvious. Until he said, I hadn't realized it myself. If I'd had to write an article on Jack right then and there, I wouldn't manage three paragraphs. "No, I don't know much."

He sighed, exhausted but a bit excited. He wanted to be the one to tell me. He wanted to be the one to shape this.

"Okay." He laid his soft hands on the table. "I'm sure you know about the writing workshop, right? Hell, it isn't even a workshop, not officially. But you know about it? The basics."

I nodded and wrote.

"Of course you do." He eyed me. "You're seeing Rose now, right?"

I fought off a blush and nodded again.

"Well, you know, be careful." He hesitated and gave me a searching look. "Anyway, so, you know, people joke it's a bit of a cult, CWC, the Creative Writing Cult. We eat the same things, talk the same, walk the same, take the same classes, all that. But people talk about it like it's a joke, you know. Like 'Oh, Sylvia's cult, haha,' but it isn't a joke. It's real.

"Take me, for example, I didn't get in at first. I got into the university but not into her program. I got like waitlisted. They thought the first pieces that I sent in weren't good enough. They told me to write some more, and they'd keep me in mind. So, I did. I took two weeks off school, pretended I was sick, fought with my mom, broke up with my girlfriend, a whole thing. I was possessed. But I wrote a few good stories. I sent them in, and they still had a spot, and they took me."

He smiled to himself. It still had a hold on him. He still loved that rush, that acceptance.

"Anyway, fast forward to orientation, and I'm hanging out with this group of guys. None of us knew each other, and we just got lucky and met and clicked. We liked the same movies, played the same video games, listened to the same music. So, we're pumped, and we're all set to room together until I get pulled aside on the second day by this guy, he's an upperclassman who's like helping to run the orientation. He tells me I'm in the wrong place. He pulls me, like grabs me by the arm, and drags me off to a different room where there are nine other incoming freshmen and two upperclassmen, and they tell me I'll be rooming with one of the people in that room. They tell me what classes I'm to register for. Tell me I'm to eat with the people in that room and only the people in that room. That I don't need to worry about making other friends, these are my friends."

"They said all that?"

"Yes."

"You ever see those other kids again?"

"Once, on campus, but I just kept walking. It wasn't…as a freshman, you weren't supposed to even interact with students outside the workshop. You were supposed to focus on your writing and reading. You had the other people in the workshop, but that was it. That was your friend group. Then, when you're a sophomore, you can do a little socializing. Just a bit. See." He nodded to my notebook and waited until I started writing to continue. "Every incoming freshman gets paired with a junior. They're your guide. Freshman year, you associate with your fellow freshman, a few sophomores, and your guide. That's it. Then when you're a sophomore, you can ask for permission to hang out with people outside the workshop. We called them SOs. Sanctioned Outsiders."

"Ask permission?"

"I know. It sounds crazy. It is crazy. But when you're in it and see all the former alum who are published and winning awards, you think it's for the best. You think the program works, so who are you, some idiot teenager, to question it."

"Did anyone ever, you know, disobey the rules? Make a friend they weren't supposed to?"

Tyson bit his lip and nodded. "A kid in my class did. I assume someone in every class does."

"What happened?"

He pulled at the brim of his cap, pushing it down and bringing it back up. "Well, uh, he started dating this guy who was outside. It was just a few months into freshman year. He met him in this history class we all took. I knew they were hooking up, and it seemed all right, so I didn't say anything, but someone did."

"Do you know who?"

"I have my suspicions." He averted his eyes. I knew. He thought it was Rose. "Anyway, they found out. Then they questioned me and everyone else in the class about it."

"Who questioned you?"

"Some upperclassmen. This girl, sorry woman, who I was terrified of. She's a prominent writer now. Anyway, I told them I'd heard about it but didn't say anything because it wasn't my business, you know. But they didn't like that. They gave me the silent treatment. Everyone. The whole workshop, my class, upperclassmen, everyone. Even my guide. No one spoke to me for a month."

"What happened to the guy who broke the rule?"

"And that's tough, you know," he said, ignoring my question. "Freshman, new school, and you're alone except for these people. Then they freeze you out… It's messed up. You get bad thoughts. Go to dark places."

He rocked in the chair and sat on his hands. I waited, letting him catch his breath. Anxious not to let this drift into a therapy session. "The student who broke the rules, what happened to him?"

"Oh, he was gone. Out of the program."

"Just like that?"

"You wouldn't think it's that bad, you know, the silent treatment. It sounds like some kid stuff, but it's brutal. It destroys you. When they spoke to me again, I cried. It was the happiest day of my life. It was cruel, but it worked. I was in. I wouldn't break rank for anything. Like, I didn't, you know, have much experience when I came here. I was looking forward to that part of college. See if I could, you know, find a girlfriend. And I had some girls flirt with me in classes, but I wouldn't even talk to them. I was that committed. Nothing was worth giving up the workshop. It was my life."

"And where was Sylvia in all of this?"

"Sylvia?" He pulled away from the table, rolling his head to crack his neck. "Well, you know, freshman year, you take that lecture with her, and you see her a few times. Then she has you work these events, like waiting tables or parking cars or whatever, but she won't even look at you during those. You're the help."

"Did you volunteer to work those events?"

"Volunteer? It wasn't like that. If anyone asked, I'd say I volunteered, but…no. They would tell us there was an event, and we'd show up and work it."

"No pay?"

He shook his head and laughed. "It was a learning experience. Same as when we went to the store for her or mowed her lawn or did whatever she needed doing."

"Mowed her lawn?"

He shrugged. "No, you don't deal with her much, not until you're an upperclassman, and even then, only if she likes you. You know, they talk about the success rate of the workshop, but it isn't like that. Most of the alums are just, you know, in debt. She and the admin hype the successes. Carol Wang, Frank Pruitt, Jennifer Brim, but there are more of the others. More like me."

"And during the program, she spends time with the Wangs and Pruitts and Brims? The ones who she thinks will make it."

"Or she spends time with them, and because of that, they make it."

I wrote and circled this line, fixating on it, bleeding ink

through the page. "Then it's very competitive to be one of them? One of her people?"

"It's insane. Cutthroat. And that's the thing, you know, you're in this bubble, and the people in there with you are looking for any chance to ruin you. I know people throw around the word toxic a lot these days, but that's what it is. A zero-sum game, you know."

I scanned my notes, searching for a pivot. "Tell me about these 'Sanctioned Outsiders.' Say we met when you were a sophomore, and you wanted to hang out with me. What would you do?"

"Well, I'd go to my guide—"

"Before we even met?"

"What?"

"Well, if you can't talk to me before you get the okay from your guide, how would you even know to proceed? Like, how would you know I liked you?"

"I wouldn't. Maybe some people are, you know, feeling things out before they ask for clearance, but it's risky. Most people in the workshop just date within or nothing."

"Wow, that's bleak."

"You're telling me." He looked down at his hands and ran a finger across a gash in the table.

"So, what was the sanctioning process like, if you even know?"

"I know. We all know. Once you're a junior, you become a guide. Then you learn. My novice—"

"Novice?"

"You know, like a learner. Underclassmen, that's what we call them. Novices. So, mine was a kid named Theo. Good kid, good writer. Artist, too, graphic novels, comics. I thought he had real talent. We got close fast. You know, that's just how it goes at college. He wasn't clicking with the other kids in his class, so I was kind of his outlet.

"Anyway, Theo came to me one day in the spring of his freshman year. He said he'd been kind of talking to this girl.

She's from the town next to his, and they met at a party over winter break. Now, as you can imagine, we don't have the same control over break, but it's still forbidden to associate with people from the university or take up any serious relationships. A one-night thing is fine just don't get tied down. But that's not how love works. So, Theo's all excited telling me this, telling me how he thinks she might be the one, how he's crazy about her, how he can't believe she likes him, all that good stuff. And my heart is breaking because I know what I've got to do."

Tyson's head dropped. He raised his fingers to the bridge of his nose and pinched, an all too familiar movement.

"What did you do?" I said, afraid of the answer.

"What'd you think I did? I'd just had a piece published. Sylvia had read it, she'd liked it. She'd talked about it in class. She'd asked to see my novel. My novel. I was on the cusp." He took hard, rapid breaths in, panting like a dog. "And I knew, if I warned Theo and they found out, then she would find out, and that would be it. I'd be done, out of the workshop. I couldn't risk it. I knew I was already in trouble just for having my novice break the rules like that. I was supposed to be watching him. I was supposed to have him trained…so I ratted him out. And he was gone, and I was on a kind of probation."

"Did you…fight for him? Push back? Anything?"

His hand was wrapped around his forearm, his nails digging in. I saw a trickle of blood escape and decided not to press. I wasn't there to judge him. I was there for information. "Probation? What does that entail?"

"No submitting for publication, extra editing duties, extra screening of new applicants, can't read any of Sylvia's drafts, no one reviewed my work for a month. Things like that. No peer editing was the worst of it. You grow to need that. The recognition or even the criticism. You get hooked on it. Aside from that, I got some mild freeze out. They went to the bar or to see a movie a few times without me."

"That must've stung."

"You know, yes and no. I thought I deserved it. In a way,

I thought I was getting off light. After a month, I was back. Lower in the pecking order, but still there."

I remembered the subject of our interview. "How did Jack handle all of this?"

"Jack." He reached for his cold, terrible coffee and drank it all down. "Well, Jack was her favorite. Jack and Rose. Fucking *Titanic.*"

"*Titanic?*" I said before realizing. "Oh, like the movie?"

"That's what we called them. They even looked a bit like them. You know Rose with the hair and the, well, you know. And Jack was long and beautiful and graceful, effortless in his charm. When he wanted to be, at least. The nickname fit. And they were the best, special. I don't think I ever read anything by Jack that I didn't think could be published unedited. Rose was good, too, don't get me wrong. I always thought Rose would be more successful. She's driven, and she's got that look. Pedigree, I guess. But it was so natural with Jack. He'd sit in a room for two hours, not even, and come out with a perfect story. You'd read it and be furious that he'd thought of it instead of you. Furious and jealous and amazed.

"So, he was Sylvia's favorite. She loved him. I mean, we all did, but it was something for her to take notice. It started when he was still a novice. I think she had a one-on-one with him when he was a freshman. That never happens." He waited, trying to figure out how to word his next statement. A writer hard at work. "Let's just say if I, you know, if I ended things, she wouldn't be publishing my book."

"You don't know that," I said and regretted it.

"I do. My book wouldn't make any money anyway. Jack's will make them plenty."

"The money's going to charity."

"Hah, maybe they'll give a little to a charity to save face. The money's going to the workshop and Sylvia and to…the people who worked on it."

He looked out the window, drifting away, making it clear this part of the conversation was over.

"I heard he'd get a bit moody when working on something?"

Tyson nodded and wrapped his arms around his ribs, hugging himself, smearing blood across his forearm.

"Is everything all right?" I leaned forward, out of my seat, and put a hand on his shoulder.

"Yes," he said, shaking me off and coming back to life. "I'm fine. I just...look, you promise you'll see this through? Because if I put this out there and you hang me out to dry...I don't know...I don't know what I'd do."

"I'll see it through," I said, and, in that moment, I believed I would.

He shifted his weight in the chair, still edgy but accepting my promise. "Sylvia did... Well, she took an interest in some of the students that went beyond." He swallowed hard, and I could already see where this was going.

"Sexually?"

He nodded and glanced over his shoulder. "I didn't, I mean, it's crazy, but I used to be jealous about it. She's older, but there's a, you know, power to her. I mean, you've met her, right?"

I nodded. I knew what he was talking about. She had a magnetism to her.

"So, when I wasn't, you know, picked, I felt jealous, passed over. It's so stupid. Worse than that. It's offensive. I hate that I felt that way."

"It's understandable. In that environment, anyone would feel that way."

"I guess." He looked up and, for the first time, conveyed a warmth toward me. "Anyway, she started with Jack right away. He bragged about it at first. Talked about her sucking his dick and things. You know, just to the guys. I don't know what was true and what wasn't, but I know she was with him from the start. At first, I didn't know if it was like a relationship thing or just sex. I guess I still don't know. I know he spent a lot of time at her place, and I know a few of the upperclassmen were close with him. He said sometimes she'd have a bunch of people over at once, and they'd all, you know, hook up. He said he was into it, talked about it like it was the greatest thing in the world. But, you know, people rationalize that stuff. And I mean, even then, I was thinking, like, what kind of consent can there be in a situation like that?"

He looked at me expectantly as if he thought I could answer the question. "I don't know. I don't think anyone knows."

"Right, well later, last year, when I was in her good graces, I got invited to one of the parties." His hand trembled, and he used the other one to stop it, but the tremble just passed to his leg. "Let me tell you, there was no consent in that room. By walking in, you agreed to it all. I'm not, you know, I don't like to think I'm closed-minded, and whatever consenting adults want to do is fine, but that was something else. That was about... power."

"Can you describe what happened?"

"There were eight of us, two novices, the rest were guides. Sylvia instructed and watched. She'd tell you to, you know, stick something into someone or hit someone. It was a lot of physicality. No tenderness, no decision, no arguing. You just obeyed. The two novices, we called them supplicants when they were there. Anyway, they were, well, they were in the center of the room, and they were tied up and gagged. I saw them crying, tears running down their faces while people... It was rape. I don't care what they said or what they say now, that was rape. And I was part of it. I'm a... I was a part of it."

He dropped his head and began to sob. I let him go. I didn't know if he deserved my compassion. I had questions, but I wasn't sure I wanted them answered. I was afraid of those answers and happy to live for a few more seconds in a world where they were still questions.

"What did the supplicants say after it was over?" I asked after his sobs had slowed.

He pinched his nose, hard, and laughed. "After? It was insane. She ordered pizza. We took turns showering, and then we went into the kitchen and ate. We joked and talked about books like nothing happened."

"The supplicants ate with you?"

"They were shaken up, but, yes, they ate. They were both covered in bruises and cuts, but they laughed and tried to be part of the gang. I don't know if it was their first time or what. I don't know if she always did it or if she started with Jack or—"

"You think this happened to Jack?"

"I know it did. I was hanging out with him and Henry. It was back when they were together. We were drinking, and I made a stupid joke about wishing I could hook up with a hot older writer, you know, just messing around, and Jack broke down. Started crying. I told him I was sorry and offered to leave, but he told me to stay, and then he talked about it. About the group stuff but also the stuff with just Sylvia. She'd...she'd abuse him. He said she locked him in her bathroom once for three days. She had a dog collar and a chain and would walk him around. She'd bring him out when she needed him. When she or the group wanted to.... It was awful. He survived by drinking sink water. He didn't eat anything. People thought he got moody because of the writing, but it wasn't that. He got like that when she was abusing him. Or maybe she was always doing it, I don't know, but it wasn't the writing that messed him up. It was her."

"Do you think that's why he—"

"There isn't a doubt in my mind. The night he, well, that last night he was coming from one of her parties. I know we said we were coming from the diner or something, but it was from Sylvia's."

"Lisa said that you'd bee—"

He didn't hear me, just kept going. "He'd been at her place, we were all there, it was a rough night. He left in a state, crying, yelling at Sylvia about something. I couldn't make out the words, but he was upset."

"Did you ever...did anyone hear what it was about?"

He shook his head. "No one said anything to me. Maybe someone...I don't know."

"And then later, did you know where he was or you jus—"

"We just stumbled on him. He was wandering around and then, well, you know the rest."

I got this down and waited, trying to see if there was anything else to ask about that night. I decided there wasn't. "Is this still going on?"

"Yes, at least it was last time I checked."

"Did you participate in others?"

He nodded and looked down at his hands. "You had to. It was part of it. I didn't…I wanted to stop, I swear I did, and I wasn't, you know, the most enthusiastic, but once you got brought in…there was no way out."

"And Jack, did he participate in these? Not as a supplicant, but on the other end."

"He was one of us."

"Was he enthusiastic?"

"We had to hold him back a few times. It was…he'd get carried away."

"Henry?"

He nodded.

"Lisa?"

He paused, swallowed, and nodded. "I went because of her," he said and stopped and shook his head. "That's not true, sorry, I went because of me, but I wanted to stop, and she… she said I couldn't. She said, well, she said a lot of things. They all did. Don't tell her I told you that. Don't tell her I told you any of this. Please."

"Of course not. No one ever…I mean, you'd think someone would've talked. Someone who wasn't, you know, a success."

"Like I said, I don't know if it was always like this or if she just started, but I know none of us would ever talk. It wasn't… you were part of it. And you, you know, were culpable. I think a lot of them see it as just sex, or that's what they tell themselves. Even some of the supplicants, they talk like they like it. I don't see how you… I mean, I know everyone has their thing, but like

I said, there was no consent there. It wasn't even sex. It was just dominance and abuse."

"Who?" I knew the answer before asking it. "Who said they liked it?"

"Like I said, Jack, but also"—he lifted his head—"Rose."

"And she—"

"Yes."

"Enthusiastic?"

"Very."

I felt the hot trace of tears rush down my cheek. Tyson looked away, and I shook them from my face. I looked down, and two had fallen on my notes, leaking through to the previous page.

38

"I don't care," he said when I repeated that I'd keep him a confidential source for as long as he wanted. "Do what you have to when you write the article. Just don't tell Lisa that I, well, you know. I don't care about the rest. Not anymore. I'll never be inside again anyway."

I was standing, prepared to leave. Eager to talk to the others, to chase down the story, to ride the high. But I stopped and sat back down.

"You two aren't…"

"What? Together? No, not anymore. Not since I left the workshop. I don't think I'm considered worthy. Not of her or the group."

"You think they told her to end things with you?"

"I don't know, could've gone either way. Maybe she decided to end things once I wasn't going to be…or maybe they told her I wasn't worth it. Either way, I don't think she lost sleep over me. Our whole relationship…I was just convenient. Just there. I see that now."

"I'm sure that's not—" He turned and looked at me, full of hate. I stood up and placed a hand on his shoulder. He shrugged it off. "If you need anything, you have my number. I'll be in touch."

He moved back to the window.

"Listen," he said, lowering his voice. "Be careful."

"What?"

"This…be careful who you trust. Careful what you believe." Paranoia.

"Thanks," I said with a half-smile.

"I'm serious. You don't know what they're capable of."

I thought of the heavy footsteps that now followed me. Of the feeling of a camera on me as I walked across campus. I thought of the big-eared woman and the sunken-eyed man. Nothing definitive. Nothing solid. Just a feeling. "I'm sure they wouldn't—"

"They would."

I said nothing.

"Ever feel like you're being followed? Watched?"

I wrapped my arms around my chest.

"Me too. Maybe that's just how everyone feels. Maybe it's just the world we live in. But maybe not."

We heard movement downstairs, a child screaming out, and a mother trying to control them in a desperate, hushed voice.

"The fire," he said. "They know how it started?"

"The fire?"

"Anyone can light a match. And it sends a powerful message. Or, at the very least, it's quite the distraction."

I said nothing. I didn't want to believe it, to entertain it, but the thought was planted.

39

I checked my phone after I was out of the café. I had three messages and two missed calls, all from Rose.

Hey, where did you go? If you're getting food, can you bring me an XXXXL coffee!

Hey, for real though, where are you? I'm getting worried lol.

Tess, call me. What's going on? Are you all right?

I could see her pacing around her apartment as she wrote the texts, staring at her phone, waiting for a response. She wasn't the kind of person accustomed to waiting. A thrill ran through me at the thought of this woman being tied in knots over me.

I went to call but stopped myself. I'd never make it. I'd explode or collapse, I didn't know which. Instead, I texted her.

Hey! Sorry! I had to run out for this thing for the paper. I completely forgot about it! I'll be back later!

The ellipsis appeared to show she was typing the second my message landed. Again, I found myself delighted at the hold I had over her. Delighted and disgusted in myself for that delight. My emotions bounding from love to hate and back.

Ok… we have that interview with Vivian Morris at 6. We need to prep first. Be here at 4?

I'd forgotten about Vivian. She was a cable news host from a network on our side. I was scheduled to go on, she'd show our recordings and ask me about what it was like on campus. Rose and I had done some trials the night before while drinking.

I'll try. I don't know if I can get out of this. I'll be ready at 6 either way. Sorry.

I felt sick for apologizing, dirty. I hated how much I still wanted her, how nervous I was that she was angry with me. That this might cool her off.

But I couldn't think of that. Not then.

I texted Henry.

Hey, Henry, it's Tess. Can I swing by, or can we meet somewhere? I have some follow-up questions about Jack.

I'd debated reaching out to Lisa first, but the order of operations was important. Henry might not tell Lisa. He might not tell anyone. Might. After Lisa, it would be over. It would be out there. She'd talk without hesitation. And then I'd have to confront Rose.

Sure, come by whenever. I'm just reading.

I was already on my way. I'd be at his door in a few minutes. I checked the time, 2:30. My phone vibrated, Rose.

Ok, I guess. This is a big deal, Tess. National exposure. Your little college paper story can wait.

I gripped the phone and had the sudden urge to scream. My *little college paper story.* She'd see. She'd find out.

Of course, she was right. Even that story, which felt huge, paled in comparison to the interview. That interview would be seen by millions of people. It would make me a presence. It would establish me as a national figure in the fight against fascism.

But it would have to wait.

40

I checked my phone before I knocked on Henry's door. I'd already texted him, letting him know I was there. This couldn't run over. I had to keep to a tight schedule. Any minute Tyson could break down and tell Lisa or Rose or even Sylvia, and then it was over. I needed to get through the interview, and the one with Lisa, before that happened. I needed to get to them before they could coordinate. Before they could strategize and quash this.

Henry peered out of the door, searching the hall for Rose. Our eyes met, and he could tell.

"No Rose?"

"Not for this one," I said.

His head and shoulders dropped. He knew why I was there.

"I'd prefer if you not tell her I'm here," I said. "We have to talk about some things, and I'd ask that they remain confidential."

"Until you publish them." He turned and walked inside, leaving the door open for me to follow.

I sat on the couch, and he in his chair. There was no offer of coffee or water or anything. All the warmth our previous conversation had ended with was gone, a distant memory.

I placed my phone on the table and set it to record. I went to begin but stopped, deciding it was best to let him start.

He took deep, heavy breaths and stared at his hands, turning them over and gazing along their ridges and valleys. His posture had collapsed from its imposing erectness, leaving him hunched and beaten as if trying to protect himself from an attack.

"You can't use my name," he said, focusing his stare on the table. "I can't...I know I'm a coward, but I can't risk it. I don't... it might not go how you think. She's not going to just lie down and die. She'll fight. And I don't know who'll win."

He stood up, lifted his chair, and walked over to the window. He opened it and set the chair down. He pulled out a cigarette, it was lime green. He lit it, holding it outside between drags, blowing the smoke through the opening.

"Well," he said. "What do you already know?"

"A lot."

"I don't want to— Ah, fuck it. What's the point? I take it you know about the parties? If you can call them that. What'd you want to know?"

"Whatever you think is relevant. Whatever's important."

"With how it relates to Jack?"

"We could start there, but it doesn't have to be limited to him." I felt the wind cut through the window and rattle around the room. It felt good, calming. I realized then I'd been stress-sweating, and I could feel it pool in every crevasse of my body.

"Jack was at them early. He was one of the supplicants."

"Supplicants? Was that the term used?" I said, already knowing the answer but wanting to pick up some momentum.

"Supplicant or sup."

"And you were never a sup?"

He shook his head and took a drag. "No, I wasn't. Jack was special. She loved him. I know you'll say that's not love or whatever, but sometimes love is like that. It isn't always a good thing. It's just a force that overcomes you and dominates everything else. It can be horrible. It can destroy you."

He paused and turned to me, tears in his eyes. He wanted me to agree.

"I think that's true. I think we've all been there. On both sides of that."

"Right, right. So, she loved him. It was a sick, power kind of love, but it was love. She never loved me like that. She never loved any of us like that."

"Was there jealousy there? Jealousy for that kind of attention, love?"

"Yes, I know it's messed up, but there was. Even after we

knew everything that was involved, we were still jealous. At first, he'd just treat it like, well, like a good thing. Like he was part of it, and we weren't. Like he liked it. And we didn't know what was happening, the extent of it, so we just…"

"He'd brag about it?"

"He was part of the older group in a way. The guides and all that. They were getting things published, and they had agents, and those things make you like a god to the underclassmen. So, you can imagine how we saw Jack. He was part of that, and Sylvia would have one-on-ones with him, and when one of her alums would come to lecture or something, they spent time with Jack. It was a whole thing. He was the one, special. He even got a story placed freshman year. It was wild.

"So yes, we were jealous…some of us still are. Some of us are mad at him. Even now. They think he wasted his chance. Wasted his talent and opportunity. They talk about it. They say they'd have switched places with him. Like even back in the day. Even when he was a sup. I don't…they shouldn't talk like that, but I don't know, I get it. Like being in this program, even having some stuff published, doesn't guarantee anything. I might wind up a professor at some mid-tier college teaching creative writing, but he never would've. He was guaranteed that life. There's a lot I'd do for that."

We sat in silence. He was hedging, but I knew what he meant. I understood it all too well.

"She took an interest in Jack when he applied for the program?" I said, shifting gears. "Or when he got here? Do you think it had to do with his talent or—"

"Before. He sent her his writing when he was in high school, sophomore year or something. He'd read *A Wake of Vultures*, and he just started sending her stories. She…" It seemed his body was trying to stop him from talking. It would pull him back, try to correct him, but he broke through. "She had him visit at the beginning of his junior year of high school."

"Did he?" I didn't have to finish the thought. I was counting in my head, how old are juniors in high school? Sixteen?

He nodded.

"Did he tell you this?"

Another nod. "When we were on the road trip. We were lying in bed one night, and we'd had a few, and I was just messing with him about Sylvia. I didn't know about all of it. You heard rumors, and I knew it was...but most of us didn't participate until junior year. And it was a running joke about how much she liked him. Anyway, he just told me. He said he'd go there once a month in high school. She'd read his work and give him criticism and stuff and then..."

"He'd go to a party."

"That's right."

"Was he upset about it? When he told you, I mean?"

"Not really. He just said it. Just put it out there. Then he told me not to tell anyone, and I could see he didn't want to talk about it, so I let it go. I was just...I was happy to be with him. And he was so closed off, so to have him open up like that, I just took it."

"Did you ever bring it up again?"

"Once. It was a while later. The morning after a party. I was, well, he'd gotten pretty rough with a sup the night before. I stayed up all night thinking about it, fixating on it, and I decided I needed to talk to him."

"Were you two still together at this point?"

"No. That wasn't...we didn't have a long run. Anyway, I brought it up. Something like, 'Are you all right? You were pretty rough on that kid last night. Does this have to do with when you supped? Or what happened in high school?' And he exploded. He told me I didn't understand it. He told me they were lucky to sup. He said he loved it. He said he still did it for Sylvia sometimes. He said it was so closed-minded of me to believe that no one could get pleasure from that. He accused me of being a bigot. He said I was just like all those homophobes condemning gay sex."

"And how long before...when was this?"

"A few months before he…maybe like three or four months before."

"Did you talk much after that?"

"Not really. He hit me a few weeks later, and then he went underground. The rumor was he was living at Sylvia's trying to finish the novel, but who knows? No one saw him."

"Were there any parties during that time?"

He nodded. "He wasn't there, not until the last one. Did you, it doesn't matter. He was at a party the night he…"

"I heard he had an argument with Sylvia? Maybe it led to…"

"Well, maybe, I mean, no one heard the argument. It was… he had another rough night. Getting rough with one of the sups. No one said anything, but I think maybe Sylvia talked to him about it after. Just the two of them, upstairs. We just heard raised voices. It could've been about anything, his novel, anything."

"But you think it was about his treatment of the sup."

"That's what I think. Maybe it's what I want to believe. Either way, he came down, and he was crying, and he just flew out the door. I tried to grab him, talk to him, but he was gone."

"Did anyone follow him?"

"No, we didn't. He was like that. It wasn't odd for him to storm off."

I couldn't write fast enough. His words were bouncing off me, swirling around in a chaotic mess, I looked down at my phone, thankful for the recording. "He'd done this before? At a party?"

"Not at a party." He dropped the spent cigarette in a cup of water; it sizzled as it hit. "But he was like that. Sometimes he'd storm out of class, sometimes mid-conversation, he was just volatile. We didn't think anything of it that night."

"And then Lisa just happened to—"

"They just stumbled on him. Or that's what I heard."

He slouched in the chair, his head resting against the shallow back. It was time to move on. "What do you mean when you say he got rough with one of the sups? I was led to believe it was all rough."

"It was. That's part of it. But there are degrees. He...there was blood. He had to be pulled back. It was bad."

"Where was Sylvia during this?"

He flinched at her name and gripped his knee hard. He lit another cigarette. "She was there."

"Did she intervene?"

"No."

"Did she say anything?"

"No. She just stood there and watched."

"How did she...in general, how did she participate?"

"Watched and instructed. She'd egg us on, always clothed, standing or walking around, taking it all in. It was eerie."

"She never—?"

"Not that I saw. She'd have private sessions. She had them with Jack for a long time. Even after he wasn't a novice, wasn't supping."

"Did she have them with others? Do you know what took place?"

His body went rigid, and he seemed to be in pain. "I think she had all the sups first. That's how I understood it. She'd break them in, make sure they were...pliant. She had regular sessions with them. Once a week, I think. They stopped once they were no longer sups. I only ever heard about her continuing with Jack and one other person.

"As for what took place, I can't swear to much, but I can imagine. A lot of the same stuff we did, just more so. Sometimes Jack would have burns or bruises or cuts. When we would...when we were together, I'd see a lot of them. Like I said, I don't know everything that happened in those sessions, but I can imagine."

I was busy writing, and it took me a minute to register all he'd said, but when I did, I felt a chill run over me. I could see the bruises. I knew them all too well. "You said one other person continued with private sessions after they stopped being a sup?"

He nodded and focused on his cigarette.

"Who?"

He turned to me and met my stare. "Rose," he said, even though it didn't need to be said.

"She was a…"

"Late freshman year, I think. She bragged about it. She'd sought it out. Sylvia likes to wait until sophomore year. They're still young, but they're committed by then. But Rose wasn't having it. She was jealous of Jack and, well, you know Rose."

I saw that my writing had begun to waver and move off the line. "And she continued?"

"She—" he said and paused and looked at me. "I don't have to."

"No, I'm fine." I held my shaking hand to steady it. "Please continue."

"We were all drinking one night, not long after the incident with Jack and the sup. He wasn't there, and we were talking about him. About how he was cracking up. We were talking about his drinking and moodiness and the stuff at the parties. Rose was defending him. She always defended him. She was saying how he was under a lot of pressure. She talked about the expectations for his novel and how brilliant it was. She always bragged about how much he confided in her. How she was his primary editor, his shadow, and all that."

"That must've annoyed people."

"Eh, kind of. We're a competitive bunch. I think people were mostly jealous. She was, is I mean, a great editor. His stuff wouldn't have been what it was without her. Anyway, she was talking about the pressure, and then she started to bring up how much strain Sylvia was under. How she was getting some heat from admin about money for the workshop and some other stuff. Rose said just enough to let us all know she was on the inside, and we weren't. She said Jack was feeling some of that pressure. She said that Sylvia would pass it on to him. So, we asked how she knew all that, and she told us. She said she still had private sessions with Sylvia. She said they'd gotten more frequent, more intense."

"More intense?" I stood, picked up my phone, walked to the window, and leaned against the wall. I didn't have to ask, he just handed me a cigarette, the same magenta one Rose had given me before the rally. I crouched down, and we smoked together. "Did she…go into detail?"

"A bit. Just how demanding and unrelenting Sylvia was in those rooms. She said it was the same as with the workshop. If you pushed back or hesitated, she'd press you harder. She talked about how…" He looked at me, and I nodded for him to continue. "How she enjoyed it. How, for a few months, they'd stopped, and she'd missed it. She had to convince Sylvia to start back up. Then she said that's how the sups felt about the parties too. She said they liked them."

I thought back on our first time together, Rose taking my hand and securing it around her neck. How she pleaded with me to squeeze harder. How I resisted and the look of disappointment on her face. And then I thought of the night before, searched my mind for clarity that wasn't there. I saw the bottle of vodka on the end table, the rolling pin on the floor, the fresh bruises on Rose's back and side, the cuts, the wire hanger, the soreness in my right hand as if I'd spent the night gripping something.

"Before that," he said, "we'd been talking about if the parties were right. If we should make a stand against them, against Sylvia. Rose told us that would be depriving the sups. She said we wouldn't understand because we weren't ever in their position, we weren't ever chosen. She said it was an honor and that they got off on it just as much as we did."

"And, in the end, you decided not to do anything to stop the parties?"

"Right."

"Do you think you would've done something if Rose hadn't said all that?"

He held his arm out the window and drummed against the side of the building. "No, I don't think so, we were just talking. No one would've done anything. No one was going to take a stand against Sylvia. No one was going to risk their place for a sup."

I checked the time, put out my cigarette, and walked back to the couch. "Do you think the parties and Jack's history with them and the fight that night and his relationship with Sylvia… do you think they contributed to his suicide?"

Henry crossed and uncrossed his legs twice, tapping a finger on the windowsill. "Suicide is…look, I don't know, but I would imagine it isn't just one thing. You don't wake up one day, happy and content, and then stub your toe and jump off a building. It isn't like that. It's a slow drip that fills the tub. It takes time. So, I'm sure the workshop and Sylvia and the parties and all that contributed. A lot of things contributed. Everyone who touches someone's life moves it. You don't think about it when you're doing it, but you leave an imprint. You shift their trajectory. A lot of people are responsible for what happened to Jack."

He'd begun to cry. You couldn't hear it in his voice. His body didn't convulse or quiver. His breathing didn't change. If he'd been turned to the window, I'd have never known he was crying.

"You can't blame—" I stopped, hearing how trite it sounded. Hearing how little impact my words would have. I fidgeted, feeling the interview was over, but unsure how to leave.

After a few minutes, his crying stopped, the tears having landed on his shirt, speckling it. He stood up and took the cup of cigarette butts. The water was yellow, and the once vibrant colors were now diluted. He took it to the kitchen, where he disposed of them.

The silence in the room clung to me. "Without a note, it's hard to tell," I said and began to collect myself to leave.

Henry spat out a scathing laugh before reentering the room. "There's a note. Somewhere, there's a note. Or there was. Maybe they destroyed it by now, but there was a note."

"Did you…how are you sure?"

"He was a writer, Tess. We write down everything. I've got thirty notebooks full of story ideas and diary entries in this room. I keep shopping lists just in case they're relevant. Half of the workshop has already begun writing their biography, the rest are working on memoirs. There's no way he didn't write a note."

"So, you think Sylvia got it? Or admin? Or what?"

"I don't know. Maybe admin. They'd want to protect her and themselves. Maybe Sylvia. Maybe someone else. But he wrote a note. Unless…"

He lowered his gaze and led me on with his eyes.

"What? You're not saying…"

He shrugged and tried to hide his evident pleasure in this line of thinking.

I felt it, too, the perverse pleasure of a morbid conspiracy. There was no evidence for it. There was no reason to believe that Jack hadn't killed himself, but it was enticing. It was just the kind of theory that none of us can resist.

"Do you ever feel like you're being watched?" I asked. "Followed? Listened to?"

He didn't answer. He didn't need to. The mirth that had filled his face a moment before had vanished, replaced by a frigid, empty stare, and that was answer enough.

41

Henry promised not to tell anyone about our conversation or my investigation. He'd been happy not to. The last thing he wanted was someone to find out what he'd told me.

I didn't text Lisa before heading to her place. I just walked. It was almost four, but I took a long, circuitous route to her apartment. I needed to think, to process.

I doubted Jack was killed, but it wasn't impossible. Maybe he was preparing to go public, making threats. Maybe a lover's quarrel. Maybe a jealous writer.

I shook my head and tried to knock the idea out of my mind. It sounded ludicrous. It sounded like the deranged ramblings of a conspiracy theorist. There was nothing pointing to it. No evidence. Just a lack of a note.

But still, it gnawed at me.

And, I'll admit, I welcomed the distraction. It was better than considering the rest of the picture, or the fire, or the sense of being followed. Better than thinking of Rose and her part in all of it. Better than admitting how little one truly knows another person. Better than thinking about what we'd done the night before and what that meant. What it meant for this story, for consent, for our relationship. What it meant about me.

I waited outside the door to Lisa's building, pretending to be absorbed in my phone, until someone came out and I could slip in. I thought about how easy it was to get into those buildings. I thought of the violent lunatics that I knew peppered the campus and how seamless it was for them to enter these buildings, unwelcomed, unannounced.

But, of course, they lived in the buildings too.

I walked up the staircase, nervous, and the now familiar sense of being followed overcame me. I stopped on a floor that wasn't Lisa's and walked down it. I heard footsteps trailing me. I turned around in a panic, fists clenched, keys poking out between my knuckles, to find an empty hallway.

I laughed to stop from crying.

Then I continued to her apartment.

My hands were slick with sweat when I knocked. Three hard, resounding thuds. I heard movement.

Then the door opened, and there she stood with her sharp green eyes and long, violent red hair. She smiled and didn't even feign a look of surprise.

"Hello, Tess," she said. "What brings you here?"

I followed Rose inside, my legs conditioned to trail her without hesitation. I took in the walls, pictures of Lisa with various authors and influential people. It was the start of a collection, still meager but growing. My stare lingered on the photo of her with Sylvia, their mirrored stares, their impersonal embrace.

I noticed the bumps and grooves on the wall, the various imperfections that make up a home. I wanted to run my hand along it. I wanted to breathe it all in. A condemned woman slowing down time as she ascends the gallows.

They didn't let on they knew. Not at first.

Lisa was waiting for me, sitting in a chair with a cup of coffee in front of her. She stood and smiled. It was full of subtext and malice. Still, I returned it; I played my part.

She offered me coffee and walked to the kitchen to retrieve it, leaving me alone with Rose and the tension.

Rose said nothing. She didn't scroll on her phone or read a book or stare out the window. She just stood and watched me. There was no need for words. She was letting me contemplate what I was giving up. Making it known that there was still a path back, I just had to take it.

And I wanted to. I wanted to rush over to her and tell her everything. I wanted to insist I wasn't going to reveal the truth, wasn't interested in exposing anything. I wanted to lie and thrash and create a world wherein I was the hero working to help Sylvia and the workshop and, above all, Rose. That I was protecting them.

I glanced over at her and blushed. She wore jeans and a T-shirt. Stripped down. Minimalist. The type of thing you wear when you want to demonstrate your natural beauty. She shifted her weight and gave a half-turn toward the kitchen, showing off her figure, emphasizing her length. I felt like I was seeing her for the first time. I felt like a girl again, full of destructive infatuation.

Lisa returned with the coffee, still wearing that same plastic smile. "Milk? Sugar?"

It was a badge of honor in the workshop to drink your coffee black. Strong coffee, uncut. Anything else was a sign of weakness.

I shook my head, faking all the confidence I could.

Lisa sat the coffee down next to a painful, rigid wooden chair. It hadn't been here last time. It'd been brought there just for me, just for that moment. A modest torture device.

How long had they known? How long had they been planning this? Had they, somehow, known before me? Had they suspected the path I'd take before it even presented itself?

They had the night before. They'd cleaned my clothes and brought them along, knowing the path my night would take. Maybe this was the same. Maybe they always knew that I'd end up there.

My mind jumped to Tyson. To him sitting in that desolate café staring out the window and trying to conceal his tears. I saw him broken, guilty, repentant. I looked over and saw Rose and Lisa. Unrepentant. Unbroken. Strong and confident in their guilt.

I took the seat and drank some coffee, burning my lips and the roof of my mouth but not flinching. This was a test of wills, and I couldn't show even the slightest trace of weakness.

"So." I pulled out my notebook and set my phone to record. Lisa looked at the phone and whispered something to Rose. They both smirked and nodded. "Do you two want to talk to me together or separately?"

They stared at me, then turned to each other and let out a joint, corrosive laugh.

"So serious, Tess," Rose said.

They each sat in comfortable, elegant chairs across from me, but they eschewed the comfort of the chairs, sitting straight, their backs never approaching the cushion. Their arms were mere inches apart, a subtle comment on their intimacy. Lisa continued to laugh and patted Rose on the arm. It was meant to excite my jealousy, to enrage me.

It worked.

I took another sip, again scalding myself, and ignored their provocation.

"What do you want to talk to us about?" Lisa asked.

"I think we all know the answer to that," I said. "I'm fine if you'd like to do this together."

"We don't have the slightest notion what you're talking about," Rose said. "We don't even know why you're here."

"So, you two were just hanging out? You just happened to be here together?"

"Yes, after you disappeared, I decided to do something. I hope that was all right. Or am I supposed to lie in bed waiting for you, trapped in my room until you summon me back into existence?"

Lisa smirked, thrilled to have our relationship cast in such a sordid light. I could see her constructing the story. She'd tell it for years, provided I became someone. She'd gather people around and explain how I was a possessive, insecure lover. She'd mock and deride me. I wondered what Rose had told her. What they'd talked about while I was conducting my interviews. Did Lisa know about the previous night? Did she know more? What intimacies had Rose revealed to her?

But I couldn't focus on that.

"If you must know," Rose said, her voice stiff and proper. It was the voice of the old Rose. The one she used with Sylvia. "I came here to strategize with Lisa about your upcoming

interview. The one you should be preparing for right now instead of running around doing whatever it is you're doing."

I said nothing. There was no point. I didn't want to spin
around with them and end up back in the same place. I didn't
want to entertain that lie.

"I don't think she believes us," Lisa said. She was bouncing
in her chair, bursting with excitement.

I looked at Rose, ignoring Lisa. I'm sure I looked sad, full
of pain. I thought I noticed a flinch, her eyes darting away, her
body trying to rebel. But it was temporary. "It seems you'd like
to do this together."

"We don't have anything to hide," Rose said.

That was it. It was over. If she'd had the humility to ask to
leave the room, to not want it aired in front of Lisa, I might've
broken. I might've buckled under that human request. I might've
taken the opening to forget everything I'd heard about Rose. I
could've buried Sylvia but left Rose out of it. But she wanted it,
she'd picked her side.

I reached for my coffee. It no longer burned my lips or
mouth. I'd grown numb to the heat. I drank it down, all of it,
and slammed the cup on the table. Then I scanned my notebook. "When was the first time you each participated in one of
Sylvia's parties?"

"What, like served?" Rose said. "I was a freshman when I
began to work her parties. I think Lisa started at the same time.
Is that what you want to talk about? Catered affairs?"

"Not those parties."

Neither of them moved. They stared back at me. They didn't
seem surprised or confused. They knew what I was talking
about, but it was up to me to speak it into existence.

"Are you going to act like you don't know what I'm referring
to?" I said.

"I'm afraid you'll just have to be more specific." Lisa took
a sip of coffee and shrugged. "Sylvia is a gregarious woman
who's quite in demand. She has many parties. I think I attended

my first as a guest when I was a junior. Is that what you're asking about?"

I waited, trying to see if Rose would add anything. Trying to gauge their resolve. Would this be their stance? Would they claim that they'd never participated in these ritualized rapes? Would they claim they never happened?

"I've spoken to two sources who have confirmed the parties. Since you're insisting on taking this line, I'll detail them. They were sex parties wherein several upperclassmen engaged in sexual acts with underclassmen, supplicants, as they were referred to. Sylvia would direct the actions. She held private parties with the supplicants, where she also performed sexual acts on them. I have separate, confirmed sources who have stated that you both participated."

Their faces mirrored each other. Calm, stone, not quite a smile but not a frown either. They made it clear that this was all expected. They were prepared for this.

Lisa leaned toward Rose, her lip nearly touching Rose's ear. I could feel her whisper rush over me, causing me to shiver. I couldn't hear the words, just dulcet tones scratching against my brain.

Rose's face dulled and then returned with more vibrancy than before. She nodded and looked at Lisa, tapping her on the upper leg. My mind seared. I saw them embracing. I saw them rolling around, caressing. I felt Lisa replace me.

Rose whispered something in response and then turned to me. "We know the encounters you're referring to." She looked at me as if we'd never spoken before. As if she hadn't told me she loved me. It was all erased. All evaporated into the recent, distant past. "They were consensual. It isn't appropriate to describe them as you have. Consensual acts of intimacy between adults are no one's business but the participants. This effort to shame us for our sexual predilections will not work and, honestly, is quite offensive."

Lisa beamed and reached over, patting Rose's hand, holding it there and meeting my gaze.

It was the answer I'd expected. It was the answer I'd wanted. I hadn't mentioned consent. I hadn't accused them of anything illicit. I'd asked them to confirm the parties, which they had. "I didn't mention consent or cast aspersions on these encounters. However, it's interesting you mention consent. Was that something that worried you about these parties? The lack of consent?"

"Well, I think consent is often something people are concerned with in today's society, and, as you emphasized the underclassman aspect of it, I wanted to head it off."

"So, you'd acknowledge that a power dynamic existed in these parties that could be seen as a lack of consent?"

"No, I would say the opposite, which is what I did say."

"You wouldn't say that a power dynamic exists in your workshop? You'd say underclassmen—novices I believe is the outward-facing term—aren't at the bottom of a hierarchy?"

"Well, of course, there's a hierarchy, but it's not as you're making it out to be. They're learning. They're eager to be in this program, we all are, and it goes both ways. I learn a great deal from my novice."

"Yes, but we aren't talking about the academic pursuits of the workshop. We're talking about the sexual expectations."

"There are no expectations," Lisa said, reminding us of her presence. "There are opportunities. You can partake if you'd like to, but you aren't required to."

Rose's eyes darted away as she said this.

I scanned my notes. "We can come back to that. What about the restrictions on fraternizing outside of the workshop? I was told underclassmen aren't allowed to make friends or have relationships outside of the workshop. Is that true?"

"Of course not," Lisa said. "That's a ludicrous claim. Who told you that nonsense? I thought you were smart enough to see through something like that."

"I won't reveal my sources, just as I won't reveal you."

"You can tell anyone anything I say in here. I don't need to hide behind anonymity like a coward."

"Rose? Do you agree with Lisa? Is this an inaccurate portrayal of the workshop?"

She paused and ran a finger along her jeans before answering. It was a nervous movement, full of trepidation, and seeing it, I wished I'd come to her first. Alone. It was the first time I'd even thought of it as a possibility. The first time I entertained the idea of trusting her with this.

"Of course, I agree with Lisa," she said. "It's true that the workshop can, at times, be rather insular, but that's a result of the rigors and closeness of the program. It's hard for us to find common ground with people outside the workshop. They don't seem to grasp it. They don't understand, and as a result, they demean it and lash out. They destroy those relationships when they do this, and we learn to look inside, not outside, the workshop for love and support."

It wasn't even veiled. It was as blunt as a hammer.

"But you admit that it's a rather insular group?" I clicked my pen, spun it around my finger, and clicked it again, pushing past the searing pain that was radiating through my chest.

"Of course," Rose said. "It's a demanding and prestigious program. I assume many similar programs are the same. It comes with the territory. We read the same things, discuss the same ideas, pursue the same objectives. It's natural that we would be close."

"Okay, how about this. Let's say when you were still a novice, your guide came to you and told you to do something. Would you have done it?"

They breathed in together, a shared, deep, steadying inhale.

"That's a vague question," Rose said. "If my guide came to me and told me to read a short story or change something I'd written—say shift a story from the first to the third person—I would, of course, try it. That's what a workshop is. You work with people on your writing. You take criticism and suggestion."

"What if they told you to do something outside of your writing? Let's say in your personal life?"

"Again, a vague question. If they told me to cut back on my

drinking or start waking up earlier, I would take that advice."

"What about in a relationship?"

"What do you mean?"

"What if they told you to stop seeing someone?"

"Well," Rose said. Lisa grinned and leaned in, whispering something in her ear. Rose turned, seemed taken aback, but then smiled. "It would depend. Your guide becomes a close friend. It's an important relationship. If my guide sat down with me and explained how a relationship I was in was toxic, if it was affecting my work and my life in adverse ways, if they expressed concern for me and my well-being due to this relationship, I would heed that advice."

Lisa followed Rose, sure not to allow a chance for me to respond. "Like, let's say she was in a relationship with someone who was attempting to destroy everything she worked for, everything she believed in. If they were sneaking around behind her back, interviewing friends of hers to create some false narrative that would destroy her life. If that was going on and her guide told her to get out of that relationship, I think she would listen."

Rose flinched and fidgeted in her seat.

"So," I said, "you would say that the workshop has an input on your romantic relationships?"

"In the way any friend does," Lisa said. "We're a close group. There's nothing wrong with that."

"Have there ever been instances where you felt the group crossed the line? Situations that gave you pause?"

"No, we know what we're signing up for. Everyone knows it's involved, intense. The workshop becomes your family. And in spite of, or maybe because of that intensity, there are thousands of people who would give anything to take our place. You have to be a little mad to be in the program, that's part of it. Genius and madness flow from the same source, after all."

"Rose?" I asked, again ignoring Lisa's cult speak. "Ever an instance that caused you to pause?"

"Well." For a glimmer, I saw her again. I saw the Rose I knew. The Rose I loved. I saw the person behind the shroud, and then she disappeared. "No. I wanted to be part of this workshop more than I wanted anything. It was my dream. That's how it is for all of us. It's like Lisa said, you know what you're signing up for, and you're eager to do it. You learn to accept all that is asked of you because you know it'll help. You know it'll make you a better, more successful writer."

"If—" I hesitated, unsure if I should ask. I knew I had to get there, but there were more tactful ways. Then I looked up and saw Lisa grinning at me, saw her put her hand on Rose's upper thigh, and my hesitancy vanished. "If Jack were here in this room now, would he agree? Would he say that he knew what he was signing up for?"

"Excuse me?" Lisa stood up and sat back down and stood up again. The anger was performed, but it would sound convincing on the recording. "How dare you? How dare you do that? You didn't even know him. Don't use his memory to advance your crazy conspiracy theories. You have no right. That's disgusting."

She slammed her feet and paced around. Then she sat back down. It was overdone, manufactured, but that was the point.

"Why do you think he didn't leave a note?" I'd been waiting to unleash this question until they were worked up, unsettled. Perhaps I'd learned more from Richard than I cared to admit.

"A note?" Lisa said.

"Yes, people often leave a note when th—"

"Often? You don't even know what you're talking about, do you?" She laughed and shook her head. "Do you know what percentage of people leave a note?"

"I, uh—" I should've researched it but hadn't.

"Around one in four. Hemingway didn't leave a note. And what is it that you're suggesting here? That we somehow found the note and disposed of it? Or that he didn't kill himself? Which is it, Tess?"

"No, neither." I felt as if I were standing in the middle of a frozen lake with the ice cracking beneath me, too far from shore to make a run, terrified to move and make it worse. "I just—"

"You just what?" Lisa was standing now, a few inches from me, hovering.

I didn't know if this outrage pouring off her was real or fabricated. I couldn't tell anymore. It all seemed indistinguishable, a viscous mass of truth and lies.

Rose leaned forward and grabbed Lisa's arm, ushering her back to her seat. "Tess didn't mean that, Lisa, you know she didn't. She…I don't know, it must've been something someone told her, put in her head."

"She shouldn't have believed it."

"Yes." Rose turned and looked at me. "You're right, she shouldn't have."

"And she shouldn't be bringing him up like she knew him." Lisa was pouting now, like a child who got what they wanted but still isn't satisfied.

"She's right, Tess, it's not appropriate of you to bring him up like that. What happened with Jack was a tragedy, and we're all still grieving. For you to dredge that up and toss around these veiled accusations for some article is inappropriate. It's tactless. It's beneath you."

I swallowed and waited to let their outrage, genuine or otherwise, dissipate.

"It's true I didn't know Jack," I said. "I wish I had. He sounds like he needed a friend. All I'm trying to do is find out what happened. I don't set out with an objective when I start to research an article. I don't have a narrative I'm trying to force. I'm just here to see what happened. People came to me. They told me their stories. They talked about how Sylvia locked Jack in a bathroom for three days. How he had to drink sink water. They talked about how she walked him around on a leash like he was a dog. They talked about how he was still in high school when she started abusing him. They talked about how he later went on to abuse other supplicants. They told me that the night he killed himself, he abused a supplicant, had a fight with Sylvia, and ran out into the night in tears. I didn't make these things up. I didn't want to find them. I didn't want to find out about the role you two played in this. I wish I never learned about any of this. It's disgusting and disturbing."

I ended there, wiping a tear from my cheek. Rose had looked away when I mentioned Jack being locked in the bathroom, and her gaze hadn't returned.

Lisa hadn't looked away. She'd held her eyes on me. She was quivering with rage. "You don't have a narrative? That's what you're saying? You didn't have a narrative in mind when you interviewed Jason? How about Richard? Did you go into that with an open mind? Did you want to hear his side?"

I didn't answer.

"That's what I thought. We all have an angle, Tess. We all have a narrative. Don't act like you don't. Do you know who else had a narrative they were trying to push? Those losers who talked to you. Let me guess, Tyson, that sniveling coward. I can't believe I let him inside of me. And who else, let's see, well, you're not a real investigator, so it must be someone on campus. Someone you already spoke to." She turned to Rose, who was still looking away, trying to make herself invisible. "You introduced her to Henry, right?"

Rose didn't move. She seemed catatonic. Maybe I'd been too hard, pushed too far. Maybe she was more fragile than I'd thought.

"So, Henry and Tyson." She spat. "Cowards. Liars. Do you want the real story? Since you don't have a narrative to push, you must want the real story. Tyson just had a collection of short stories rejected from every publishing house he sent it to. Sylvia told him not to send it out. She told him it wasn't ready. She told him it needed more work. But did he listen? No. He's a man. They never listen. They hear what they want. He just couldn't accept that he wasn't quite good enough. He never was. He barely even got into the workshop, and he never could handle it. Couldn't handle the work and couldn't handle that his writing just wasn't good enough. He knew it wasn't. He talked to me about it all the time. He told me he was worried he didn't have it in him. That he'd never make it." Here, she leaned in and lowered her voice, mocking a secret. "And you know what, he was right.

"As for Henry. He used to fuck Jack. Did you know that? What am I saying? Of course, you did. He tells everyone. It's the only impressive thing he's ever done. So, he and Jack had a little thing, and it meant the world to Henry and didn't mean anything to Jack. It was just a thing to do. Henry was just around. Then Jack was done with him, and it crushed Henry. He went to pieces. And you know who was there for him? Sylvia. Sylvia and Rose." She turned to Rose and put a hand on her arm. "They comforted him and took care of him. They listened while he cried about Jack.

"But he didn't get back to writing. He hasn't written a thing of quality since they broke up. If you can even call it a breakup. Jack never saw it that way, but that's not the point. Almost two years without a thing written. Henry lost the drive. And you need that. More even than talent. Writing is more perseverance than talent. He's not the first to lose it, and he won't be the last. So, after two years of waiting, Sylvia told him he was done. Out of the workshop. He wanted to do another year, but she drew a line. His book is supposed to be finished in a couple of weeks, and he's not close. So, he won't graduate from the workshop."

She stopped and panted a bit, gasping for breath as if she'd just run a marathon. She kept her hand on Rose's arm and caressed it.

"So, those are your sources," she said. "Two people with ample reason to smear Sylvia. Two people coming off crippling news, their lives in pieces. And they both blame her and the workshop. These are your sources, your only sources. Does that sound reliable to you? Do they sound unbiased? Did you see any evidence to support these outlandish accusations? How about this, if someone else came to you with this, would you trust them?"

She leaned back in her chair and sighed with satisfaction.

"And not that it matters to me," she said, "but is this really where you should be putting your energy right now? With fascists marching through campus, setting fire to buildings. To your building. Threatening you. Is this where your focus should be? Letting two failures lead you around on a wild goose chase."

I stared down at my phone, wishing I'd never set it to record. Wishing I'd never even gone to Lisa's. The story was cleaner before. I could've published what I'd found without this shadow hanging over it.

My stomach fought itself into a knot as I sat and thought.

Neither of them spoke. Rose continued to stare off into the distance, her back half turned to me. Lisa stood, went to the kitchen, and returned with a fifth of something. She poured some into her cup and did the same for Rose, letting that pour run a bit longer. Then she put the bottle on the table and took a sip.

She might have been telling the truth. I didn't have any evidence aside from those two sources, who were far from unbiased. The program was cutthroat. The stakes were enormous, and that often created an environment where a lie could fester. Maybe they coordinated with each other. Maybe they embellished. Maybe consensual orgies were going on, but nothing untoward.

I thought back on those interviews, the pain in their voices, the scars that shone through them. They felt real. Lisa felt like a lie.

But perhaps I just wanted the story to be real. Even with all the implications, even with Rose being involved, maybe I longed for it to be true. It was scandalous, sensational, viral. It would increase my fame.

I flipped through my notes. I looked up and stared at Rose. I willed her to turn to me, to show me something. I thought of the consequences if this wasn't true. Thought of what I was giving up. Her. Our imagined future. Everything.

Then she turned and met my eyes. She'd been crying, her

face drained of its familiar hue. Even her hair seemed to have given up, lost its bounce, flattened out, dulled from its accustomed fire to a soft simmer.

"Lisa," she said. "Can you give us some privacy? Go for a walk or something? Tess and I need to talk."

Lisa feigned outrage but agreed. "Okay, how long?"

Rose didn't move her eyes off me. They were weak but insistent. "I'll text you when we're done."

Lisa paused before leaving. She stared at Rose, a bit frightened. This hadn't been in their script. This wasn't scheduled. This wasn't part of the plan.

I began to sweat. Nervous excitement welled up in me. Maybe she'd decided to come clean. Maybe she'd decided to side with me, weighed the options, and opted to change teams.

After the door closed, Rose stood and walked around, searching for something, a phone or camera, something meant to record us. She found nothing. Then she went to the door, careful not to make a sound on the old wood floors and swung it open. The hall was empty. We were alone.

She pulled her chair and moved it toward mine. I saw the softness return to her. I saw the person I loved sitting across from me.

She lifted the bottle and poured some into my mug. She raised hers, and I followed. We both drank. Then she reached out a hand and cupped my cheek. She held it there, and the world opened up to me, and I fell in. She reached over, picked up my phone, and stopped it from recording. Then she sat back and took another drink.

"Sorry about Lisa," she said. "She gets excited. We all do, I guess…this wasn't the way to do this. You should've come to me first. Instead, I had to hear about it through the grapevine. How do you think that made me feel?"

"I'm sorry. I should've…you're right."

"We could've talked this through. It didn't…we could've worked together, found a real story. One that holds. But now this…Sylvia's upset. I'm sure you can understand that. She's already been in touch with a lawyer. If you try to run this, well, she's ready to talk to admin. They'll shut it down. This is a bad look for everyone involved, including you. It'll destroy your credibility, which is already in question, and with this…there's no coming back from this, Tess."

She was right. I'd been knocked down by Richard, but this would end me. He was a crazed, right-wing zealot. No one held it against me that he hated me. That was life. It was, if anything, a badge of honor. But this would be different. Sylvia was different. She was royalty.

"I thought it was solid," I said, doubt consuming me. "They corroborated the same things. I didn't lead them. They had the same stories. How could they have managed that?"

"They planned it, and there are…parts that are true."

"What parts?"

"Well, Jack was at Sylvia's that night. And he did leave upset, but it didn't have to do with the parties or anything. She was telling him he needed more work on his novel. I'd made some suggestions that he'd fought against, writers always do, and he was emotional and left."

"Do you think that…" I stopped myself. "You know that's what they argued about?"

"He'd been complaining about it for days. I didn't hear the argument, but I'm sure that's what it was about."

"What other parts are true?"

"The parties, I guess. Things happened that were on the edge. That's how those things are. You're trying to find your boundaries, push them, and sometimes, maybe, we pushed too far."

"What they told me was way past any boundary."

"I know that's how it looks. I know it seems horrible, but you weren't there. Most of the time, they weren't either. I was. I had my boundaries tested. I liked it. Now I know what gets me off and what doesn't. I've found out things about myself that I never would've otherwise. I know how it sounds, but it's the truth. And the people in those rooms, they wanted to be there.

They wanted to find out the same things about themselves. If that isn't consent, I don't know what is."

She drummed her fingers on the arm of her chair.

"Think about us," she said, softening her voice.

I already was. I saw the rolling pin, the bruises on her back, the blood, the wire hanger. I felt my hand around that wooden handle. I couldn't remember all of it, but I could feel it. Feel the urges, the longing, the excitement. I wanted more, and I didn't know how to process that want.

"Think of last night," she said. "We...that was consensual. I know you might not remember everything, but I asked for it. You were obliging me, not the other way around. And we didn't stop every minute to ask if it was all right. That would've ruined it. We just agreed going in and let our desires take hold. Is there anything wrong with that? Was there anything wrong with what we did?"

I didn't answer. I couldn't, and she knew it.

"No." She ran her finger across my forearm and then traced the nail down the back of my hand. "We're consenting adults. There's nothing wrong with us exploring our desires. That's what trust is. That's what a solid relationship is built on."

We sat in silence for a long time. We heard birds outside and the constant noise a university in early spring gives off. Conversations being had, friendships being formed, jokes being told. People were falling in love and getting into pointless, pretentious arguments. Life was going on, unaffected by the world and all its complications and horrors.

"But how could you know what they wanted?" I asked. "No one would ever be willing to say no to her, to you, to the workshop. How can that ever be consensual?"

"I see that, but, and I know how this will sound, but it doesn't matter. I can tell you what happened in those rooms, I can tell you I know it was consensual, but I'll never be able to prove it. And neither will they. And at the end of the day, that's what this is about. It isn't about what happened, it's about what you can prove. You need this to be iron-clad, bulletproof, and it isn't."

My stomach contracted, and I felt the liquor rise through my throat. I tasted the acid and forced it back down. This wasn't what I wanted. I didn't want ambiguity and gray areas. I wanted her to tell me it was all made up. I wanted to be told that she'd never participated in what they described. I wanted to hear that, even if it was a lie.

"Do you know how we found out?" She sat back in her chair. "About your investigation. They each came to us. Tyson called the second you left the café. He thought Sylvia would help him out with his book if he brought this to her. He cried and begged. He said he'd renounce it all, claim he made it up. Claim you were lying. Henry did the same. You left, he called. He wanted another year in the workshop. They both told us everything. Everything they told you. They were just using you."

"They called you?"

"Yes." She straightened up and crossed her legs. "Because they're desperate, and they still love the workshop, and, as Lisa put it, they're cowards."

"I heard…someone told me that the workshop was ready to stop the parties. Jack got rough with a sup, worse than usual, and everyone talked about ending them. Putting their foot down. Going to Sylvia. They told me you…they said you fought to keep the parties going. Is that true?"

"Tess, does that sound like something I'd do?"

And there it was. That was the ultimate question. I had to choose. I could believe that she was capable of all those things, or I could believe she wasn't. It was a question of faith, not fact. "So, nothing like that happened?"

"Jack got rough with someone. It was bad. He was going through a lot, right after that was the fight with Henry, and then he went into a kind of hole for a bit."

"What do you mean got rough?"

"He shut himself off." She ignored me. "Built a wall. He talked to me and Sylvia, and that was it. He was finishing his book and rewriting a section. Every week, he'd give me pages to read that were unbelievable. Polished, confident. It's one of the best things I've ever read. Anyway, he just lived and breathed it. There was nothing else. And then he finished, and, well, there was nothing else. That's what happened. That's why he…"

She stopped, lowered her head, and fought back tears. Then she stared up at me, her eyes glimmering, the sunlight pushing through the window, coating her face.

"We should've seen…we should've seen what was happening, done something. Stopped him from writing for a bit, forced him to focus on therapy, made him go out. I don't know, something. But we were all in it. The book was so good, and we thought it was helping him. We thought he'd come out of it. He always did with a story. But this time… I blame myself for Jack. Sylvia does too. We pushed him, and we were there at the end. We could've helped him, and we didn't."

Before I knew what was happening, I was comforting her, my hand on her arm. "Don't, you can't blame yourself. It isn't your fault. There's only so much you can do. Suicide is a culmination of things. It's a slow drip that fills a bathtub over the course of a lifetime. It's never just one thing. You can't blame yourself."

I didn't know if I believed it, but I knew I needed to say it. I'd picked my side. I'd done it the first time I saw her. That was it. I was hers, and she knew it.

"I know," she said, pulling back her tears like they were on a string, resting her hand on mine. "I know, thank you. It just hurts. It's hard. I think you're right. I don't think it's ever just one thing."

We sat in silence for a minute while she let this sink in.

"Rose." I didn't know how to broach it. "I know this is going to sound… The fire, it wasn't—"

"What, Brando?" she said, choosing not to understand my question. "It's possible, but I'd say Richard is the mo—"

"Not Brando. Sylvia. The workshop."

She stared at me. She wasn't outraged, she wasn't appalled. She was flat, even, calm. "Of course not, Tess. We'd never do something like that. Why would we—"

"To shut me up. To scare me off. To distract me, take my attention off the story about Jack. I don't know. I just—"

"Who mentioned this?"

"No one."

"Who?"

"I don't know, just something Tyson said. I just can't…I don't know what's up and what's down anymore. I feel like I'm being followed. I keep seeing the same faces, feeling footsteps behind me. I think people are watching me, listening to me."

She hugged me, placing my head on her chest, cradling me. "Shhhhh, it's okay. It's going to be okay."

We stayed like that for some time. Her holding me, rocking back and forth, running a hand over my hair. It should've been absurd, comical even, but it wasn't. It worked. I felt better.

"I can't publish this article," I said. "She'll destroy me."

"You can't write that article." She sat me down and placed her hand on my knee. "But you can write a different article. You can interview me and Lisa, and Henry again if you want. You can interview us about Jack. Sylvia even said you could talk to her."

My head jerked up. "Sylvia?"

"It's her idea. People know you've been thinking about an article on Jack, it's perfect. His book is getting fast-tracked. It's going to be published by the end of the year. You can write an article, and we can release it right before the book. The definitive piece on Jack. We'll get it in a national publication. It'll be perfect. You'll do a wonderful job. I know you will."

I ran my hands over my face and up to my hair. I let my palms rest over my eyes and pressed.

"In the meantime, you can write about what's important," she said. "Like Lisa said, fascists are marching on campus. You're a leader in the fight against them. They set fire to your building. They've made threats against you. Hell, it sounds like they might be spying on you. That's where you need to focus your energy right now. Not here."

Lisa's words coming out of Rose's mouth. Or were they Lisa's? Or Rose's? Or Sylvia's?

"Sylvia's on board with this?"

"It was her idea. She likes you. She wants to help. No one wants this to go the other way, Tess. I told her, I said you were good. I told her I loved you. I told her you just had bad information and were following the story. She understands. She knows how it looks. She wants to help. She was…we were going to tell you about all this next week anyway."

I hugged myself. I was scared and tired, and there were no more moves to make. My mind was stumbling toward the finish of a long race, exhausted, unable to make a final push. All that registered was her saying she loved me. She said it in the present tense. She still loved me. Or she wanted me to believe she did. It was shameful, but it appeared that was all that mattered to me. I'd thought there was no way back for us, but she seemed to feel we'd never ended.

I nodded, and Rose clapped her hands. She poured me another drink and one for herself. We toasted and drank. It tasted bitter and caustic going down, but once there, it was warm and soothing.

"Okay," she said. "I'll let Sylvia know, but first, we need to prep for this interview. Vivian Morris is a friend of Sylvia's, and she gave us the questions in advance." She adopted a playful tone, as if the conversation we'd just finished had never happened. "Nothing nefarious or unethical in it. It happens all the time. She just wants you to have time to prep. Like an open-notes test."

I wanted to ask if I'd have gotten the questions if I hadn't agreed to Sylvia's proposal, but I knew the answer to that.

"Here." She laid out pages of notes. "Take a look at this. Lisa and I have been doing some outlining and research for you. Just some historic examples to use if you want. I'm going to call Sylvia and tell her about the new article. And I'll let Lisa know she can come back. She can play Vivian in a mock interview."

She was excited, bouncing from one leg to the other. She

headed into the bedroom to make her calls, not wanting me to hear what she said.

"Oh." She poked her head around the doorframe. "One more thing. Richard's having an interview on a different network at the same time. Grayson Jackson. It shouldn't matter, but I wanted you to know if he...I don't know, just thought you'd want to know."

I nodded, unsure what to make of that information. Unsure what to make of any of it. Then I began to read the notes.

42

INTERVIEW BETWEEN TESS AZAR AND VIVIAN MORRIS:

Vivian: Tess Azar, wonderful to have you here with us.

Tess: Thank you, Vivian, the pleasure's all mine.

V: Well, given the nature of this situation, I'd like to get right to it. We just showed some videos of the chaos at your university in recent days. What did it feel like when you saw that mob marching through your campus, chanting those vile slogans?

T: Catastrophic, like the world was collapsing around me. When you grow up in this country and go to a university like ours, you imagine these things won't touch you. You imagine you're insulated, but you aren't. No one's safe from this.

V: When you say, 'safe from this,' what are you referring to?

T: Well, fascism, for one. The alt-right and their fascist tactics. But also the hate and fear. You know there's hate. You see it online or in the news, but you imagine it won't get to you. As children, we're told that those things—fascism, Nazism— are history. They're like ghost stories or something. And you believe that. And then it's marching through your campus, and you realize it isn't history. It's the present. It's the future. And that realization is terrifying.

V: What did it remind you of? Historically or otherwise.

T: Well, of course, the fascist movements of the twentieth century come to mind. I know the right likes to roll their eyes when we compare them to Nazis, but I'm not sure what other comparison works. They have a uniform. They have a hateful, regressive ideology. They march. They chant. They're fueled by bigotry and unrest, and strident nationalism. They're almost all white men. And they have a boisterous and, as much as it sickens me to say, perversely charismatic leader who's grown their movement with shocking speed. It's easy to look at this and try to dismiss it as a bunch of isolated people on the fringe, but that's just what they said in the late Weimar Republic, and look what happened there.

V: You feel Richard Welch, whom you've interviewed more than once, is charismatic?

T: I find him and his rhetoric repugnant, but charisma isn't reserved for those we agree with. Charisma is the ability to entrance people. To pull them toward you. It's a magic trick of sorts.

V: A magic trick, that's an interesting way to put it. Almost like a spell. Do you feel many of his supporters would not believe these things if they weren't coming from him?

T: I can't say for sure, but that's my suspicion. In times of distress, people long for a strong leader, and often, someone like Mr. Welch appears to parade himself forth as such a leader. It doesn't matter that they aren't actually cut out for it, just that they appear as such a leader. We've seen this time and time again in history. And I don't think you could argue that we live in anything other than a time of distress. For people like us, that distress manifests in a different way than it does for Richard's followers, but it's all a response to the same things.

V: What would you say is their primary concern?

T: His supporters?

V: Yes.

T: Well, that's hard to say. At the core, they feel the world has passed them by. They sense the inequity that's so pronounced in our country, and for the first time in generations, they assume they'll be worse off than their parents. They're likely correct in assuming this. For some of us, we channel our outrage toward the systemic issues that have caused these inequities. The wealth gap, systemic racism and sexism, climate, things like that. For Richard and his supporters, it's different. They blame liberals, and feminism, and minorities. They feel those groups are striving to replace them. They feel things were better in the past. And, above all, they're angry. Angry at everything and nothing.

V: And Mr. Welch taps into that anger.

T: Yes.

V: Do you think there's something that has primed them for this? Were they predisposed to see his point? Or is it just his charisma?

T: I would say they were predisposed. I don't want to put this all on the internet, but it's played a part. The Overton Window has been shifting for years, and if you spend a great deal of time online, you see a different world. You see a world where it's acceptable, encouraged even, to joke about mentally ill people or queer people or women or minorities. And once those ideas are played for jokes, you begin to entertain them seriously. This is harmful for people whose primary social interaction is online. They're isolated, they're alone, and then someone comes along and offers them a group of friends, a movement, a purpose. All they have to do is join, agree, march through campus chanting hate, and then they're part of something. That's a godsend for the scores of lonely men sitting at their computers, full of rage.

V: Fascinating. I can't believe you're just nineteen. So knowledgeable.

T: Thank you, you're too kind.

V: Now, I would be remiss if I didn't mention the controversy surrounding your article. Mr. Welch accused you of twisting some of his words and released a recording of the interview that supports his claims.

T: Thank you, Vivian. I appreciate the opportunity to address this. The recordings he released were doctored. He recut them to fit his false narrative. Yes, I used his quotes in my article. No, they weren't in order. That's how you write an article. No journalist simply publishes transcripts. I didn't misquote him. I have recordings of all my interviews. I didn't misrepresent his opinions. I didn't twist his words. He gave an interview full of hate and violence, and he's now unhappy with how that makes him look. That's his problem, not mine. I stand by my article, and so does my paper. We have lawyers who are working on a suit against him. He's attempted to smear my name and destroy my reputation, but it won't work.

V: Very well put. Now, he released a recording of a second interview you did as well, though I believe you haven't finished that article yet. Is that correct?

T: That's correct. I assume his hope was to get out in front of that article. Take the sting off it. I'm sure he knows how radical he sounds in the recording. I'll still be writing the article. It'll cover the violent attacks perpetrated by Richard's men in the aftermath of his rallies, as well as the march and rallies themselves.

V: Well, I, for one, look forward to reading it. Let's see, we haven't covered the fire. The university is noncommittal on the cause of the fire. What are you hearing?

T: From the university, I'm hearing the same. They won't make any statements on the cause. It's all speculation at this point, but I have an opinion.

V: And that is?

T: I believe it was arson perpetrated by one of Richard's followers.

V: What leads you to believe this?

T: Richard's speech that night was about a man who set fire to his farm in an act of defiance. Richard also railed against our paper in the days leading up to and during his speech. After he finished speaking, his supporters marched off with torches to spread hate and fear across campus. The fire was isolated to our paper's office. It's a clear line. Also, and I was going to save this for the article, I saw one of his people, someone I know he's close with, handing out torches.

V: Wow. Handing out the torches? One of his people?

T: Yes, I've seen him with Richard before on more than one

occasion. He's one of his close associates. To me, this whole thing is very reminiscent of the Reichstag Fire. During Hitler's rise, Germany's parliament building was set on fire. Some people believe the fire was set by the Nazis themselves. I'm not a historian and cannot speak to the veracity of these claims, but I believe Richard learned from this moment and set fire to his enemy's building.

V: That does seem logical. The evidence connecting him to it is convincing, a clear line, as you say. Hard to see what else could've happened.

T: Also, another of his supporters, Jason Cooper, wa—

V: Is this the Jason Cooper who recorded women having sex with him and uploaded those videos online without their consent? That Jason?

T: Yes, one and the same.

V: He's one of Richard's supporters?

T: Yes, I saw them together after one of Richard's rallies.

V: Unbelievable. Predictable but still unbelievable. But I'm sorry, you were saying…

T: Yes, well, Jason was also at the rally handing out torches, so I think it's safe to assume that Richard was aware of what would happen after his speech.

V: I don't see how anyone could reach a different conclusion. Unfortunately, I believe that's all the time we have. It was fascinating speaking to you. Again, I'm floored by your knowledge and poise. I'm sure this is the beginning of a long, illustrious career, and you'll have to come on again.

T: Thank you. It was a pleasure. I'm an enormous admirer of your work. I would love to come on again.

43

INTERVIEW BETWEEN RICHARD WELCH AND GRAYSON JACKSON:

Grayson Jackson: You were just watching a clip of our next guest, Richard Welch, giving a speech at his university. Richard, great to have you here with us today.

Richard: Thank you for having me, Grayson.

G: Well, I think we should get right to it. You've been a recent victim of some savage attacks by the left.

R: That's true. They've attempted to smear me and destroy my reputation. Nothing new there.

G: But you've handled them masterfully. What made you release the recordings of the interview you had with that woman? Tess something, Azul, Azure…

R: Something like that. I can't say I remember. She's just one of many people on the left who have attacked me for my beliefs. I decided to release the recordings because I'm tired of the liberal media manipulating and twisting our words to fit their narrative. Anyone who says anything they disagree with, anyone who points out the issues in our society, is attacked. They don't care about facts, they don't care about the truth, they only care about their narrative.

G: And what is that narrative?

R: Well, the erosion of our nation's morals and structures. They like to pretend those things don't exist, but they do. They're what built this nation, the greatest nation that has ever existed. The left wants to destroy those morals and structures and, in doing so, destroy our nation.

G: And what would they like to replace it with?

R: They make that very clear, communism. They can mince

words all they want, call it socialism or racial justice or something else, but it boils down to the same thing, communism. They want to eliminate private property. They want to take all the money you've spent your life earning, and they want to give it to lazy people and immigrants.

G: That's so true. Very well put. It's incredible how blatant they are about this. They don't even try to hide it anymore.

R: They don't. It's the same with their anti-men, anti-white, anti-straight, anti-America agenda. At my university, you have to apologize for being a straight white man. I've actually been told in class to apologize for that. Because my ancestors allegedly did something to someone else's ancestors. You know what my ancestors did? They built that university. They built this country. And if you don't like it, there's the door.

G: Exactly. I'm tired of having to apologize for who I am. I'm white, I'm straight, I'm a man, I'm a proud American, what's wrong with that?

R: Nothing. You should be proud of that. They're allowed to be proud of who they are. They have gay pride marches, Black pride marches, woman's pride marches, trans pride marches. You name it, they've got it. Except us. And my followers tried to march one time, and they got assaulted and accused of being Nazis.

G: Outrageous. They call us Nazis.

R: It's just projection. They know they're the real fascists. The Nazis were the National Socialist Party. It's always been this way. The left are the actual fascists, and they've just twisted history to make it seem otherwise.

G: Very true. Very true. Well, I thought releasing the recordings was a masterstroke. Your points on it are coherent and honestly mild. I would've been harsher. And then you read the article, and you see how the left twists things around to make you look extreme.

R: Exactly.

G: And there's nothing extreme about what you're saying. My audience agrees with you. You're simply asking to be able to gather and discuss your ideas. A right they extend to every other group, no matter how radical and violent. And now I hear they won't allow you to hold these gatherings anymore, is that correct?

R: Yes, Grayson, that's the case. It's a tragedy. We're no longer allowed to gather in public, and I'm no longer allowed to give speeches.

G: And what was their reasoning for this?

R: Well, after a previous rally, a few of my supporters were assaulted and fought back. Look, you know, my guys aren't going take that sitting down, someone hits them, they'll hit back. And they hit harder and allegedly hurt someone.

G: Someone who attacked them?

R: Yes, they got attacked and fought back.

G: And somehow, we're the bad guys.

R: Well, Grayson, we're conservatives on a liberal campus, and, in this nation, that always makes you the bad guy.

G: Very true.

R: The same thing happened after my next rally. These liberal fascists attacked my supporters, and they fought back.

G: This was while they were marching, correct?

R: Yes, that's correct. Now I wasn't a part of that march. I didn't tell them to march. I didn't, as some people are claiming, pass out torches. But that being said, I don't disagree with what they did. I think they maybe should've used different language, but everything is off-limits these days. You can't say anything without triggering the liberals.

G: The PC police have made it impossible to speak your mind. And yes, I agree some of those chants could be seen as controversial, but if you listen to the words, there's nothing wrong there. There's nothing offensive in what they said.

R: Of course not. And I don't even think my supporters knew the history of those chants. They just found them online somewhere and used them. My people aren't violent. They aren't hateful. They're angry. We're very angry, but everyone should be angry.

G: Agreed. And you didn't lead this march, you weren't a part of it in any way?

R: No. I was there in spirit, of course, but not a part of it, no. I was long gone by then. Watching the video, though, I kind of wished I was there. Seemed like a good time.

G: You and me both. I was thinking the same thing when I was watching it. Those seemed like passionate, levelheaded patriots just trying to take their campus back. Their country back.

R: And we will. This is just the start.

G: I know it is. Now, not because I believe it, but because I have to ask, the fire?

R: Just ridiculous. It was an electrical fire. Or that's what their official line is right now. I have my suspicions, but an electrical fire seems possible.

G: Suspicions?

R: Well, it's just my opinion, but I think it's a little too convenient. My people are marching peacefully across campus. They have some torches with them. I know they would never set fire to a building. I mean, Grayson, you know our people. We're on the side of law and order. We're not the vigilantes. We're not the terrorists.

G: No, we're not. They're the terrorists. History has shown that time and time again.

R: Exactly. And if there was a trace of evidence that it was us, you know they'd have me drawn and quartered by now.

G: Without a doubt.

R: So, if not an electrical fire, which seems a bit convenient, then what? I'm thinking that they set the fire. I'm thinking one of those liberal, feminist, socialist, fascist lunatics set the fire when they saw my people marching. They picked a building that they thought we'd target, they set the fire, and now they're pointing the finger at us.

G: Wow. That seems very logical. It's just what they'd do.

R: They know we won't commit an act of violence. They know we won't stoop that low, so they do it and blame it on us. This is the same thing that happened in the Weimar Republic in Germany, do you know about this?

G: I do but run through it for our viewers.

R: Well, in Germany many years ago, there was a fire. Someone set their congress building on fire. And who set the fire? A communist, of course. Who else? But the left couldn't allow that, so what did they do? They did what they always do, they lied and blamed the right. And to this day, you have people who believe that lie. And now they're doing it again, and the scary thing is, it's working. People think we had something to do with this, just like they blame us for the violence on campus. And now we can't hold rallies. We can't gather. But they're having a rally and a march tonight.

G: They're allowed to have a rally and a march, and you aren't?

R: Yes.

G: Well, I wish I could say I was surprised. Such a typical double standard, appalling behavior. Unfortunately, that's all the time we have tonight. I'd love to have you on again soon to fill us in on this situation and to just discuss the state of liberal fascism in the country.

R: I would love that, Grayson. Thank you for having me.

44

I felt like a fraud when the interview ended. The heavy lights burned my made-up face. Borrowed clothes, I don't know whose they were, Rose had simply made them appear. They were formal and expensive and rubbed my skin raw with my every move. I was an imposter, reading someone else's words, wearing someone else's clothes, living someone else's life.

"Glad we could make this work," Vivian said through the monitor, her eyes stuck to her notes. "Sylvia spoke highly of you, and I'm pleased to say she was correct. She's usually a good judge of character."

"Yes."

"You know I went there, right? Not Sylvia's program. I could never do fiction. But I was there, I knew her." She looked up and into the camera, meeting my eyes. "She's a great person, lots of friends. I'm glad you're one of them."

And that was it. The video cut out, she was gone, and I was left alone in a windowless room with the spotlights shining on my face, wondering what I'd just agreed to.

Rose was buoyant on the walk back to her apartment. I don't remember discussing where we'd be going or what we'd be doing. I just followed.

"That was great," Rose said again—she'd been repeating this phrase every few silent steps. We were passing the burned-out skeleton of Clinton Hall. We both looked at it but didn't break stride. We were already used to it. It's amazing how quickly we grow accustomed to a new reality, no matter how horrific.

"I guess so." On the ground was a charred brick. I nudged it with my foot, and a part broke off.

Rose was a half-step in front of me, leading but glancing back at timed intervals to ensure she hadn't lost me.

For a moment, her shoulders dropped, and her back relaxed.

She unclenched, and I could see an ordinary woman. I could see myself in her. She felt my stare and straightened up, re-clenched. Her aura returned in an instant.

She slowed her stride and linked her arm through mine. "Look, you did the right thing. I know how you journalists are, obsessed with the story and all that, but you did the right thing. It wasn't even…and it never would've seen the light of day. All that would've happened is you would've set yourself on fire. And for what?"

I listened for the heavy sound of following footsteps. I scanned the oncoming crowd for the big-eared woman or the sunken-eyed man. They were everywhere. Every face. Every person that passed.

I focused on the ground. I reverted to my childhood ambition of never stepping on a crack. I had to plan, focus not on the step I was making but on the next and the one after that. I had to adjust my gait, sometimes shortening, sometimes lengthening. It wasn't as easy as it seemed, and Rose's long, quick strides made it harder.

"So," she said, "I think we should work on an email for you to send to Tyson and Henry. What kind of correspondence have you had with them?"

This required a response. I shrugged, hoping to avoid my reckoning for as long as possible.

Rose stopped, and I braced for impact, but none came. I turned and saw that, somehow, we'd arrived at her apartment. The silences must've ranged on for longer than I'd thought. Or else time had sped up. I wouldn't be surprised by either.

She gave me a weak, pitied smile before we headed inside.

I kept my eyes on my feet as we climbed those now familiar stairs. If I looked up, I'd see her. I'd see her body. I'd see her presence, and pleasure would leak in. I knew that was where this led, but I needed to suffer a bit longer. I needed to feel the weight of my betrayal, my cowardice. I needed to serve my penance.

The second her door slammed behind us, my eyes ran

around the apartment, from one curated piece to the next, each dripping with the past. I landed on a corner of the wall, an area devoid of any hangings, any culture, any beauty. I settled there, hoping to avoid the intoxicating trappings.

"What did your emails say?" Rose asked. "What did you text? What do they have in writing? What are you staring at?" She grabbed my elbow, spinning my body toward her. I felt my head go light and my stomach flutter. I longed for it to be a different spin, to be foreplay.

I met her eyes, cold and furious. "Nothing, all right. I didn't send any emails to Henry. I sent one text asking if I could talk and showed up at his door. And Tyson texted me saying he wanted to meet." I wished it wasn't true. I wished there was a trail. I wished I'd sent them the recordings or confirmed the story. Then I'd be locked in. Then I couldn't continue down this coward's path. "There's no trail."

"Did they record the interviews?"

I shook my head.

"You're sure? You're positive that the recordings you took and uploaded to the cloud are the sole copies. There's no way they were recording you without you knowing?"

I didn't respond.

She broke out in a smile and walked into the other room without a word. She was giddy, childlike in her joy. I hated how much it made me love her. How much I reveled in the fact that I'd caused that joy.

I stared up and saw the painting. The one I'd been so enamored with that first morning. The one she'd tested me on. I stared at the father and son in the foreground, I saw their eagerness. I was convinced now that they longed to join the violence behind them. I felt that pull. In the moments following the painting, I knew they'd be chasing after the mob, laughing, primed to be a part of it.

She sat down at the table and motioned for me to join her. She opened my computer and began to type. There was nowhere else to go.

"Now look." She pulled out the seat for me. "We need to delete these recordings."

She already had them selected, moved into their own folder. Somehow, I hadn't realized that she'd heard the recordings the second I clicked stop on my phone. They uploaded to the cloud automatically. She had probably been on my computer when they came in. She'd listened to them. That was how they'd known. I was the leak. Not Tyson. Not Henry. Me.

I should've been irate. I should've railed against her and her duplicity. I should've talked about privacy and boundaries. But I didn't. I wasn't angry. I didn't feel violated or betrayed. I felt relief.

"These are the only ones that mention the…" She danced the cursor around the screen. "That we need to clean up. A few others mention Jack, but nothing on them is damning. We want to keep those. No use pretending you weren't researching his death."

She clicked off the folder and into another with the rest of my recordings. She'd been busy—labeling, cataloging. I scanned the screen and caught it. *First Date with Rose.* I'd never even thought…when I gave her access to my computer, to my cloud, to all my recordings, I'd forgotten about that one.

All my righteous indignation was gone. All my anger, my rage, my doubt were replaced with shame.

"Rose," my voice just above a whisper. "I'm so…"

Her eyes ran across the screen, the cursor moving with them. She hovered over the file. "You don't have to—"

"I do, I…I'm…"

She reached over and held my hand. "You didn't know me. You were on a story. It's one of the things I love about you. You're so focused, diligent. I won't say it didn't…it was surprising."

"I'm so, so—"

"You don't have to be. We do what we need to. I'd have done the same. It's in the past. Now, I think it's best if you do this." She angled the laptop to me.

I nodded and dragged the folder to the trash. I took the recording from our first date and did the same. Then I emptied the trash, a permanent delete.

"Good." She patted my leg and turned the computer back to her. "Now, I understand that this next part is uncomfortable. I get that you might not want to be the one writing this out. That's fine. I can write it. You just tell me if anything looks wrong to you. Okay?"

I said nothing. This was happening. I could thrash and struggle against the inevitable if I wanted, but it wouldn't change anything.

Dear (Henry/Tyson),

I hope you're doing well. I'm reaching out to discuss our recent interview. I want to begin by telling you that I appreciate you taking the time to share your version of events with me.

I have done some further research and have found your stories not to be credible. Memory is a tricky thing, and we cannot rely upon one eyewitness account in journalism. I take pride in confirming and re-confirming all my sources before publishing a story. Your story did not stand up to that scrutiny.

I apologize for any difficulty this process may have caused you. As promised, I will not reveal what you've told me to anyone. I will not confirm with anyone that you volunteered yourself as a source for this story.

Thank you again for your time and understanding,
Tess

"We just can't predict the future," Rose said after she finished. "If they want to throw this email out there in a year or five years or fifty years, we want it to be as bland as possible. You checked out their story—a story that we avoid mentioning the content of—and found that they weren't credible."

"What happens if the story breaks? If someone else gets it and it runs and is proven true?"

"That won't happen."

"But what if it does?"

She leaned down, forcing her head into my eye line. She grabbed my hand and held it. "If that happens, which it won't, I'll be there, and we'll get through it. We'll claim you got pressured or checked it out with other sources who contradicted their stories. We'll say that you were coming off the Richard thing, still in the middle of it, and you didn't have the time to deal with this. Didn't have the time or capital to fight this fight. Or we'll just claim it was a different story, and you didn't know. If that happens, we'll figure out something, and you'll be fine."

I hated myself at that moment. I still hate myself for it. I always will. She was so calculating, so cold, so indifferent to the victims she knew existed. But she also had a point. And my hand felt at home in hers. And her hair fell over one shoulder, a trail of fire illuminated by the chandelier. I loved her. I always would. I'd follow her to whatever precipice she took me to. I'd step off into the dark unknown if she said.

I hit send.

45

I was sitting by the window, drinking, smoking my fourth consecutive cigarette, staring at the painting, falling into it. There was always something else to focus on. Always another figure to create a backstory for. I think I'd have stared at it and drank and smoked for days if it hadn't been for a knock at the door.

I didn't move. I felt my heart seize up. I thought it was the police. I thought it was Henry or Tyson. I thought it was my reckoning.

Rose checked the peephole, smiled, then swung the door open and ushered in the cloaked figure.

"Can I take your coat?" Rose said, in her clipped, formal tone, her posture stiff.

"No, no." The figure's head was covered in a scarf, their rain jacket buttoned to the top. They wore oversized, dark sunglasses despite it being night. But none of that obscured them to me. It was Sylvia. Who else would it be?

"Coffee? Tea? Wine? Whiskey?" Rose said.

Sylvia took off her scarf and glasses. "Whiskey? We've talked about this, Rose. That alcoholic writer stuff is passe. It won't work. Not now, not for a woman."

"I know." Rose's shoulders fell with her words. "I...I just..."

"I wanted the whiskey," I said. "She hasn't had any." It was a lie, but what did that matter? What was this lie compared to the others that had been and would be told?

Sylvia peered around the corner toward me. She kept her coat on and held her scarf and glasses in hand. She wasn't settling in. This visit was temporary. "I'll take a whiskey. Neat."

Rose rushed to the kitchen, flung open a cabinet, and broke a glass in her alcohol-soaked haste. "Sorry." She didn't move to clean it.

Sylvia paused in front of the painting and gave it a brief

study before continuing toward me. She wanted me to know she was calm, that none of this had rattled her. She stood in front of me and smiled, her lips curling at the edges, her teeth hidden. There was disgust in that smile, vitriol, but she still went through the motions.

Rose darted out from the kitchen, and I heard the soft, clawing crunch of glass under her bare feet. She internalized a muffled cry but didn't break stride, leaving a dotted trail of blood in her wake. Then she stood in front of Sylvia, bleeding, holding it in.

"A little full for my taste," Sylvia said. She rested the glass on the windowsill.

I lit another cigarette and was careful not to offer her one.

There was a tense moment of silence where I wondered if she might attack me. I saw it. Saw her reach out, grab hold of my hair, and pull me down. Saw her scratch and gouge and bite. Saw her kick and spit on me. A part of me longed for it. Longed to have it out, in the open. A physical representation of the conflict.

"Well," she said. "I know it's been a rocky day for you. I saw your interview with Vivian. You did very well, but we can get to that later. I hear we have some other things to discuss first."

She turned and stared at Rose, who nodded and walked over to me. "She wants to see that your phone isn't recording. She'd rather it not be in the room."

"My phone?" My words blended together, and I realized I was feeling the whiskey. "She doesn't trust me?"

"Tess, come on," she said, still pretending that Sylvia didn't know what was being discussed. "She just wants to be safe. You can understand that, after everything."

I smiled and shrugged and handed her my phone. Rose disappeared into the other room with it and returned a moment later.

Sylvia nodded, satisfied. "Now, I know you've heard some stories today. Stories that are, of course, complete fabrications. I'm actually rather offended that you were taken in by them. I would've thought you knew me better than that, but nonetheless, these things happen. It was who? Tyson? Henry? Both?"

I took a pull off my cigarette and held it before blowing the smoke out the window. "I'd rather not say."

"You'd rather not say? After all the trouble you caused me, you'd rather not say. Well, I'm sorry, Tess, but if we're to heal, if we're to forgive, we need honesty. I appreciate your desire to protect your sources, I do, but this isn't a state secret. This is a case where some of my students are libeling me. I have a right to know who they are so I can speak to them and sort this out."

"Honesty?" I felt the whiskey rise in me. "Honesty? You want to be honest?"

"Yes, of course."

"Okay, then, let's be honest. I'll tell you who my sources were. I'll tell you what they said, but you tell me what happened at those parties. You tell me what happened with Jack. I don't have to print it but tell me the truth. That way, at least, I know what I'm covering up. If I'm selling my soul, I want to know what kind of devil is buying it. And while we're at it, are you having me followed? Did you have something to do with the fire?"

Her false smile evaporated, leaving behind pursed lips and hate. "I'm going to pretend you didn't say all of that. I'm going to pretend, for Rose's sake. For your sake. I'm going to assume it's the whiskey and the stress. I already know who talked to you. I knew about your conversation with Tyson before you left that poor excuse for a library. And I knew you were going to talk to Henry before you even set foot in his apartment. I let these things happen. I allowed them. I know what both of those men said."

She folded her arms and lifted her chin. "Now, you don't deserve an explanation. Maybe if you'd come to me as a friend and asked me, you'd deserve one. And I'd have given you one. But this, this sneaking around, this deceit, this mistrust…but I'll give you an explanation anyway. I'll give you one because I believe that we'll be, if not friends, then acquaintances for many years to come."

She waited while this sunk in and settled over the room. I smelled the outside, the changing season, the crisp air still heavy with ash.

"Those two men told you stories of abuse," she said. "They told you stories of sexual acts that lacked consent and reveled in violence. They told you stories of a program that was more akin to a cult than a writer's workshop. They told you these things because it's how they now see them. I don't believe they think they were lying. I don't believe they'd do that to me.

"But they were lying. They were often lies of exaggeration, but lies, nonetheless. It's true that we have parties, that people explore their sexuality in the safety of my home. It's true that I'm a part of many of those parties. It's true that I have private sessions of a similar nature. But nothing was ever done against anyone's will."

"How can someone possibly give consent in those situations?"

"Consent is a difficult thing in kink. You take yourself to the edge of your comfort. You go past it. That's part of it. That's, in some ways, the entirety of it. You challenge yourself and explore your darkest desires. You find out things about yourself—not just about sex, mind you but about yourself in general—that you never would've discovered otherwise. To someone who's a mild participant, whose mind is still closed, like, say, Henry or Tyson, these things may look wrong. They may look like lines were crossed. But I ask you, would they keep coming back if they didn't enjoy it? Would someone go downstairs and have dinner and drinks and joke around afterward if they'd just been raped?"

I felt my chest contract. I wanted to push back. I wanted to argue. I knew that the mitigating factors of the program made consent impossible to give.

But I also wanted her to be right. I was tired, and this was the path of least resistance. The path I'd already begun down.

"Think about yourself. Have you ever found yourself approaching your limit and decided to keep going? Have you ever done something, sexually or otherwise, that felt questionable? Wasn't it…exciting? Didn't you learn something new about yourself?"

I looked over at Rose, whose gaze was locked on Sylvia. She twitched slightly when my eyes fell on her, like she knew I was watching her, like she could feel me. What had she told Sylvia? Was anything between us sacred? Intimate? Private? Did privacy even exist anymore?

"I know how it looks," Sylvia said. "That's why we keep it quiet. I know that it looks like I'm some cult leader who's subjecting my students to my sexual perversions. But that isn't the case. Students beg me to be part of it. Students return to this campus years after graduating and thank me for those parties. Writers you've read credit those parties as much as the program with their success. Not in public, of course, but to me, in private, they cite those parties as formative experiences."

She turned and walked a few steps, pivoted, and returned closer than before. So close I could taste her breath.

"Have you ever done something that you wouldn't want the world to know about? Something that wasn't wrong but would seem wrong to the outside? Something on the edge. Something you'd want to be kept private."

She must've known. Rose must've told her.

"Maybe you haven't," she said, reeling me back. Making me question my certainty. "Maybe you've lived a safe life. Maybe all of this is foreign to you. But if that's the case, I'm sorry for you. That's no way to live."

She swirled the liquor in the glass, holding it away from her, inspecting it. Then she placed it back on the windowsill without drinking and resumed her pacing.

"Tyson and, to a lesser extent, Henry are going through a moment of crisis. They're at a crossroads. They can work harder and get better and become something, or they can fade off into obscurity. The choice is theirs. Unfortunately, and I think this is an affliction that many people in your generation have, they wish to blame others for their setbacks. For their failures. There have always been these people, but it's quite pronounced these days. Men, in particular, seem to revel in it. Tyson and Henry have failed. That's not my fault, and it's not the fault of the workshop. Some people make it, some don't. We have a very high success rate, higher than most, but we still have our failures. These two saw a different path forward. They were told to leave, told they weren't good enough, and they decided they couldn't do it, couldn't leave. So, instead of working harder and proving me wrong, as others have done, they tried to destroy the workshop, destroy me."

"And Jack?" I felt tears welling up in me. Tears for a person I'd never met but now felt I knew.

"And that doesn't fit the narrative they painted, does it?" Sylvia ignored my question. "A vile and toxic program wouldn't instill that level of devotion, would it? The truth is their actions show how absurd their accusations are. If it was such a terrible program, such a horrible experience for them, they'd have left without all this fuss. They'd have been thrilled to get away. But they weren't. They couldn't leave."

"Jack."

"Jack." She walked to the window, took a cigarette from the pack, and held it. "Jack was sad. Much sadder than those failures. Like countless people every year, Jack couldn't take it any longer, and he let the darkness win. It's a tragedy. He was one of the best writers I ever taught. I thought he could've been... Well, it doesn't matter now."

She turned back from the window and faced me. She played with the cigarette, tapping it against her palm and rotating it.

"I blame myself for Jack." Her eyes slick with tears. "But not because of the parties. He begged me to continue with them. Begged to be part of them again, how he was before. That was his kink. That's what turned him on. At his insistence, I resumed private sessions with him, intensified them. He said it helped his writing. He said he needed it. But I had to stop. He was an addict, I should've seen it before, but I…anyway, I cut him off. I told him we couldn't go on like that. That was when he fell into the darkness. That was when we lost him.

"That was what we fought about that night. That and his novel. They were always tied. He wanted more private sessions, he wanted to go back to his old role at the parties. And he was upset about his novel. About edits we had for him. As I said, they were always tied to each other."

I reached out and extended her the lighter, but she ignored me, instead continuing to play with the unlit cigarette as she paced.

"I wish I hadn't stopped. I wish I'd kept the private sessions going, let him return to his old role, told him to ignore whatever edits he wanted. If I'd known…but that's not how it works. I did what I thought was best at the time. I stopped it, got him a therapist, told Rose what was going on. We tried to work him through it, but we couldn't. At the end of the day, if you're going to do that, you'll find a way. It's the old curse, genius and madness and all that."

I turned to Rose. She was shaking, tears streaking down her cheeks. "Is that true? Did she tell you all this? Did you two…?" I, too, was crying, whether for Jack or Rose, I couldn't tell.

She nodded. "We tried. We did what we could…it wasn't enough."

Rose walked to the kitchen, leaving a pool of blood where she'd been standing, and got another glass. She filled her glass, and we all drank in contemplative silence.

"So," Sylvia said, "now you know. Now you have the full story. If you think it should be published, if you think we'll get a fair hearing in the court of public opinion, go ahead, write it. At least now you know the truth."

46

She picked up the pack of cigarettes and returned hers, unlit, unsmoked. Then she straightened herself up and pinched the bridge of her nose with her thumb and forefinger, a familiar gesture that surely originated with her.

I turned and saw Rose doing the same.

Sylvia walked to the mirror by the door and wiped the tears from her face. She reapplied her basic, natural makeup.

The questions began to flood in as my adrenaline sobered me up. She hadn't answered everything. She hadn't even touched my accusations about the fire, about me being followed. At best, she'd skimmed the surface. And I hadn't held any of it up to scrutiny. I hadn't used my interviews with Tyson or Henry to refute her claims. I hadn't asked for proof. I hadn't pressed her in the slightest.

But I knew I never would. I didn't have it in me. All my fury was gone. I was tired, and this was the path I'd started down. It would've taken strength to turn back. Strength, I lacked. And as Rose pointed out, what would I be turning back for?

Of course, these are just the excuses I tell myself. I know what I did. I know I chose the coward's path. I know there's no excuse.

Sylvia walked back, restored. She went to the window and picked up her sunglasses from where she'd set them down. Then she turned and said, as an afterthought, like she hadn't been waiting for the whole conversation to bring this up. "By the way, I think I might be able to help you with some things."

I didn't answer.

"You've had quite the day. And even if there wasn't anything to those accusations, you did me a favor sending out those emails and deleting the recordings." Rose had already told her about that. I assumed as much, but the confirmation still stung.

"Rose and I have talked about this, and we want to help you. You're talented and smart and hardworking, and Rose has a bit of a thing for you. We think you should write an article about Jack."

She was so brazen.

"We've finished up the edits on his book. It's superb. It's with my publisher now, and they're going to publish it. Soon. I think it'll be quite the sensation. And we want you to write the definitive article on it, on him. I'll help you get it placed. We were thinking long form. You can talk to some other members of the workshop. I can arrange interviews with some former students—Wang, Pruitt, Brim, others. And it won't be all fluff, don't worry. You can hit us a bit. The rigors, the demands of the program, maybe even a shot at me."

"But you'll want final say?"

"Tess," she said, as if we were old friends, "let's not move forward like this. Let's work together. Rose and I will, of course, offer our services as editors. We'll help you with your writing and make sure the content works to tell the best story. We do, after all, have to look after Jack's legacy. And then, once we're all satisfied, we'll help it get placed."

I turned to Rose, looking for something that wasn't there. She forced a smile and then hid her face.

"We also," Sylvia said, unable to allow me time to contemplate her offer, "want to talk to you about Richard. This can wait if you want, but—"

"No, let's have it all out now."

"Okay." She gave me a sour smile of triumph. "My publisher and my agent have read your stuff and seen your video and followed your career so far. They like what they've seen and are interested in a book. Maybe a collection of articles, but maybe a more cohesive work on Richard's rise."

"And you could talk about the rise of fascism in the country in general," Rose said. "And how it's spread across campuses. How they've become a breeding ground for this far-right ideology. I could help with the research. Lisa said she'd help too."

"We also have some members of the history and poli-sci departments we could put at your disposal. And I know some people in politics who might be able to help as well. If you work on it over the summer, maybe we could have it out this year. Ride the wave of your current fame and the article on Jack right into a book release."

"A book?" I hadn't thought anything could surprise me. I hadn't thought she could see through me and pull at my strings with such ease. But of course, she could. It was so obvious. What did we all want? A book. An agent. Success. Recognition.

"It'll be a lot of work," Sylvia said. "But you're up to it. And…"

She turned to Rose, who dropped her head. "We can talk to Claire. Off the record, but she's willing to talk. Background."

"Claire?" I said. "You've been talking to Claire?"

"She's a source, I don't like her. Neither does Sylvia, but—"

"You know Claire too?"

"I know a great many people," Sylvia said. "I disapprove of her politics, but I know her family. She almost joined the workshop, but she chose a different path. Pre-law for some godforsaken reason. Politics, I suppose. I still wonder what if… but it doesn't matter now."

"Anyway." Rose walked toward me, her gait steady. "She's not… Richard's just like a tool for her. He's popular with those crazies. I'm not defending her, but I'm just saying she'll talk. Background, but still. It'll help. Maybe we can even corner that other one, what's his name?"

"Connor," I said.

"Or even Jason." She looked away from me as she said his name. "I know he's…but you never know. Claire says he had an argument with Richard. She says he might be willing to talk."

It was disgusting. Jason? We were going to use Jason as a source. Trust him.

But again, she was right. They were both right. I'd do some interviews, however distasteful, get some details from people close to him, and tell the story. Then I'd weave in some history that fits my narrative, and we send it out. It wouldn't even be that much work. So much of the heavy lifting was already done.

It was the type of opportunity people waited a lifetime for. The type of opportunity many people never get. And here it was. Presented at my feet. All I had to do was agree.

I nodded and stood up.

"Now." Sylvia was back at the mirror, disguising herself, pulling her scarf around her head, adjusting her sunglasses. "You two need to get over to that rally. Make yourselves seen. Tess, I assume they'll want you to say something?"

"I haven't…"

"We have something prepared," Rose said. "Short, blunt, but effective."

"Send it to me. I'll read it here before I leave." Sylvia walked over to the couch and sat down. "I'll make corrections and send you the updated speech. Now, it's past time you two get over there."

I checked my watch, she was right. I'd known I had to attend, but it had slipped my mind in the turmoil. They would've started by now. My absence would've been noted.

Rose pulled out her phone and sent Sylvia the speeches.

"Can I?" I asked.

Rose, startled by my voice, nodded. "I'll send it to you too. You should familiarize yourself with it. Don't worry, it's in your voice."

"Oh," Sylvia said from the couch. "After the rally, come by my house. I'm having some people over."

She didn't look up as she spoke, focused on her phone, scrolling and typing. I went to say something, but Rose pulled me through the door and slammed it closed.

47

The crowd was restless by the time I climbed the stage. They wanted to be inspired. They wanted Richard, their own version. They wanted me to mount that stage, pull them in, and fill them with life.

"I just want to start by saying how proud I am of all of you for being here. They thought they'd drive us away, scare us off. That's what the chanting and the torches were about. Intimidation. But we won't be intimidated. We won't succumb to their fear tactics."

I felt Rose move behind me, the shotty stage creaking with her every tilt. Lisa was saying something to her from the side of the stage, Rose crouched down, taking it in. She walked over and whispered in my ear. "Isaac Lieberman has died. I don't think we want to tell the crowd. It'll start a...best not to mention it."

I nodded and tapped my foot. I wanted to argue with her, tell her she was wrong, tell her I could handle it. They could handle it. I wanted to tell the crowd and console them. I wanted to be a hero, a prophet, but I had no words for that. I didn't feel it. I had no anger or sadness welling up inside me. Just anxiety.

"This, this right here," I said. "This gathering is what they'll never understand. They think that those displays of hate and violence will drive us away, but they won't. They only serve to bring us together."

Scattered applause. Nothing like Richard's. I could feel him watching this, comparing the reception, the crowd, the energy. I could see his satisfied smile.

"They think they can destroy us. Destroy our institutions, our hope. They think a fire will end decades of progress, but they're wrong."

I marveled at Rose's careful wording. Richard couldn't claim libel. He couldn't claim we were blaming him for the Clinton Hall fire. We'd say we were talking about the torches or a metaphorical fire, but everyone knew the truth.

"This is democracy in action. This is what the future looks like."

Applause, sustained but not manic. Not what I wanted. Not a tenth of what Richard could summon with a simple look.

"Fear. We're all afraid. When I was walking over here, I'll admit, I was afraid. These were the same steps I took last time when reporting on their rally. And I was scared then. I won't hide it. After it was over, they searched for me. We'd left, moved on to get a view of the march, but we saw men search us out. Men with malice in their hearts and violence in their eyes."

An authorial flourish that was lost on the audience.

"But tonight, as I neared the quad and heard your excited voices, that fear fell away."

I looked up and scanned past the audience to the edge of the quad. It was filling with men. Men in polos and khakis. Men trying to appear as if they weren't gathering, weren't connected. They didn't hold bats or torches, they didn't, on the surface, look menacing. But it was there. The message was clear.

"They thrive on fear. It's their lifeblood. They need their supporters to be afraid. They need you to be afraid. Without fear, they're nothing. Just smoke and mirrors. A bad magic trick."

I tried to meet the khakied men's eyes, stare them down, but it was no use. I landed on the man in the front. I squinted and saw a heavy gold chain dance along his broad neck. I saw him lean down and listen to the man next to him. Then I heard them laugh, it echoed out through the cold night, startling the crowd, unsettling them.

"And you know what drives out fear? It isn't anger, though, that can be useful. It isn't hate. It isn't more fear. It's unity. It's love. It's courage."

More laughter from the men in the distance. They were indifferent to my words, to our gathering.

"That's what drives away fear. And I look out at this crowd, with so many beautiful, diverse faces, and I know our courage will overcome their fear."

There was no courage out there. There wasn't fear either. Just boredom and disquiet and pockets of rage.

"We show courage in assembling like this. In spreading our message. In rejecting their future and creating our own."

In the back of the crowd, the audience began to jostle. Hurried voices shouted toward the khakied men. They shouted back. I saw Brando, his leather jacket and bursting energy.

The police, who'd been watching the scene from a safe distance, crept closer, still off to the side, watching, hands rested on their belts, prepared for action but reluctant to force it.

Everyone was waiting for a spark. It wouldn't take much.

I saw Jason smile and nudge the man next to him, showing him his phone. They both laughed. Then, with the joy of a child, Jason shouted at the pulsing mob in front of him. "Isaac is dead, you fucking cunts."

"We must…we can't…"

No one was listening to me. Their bodies began to turn toward the khakied men, toward the verbal volleying. People began to lunge at each other, the stairs serving as a barrier. I don't know who broke it, who took that first brave step, but someone did. And then they were coming from both sides. Flashing up and down, weak blows landing on soft bodies. No one knew what they were doing, a generation raised to avoid fights trying to reenact superhero movies.

I saw a woman try a spin kick and miss everything, including the step. She fell back, and someone caught her just as her head was about to hit the ground.

A khakied man wound up for a punch, slipped on the step, and only managed to bloody his own nose.

Mayhem. Pathetic, ineffective mayhem.

The police shouted into their megaphones. "Break it up, break it up. Disperse, or you will be arrested."

Our side would claim they arrested more of us. Their side

would claim the opposite. For every arrest they made, another fight would start. They'd control one area just to have another descend into violence. A hydra of rage.

An officer was coming to the stage. He wasn't in a hurry, he was moving with resigned indifference. He held up a hand, signaling for me to stop.

Brando sprinted through the crowd, pushing people aside, moving to the stage, trying to beat the cop there. His face was bloodied, but I couldn't tell if it was his or theirs. He was shouting to me, something inaudible and frantic. He wanted to speak. He wanted to incite.

"Isaac," he mouthed. "Isaac is dead."

I held the mic, my hands slick with sweat. I looked out at the pulsing crowd, the violence splintering across it. I could light the match. I felt that power. All I had to do was tell the truth, and the campus would erupt.

Rose reached over, covered the mic with her palm, and leaned into my ear. "Time to go."

I hesitated, looking into the few faces that still stared at me with expectation and hope. They were static, not sure if they should stay or go. Longing for someone to instruct them. Not just on this but on everything.

"Come on." Rose gripped my elbow and pulled.

Brando beat the officer to the stage, but Lisa met him, her shaved head glimmering with sweat under the spotlights. "You're not going up there, just turn around."

"Out of my way," he said.

"No, you're not turning this into that."

"Move." He threw his arms forward, landing them on her chest. She tumbled back, her head connecting with the corner of the stage. Blood was everywhere. When Lisa would tell this story in the days, weeks, and years to come, it was always a nameless, faceless fascist who shoved her. Sometimes he shouted hate, sometimes he groped her, sometimes he spat on her. Never was he Brando.

Two officers made their way down the stairs behind us. I

didn't hear them, but they arrived just in time to take Brando away. He shouted and begged me to help him.

"We can't be here," Rose said and pulled me from the stage, draping an arm over my shoulder to comfort and hide me.

Rose kept me hidden as we moved through the assembling police perimeter. I breathed her in, my stare fastened to the sidewalk. I felt such comfort being held like that, being taken care of. I couldn't remember why I'd ever turned on her.

"Okay, I think we're clear," she said and straightened me up. "But if anyone calls to you, don't break stride. Even if you know them. We can't... We want to be safe."

I nodded and tried to keep up with her as she started moving. She kept glancing over her shoulder, pausing before intersections and peering around corners. I felt like we were at war. Sirens blared around campus, and the sky was cast in a perpetual purple hue. We heard shouts, some of joy, some of fear.

We turned a corner and saw a group of men throwing bricks at a window. It didn't shatter, but cracks spread out with every throw. They'd get there even if it took all night.

Rose pulled me back, and we went the other way.

We saw a woman running away from a group of men, screaming, crying. We didn't slow, we didn't investigate, we just kept moving.

"Were those...?" I knew she didn't know the answer either, and I wasn't even sure of the question.

She said nothing, her eyes darting from left to right, anticipating every entry point. I could see her processing, see her mind spinning. We needed to get clear, get inside somewhere.

Rose stopped, reaching out a hand, and held me in place. "Don't move."

At the end of the path, three figures emerged. They lumbered toward us. Not in a hurry but menacing all the same. One of the men whistled a tune I couldn't pick out. Their faces and dress were obscured by the pulsating purple darkness.

Heavy footsteps. Not theirs. They were coming from behind us. They were faster than the shadowed figures at the end of the path. We turned our heads. It was another threesome coming toward us. We turned back, and the shadows had closed, their pace accelerated. The walls closing in.

"Rose, Rose, what are we going to do?"

"Don't use my name." She gripped my arm harder than she'd ever done before. Hard enough that I'd have a bruise there for a week. "This way."

We took off, leaving the path and heading into the trees. There was a volley of shouting, but I can't say if any of it was directed at us.

I tripped over a root, and Rose caught me just before I smashed my face into a tree. I didn't even have time to thank her, she just picked me up and pulled me along.

It wasn't a forest, just a small grouping of trees, and we burst through the other side within a few minutes. It was calmer there. You could hear the shouting and destruction, but it was at a distance. Something happening in a different world.

"This way." Rose hadn't let go of me since we'd started moving.

I looked at the ground, and it was familiar. I recognized the cracks, the area where a root had forced the path up, the smell of lilac.

We turned a corner, and there it was, covered in ivy and full of history. I must've known this was where we were headed. She'd told us to come by after the rally, and Rose would never ignore an invitation from Sylvia. But I hadn't been conscious of it. Not as we fled.

"Are we…" I said, unsure where I was going.

Rose stopped and dropped my hand. Her face sank. I hadn't noticed till then, but there'd been a glow of excitement in her until now. She'd enjoyed that, the run, the escape, the explosion of rage. And now it was gone, faded into the past, and she missed it. "She's expecting us."

"What…do we know…what is this?" My mouth was dry, and my hands wet. I turned and looked over my shoulder at the purple hue and the cacophony of violence. I thought I saw the pale glow of fire.

"I'm going in." She walked to the door and stopped before her hand reached the knob. "You can come with me, or you can leave. It's up to you."

I swallowed, and it went down like a stone. I tapped my fingers against my leg. "If I…what am I…what will…"

"I'll be inside." She took a step back and grabbed my hand, squeezing it. "The door's open."

Then she turned and walked inside, pushing the door almost closed. It wavered, vibrating back and forth, light from the house trickling out, charging into the darkness.

I hesitated. I paced. I walked to the door and listened. Silence. I held the knob, it was cold, and the cold traced up my arm.

I heard a rustling in the darkness behind me. I felt eyes watching me, surveilling me.

I stepped back and heard a noise above me. Muffled excitement and nerves. I moved along the vast expanse of the stone wall, searching for the sound. There was a light on in a second-story window. It was ajar, noise and light leaking out. I put my hand against the wall and felt the old house breathe.

The window slammed closed, taking the life with it, leaving me in the cold, dead night. I heard shouting in the distance and felt heat coming from campus. I walked back to the door and stood, my foot tapping against the ground, the door swaying, dancing on the hinge, living off the residual momentum that Rose had left it with.

The violence that night didn't last long. The police were ready for it, and they gained control of the quad with vicious ease. But you can't put that kind of rage back in the bottle. The fights cropped back up in dorms and at parties, and across campus. They weren't isolated to that night either. The university didn't go a week without an arrest for the rest of the semester. People were spit on, cars were vandalized, property defaced. The medical center was inundated with black eyes and broken hands. Often you couldn't tell who was at fault or what the message was. It was just chaos, for chaos's sake.

In the months and years to come, that night would change. It would take on a mystical aura. The violence would be reshaped, viewed as righteous or villainous depending on whose side you were on and who was committing the violence.

And my speech became legend. People still talk about it. People pretend they were there. People claim it inspired them to move into politics or civic action. But it's all just a rewriting of history. No one left that quad inspired by me and what I'd said. No one stood there and watched me and felt drawn to action. Those who fought, came looking for a fight. Those who didn't, left terrified and anxious. No one felt what Richard's audience felt. No one would've died for me as they'd have died for him. They chose later to remember it differently. To remember a defiant stance against the enemy, and I don't blame them. When I tell people about that night, I tell the lie too. Sometimes we need the lie. Sometimes it's all that saves us.

EPILOGUE

"JACK HOUGHTON: PORTRAIT OF A LOST NOVELIST"

by Tess Azar (excerpt)

"We almost ran out of gas in Nevada." Henry Putskin stares out the window at everything and nothing. "It was this long stretch of highway, and we were at about a quarter of a tank, and we came to this gas station that said, *Last gas for 400 miles* or something, and they were closed. Out of business. I couldn't believe it. No cell phone service either. Stranded. I shouted about how this was unacceptable. About how the state has a responsibility to have gas available. I was going on about the failures of capitalism or something, you know, typical sophomore-in-college talk.

"Anyway, Jack didn't say anything. He just sat in the car and wrote, a man possessed. I asked him what we should do, and he just pointed forward and went back to writing. That's how he was. When he was writing, when he was focused, there was nothing else. Not even getting stuck in the middle of the desert without gas while the summer sun cooked us alive."

I asked him what they did, even though it wasn't the point of the story.

"We drove—well, I drove. He kept writing. He didn't even look up. As the needle hit E, we pulled into this town, I'll never forget the name—Rachel, Nevada. And they sold us some overpriced gas, and we ate a terrible hamburger, and the whole time Jack wrote and wrote and wrote. When we found a motel, he gave me the story to read. It was perfect. It was about a man walking through the desert searching for gas. It was about climate change and our addiction to fossil fuels, but it was also about the contradictions in each of us."

"'Out of Gas,'" I said, naming Jack's first great story, the one that put his name on the map as a nineteen-year-old.

"Right." Henry dropped his gaze from the window and pinched the bridge of his nose, fighting back the tears. Everyone in the workshop does this same pinch when they talk about Jack. It's as if they believe they shouldn't be sad about it. As if it would be a disgrace to his memory to cry. "It's a great story, perfect."

It is, of course, a great story. Maybe even perfect. And in light of the recent tragedy, the story of its writing is a cautious and somewhat troubling tale.

"He fell into his work," Sylvia Lobo, Jack's mentor and professor, said. "It's the kind of drive you hope to instill in your students. Many of them float in and out. They have bursts of work and dormant periods. Many very successful writers are like this."

Sylvia, of course, would be quite familiar with the working habits of successful writers. Her program, unofficial until this year, has produced countless writers of renown. Carol Wang, Frank Pruitt, and Jennifer Brim, just to name a few. To date, her graduates have won twenty-seven major literary awards, and the number who've been shortlisted is too numerous to count. Last year, she had four of her former students place as finalists for the National Book Award. And that's, of course, without even mentioning her own vast accomplishments as a writer, critic, and thought leader.

"You don't see many with that skill and work ethic." Her face was awash in fond memories. "He was special. And not just the drive, but the quality. He was published before he even arrived here. 'Radio,' a short story about a girl and her mom arguing over what to listen to. It's a good story, not as layered or complex as his later work, but it's efficient and affecting. By the time 'Out of Gas' was published, I had no doubts about his eventual success. I was already telling people about him in literary circles."

Here she pulls back, sitting up straight, tensing all the muscles in her body. Bracing herself as if she were about to be struck. She pinches her nose.

"I blame myself. I know that people will say that's irrational, but I can't help it. It's hard not to push when you have someone like him, someone special, someone you believe can be exceptional. And with him, there was passion along with the talent. So, I pushed him. I worked him. I tried to mold him into the best writer he could be. And it worked. This novel…" She looks away and blinks back tears. "I believe it's one of the best American novels of the century. Spectacular. As good as anything any of my students have ever written. As good as anything I've ever written…but at what cost?"

When I ask the question, she tells me that she would trade the novel for him, but there's an undercurrent in her voice that makes me wonder if this is the truth.

"He believed the two were connected." Rose Dearborn, a close friend of his, who, along with Sylvia, edited Jack's manuscript, *The Bewildered and the Guilty*. "He thought you needed the darkness to write. He told me many times that nothing of worth comes without struggle. And he reveled in that struggle."

Rose has a collection of short stories, *Blood Orange*, coming out in a few months. She worked with Jack during his entire time at the university. They were paired off by Sylvia as freshmen due to their shared intensity and talent.

"I used to think that too," Rose said. "We were in a bubble together. We would write for each other more than anyone else. We'd write and send stories back and forth, editing the other's work until it was perfect. It was competitive and constructive. I never would be the writer I am without that…but it was also toxic. I see that now. We pushed each other and pushed ourselves past the point of comfort. I developed an eating disorder sophomore year after I read something Hemingway said about writing better when hungry. I became consumed by the idea. I wouldn't eat for days on end. It was dangerous."

"How did you pull yourself out of it?"

"I stopped reading Hemingway." She gave a desperate laugh, meant to hold back tears. "I got help. Sylvia helped me. Jack helped me. They said I was hurting myself and... this stung... they said my writing was suffering."

Here she did the nose pinch, a tear leaking out of the corner of her eye.

"I just wish I could've helped him like he helped me. He had his darkness. We all do, but his was pronounced. He wasn't always a saint. No one should pretend he was, but he was my friend. Closer even. A brother. I loved him, and I miss him. I wish I could've helped him. We just... He always fell into that darkness when he wrote. It was his method. But he always came out. And he was himself again. This time, with the novel, it was just too much. He was so far in it...he just couldn't come back."

Rose, too, assures me she'd trade all his work for him to be back with her. I believe her. There isn't a trace of doubt in her answer.

But I find myself wondering what we, the public, would want. I wonder what value we place on the temporary, unspectacular life compared to the immortality of art. I think of how we venerate the tortured genius. How we memorialize their struggle. And I think, not for the first time, of Achilles and the two lives he could've lived. A peaceful and happy life that would never be remembered, or a short, violent, spectacular life, that would ring out through all of history. I wonder which Jack would've picked. I think I know.

EXCERPTS FROM THE INTERVIEW FOR *THE BEWILDERED AND THE GUILTY* BOOK LAUNCH, HELD AT THE UNIVERSITY:

Tess: Hello, everyone, thank you all for joining us here tonight. I'm Tess Azar.

(Applause.)

T: Thank you, thank you. Today is a difficult day for all of us. We're both celebrating and mourning. We're celebrating this brilliant, transcendent novel that I believe will come to define our age as much as any work of art. I've read it. I know some of you have. I know many more of you are eager to. Let me just say you're in for a treat.

(More applause.)

T: But as I mentioned, today is also a sad day. As you all know, Jack Houghton, the author of this outstanding novel and several acclaimed short stories, took his own life earlier this year. He didn't live to see the publication of his novel. He didn't live to see the adulation it's receiving or bask in his triumph. We all mourn his death. I didn't know him while he was alive. I know some of you did. I know the two people who will join me on this stage in a moment did. But I think even for those of us who didn't know him, we still feel the loss. Both for the man we might've someday gotten to know, and for the work he will never go on to write. I, for one, feel that in the months following his tragic death, I have come to know him through the people in his life. Through the interviews I've conducted. And, of course, through his work.

T: I think we should view tonight as a celebration. It's reasonable and appropriate to feel pain and loss, but I believe Jack would want us to celebrate, not mourn. We have a great work to discuss. We have two brilliant women to discuss it with. Let's enjoy those things. Let's enjoy the night and, in doing so, honor Jack's life and genius.

T: And, without further ado, let me introduce those women.

T: First, we have Rose Dearborn.

(Rose enters to applause. She waves, posture erect, body clenched, smile glued to her face.)

T: Rose was a close friend and associate of Jack's. She edited almost all his stories. She was his primary, and toward the end, sole student editor. She's a fabulous writer in her own right. She'll have a collection of short stories published later this year entitled *Blood Orange*, I've read that collection, and all I have to say is when it comes out, buy it. It's excellent.

T: Our other guest tonight needs no introduction, though that won't stop me. Sylvia Lobo.

(Sylvia enters to raucous, deafening applause.)

T: Sylvia is the author of more than a dozen books. She has won countless awards and praise from her peers and readers alike. Some of her notable works are *A Wake of Vultures*, *Jezebel*, *Bubblegum*, and a personal favorite, *Chariot Races*. She's one of the defining authors of her generation, as well as one of the finest teachers of creative writing in the world. Her students have gone on to publish scores of books and won numerous awards.

(The three women stand while the applause continues, then take their seats.)

T: Well, where to begin? So much to talk about…

Rose: While the prolific use of sheep in the novel, both in dreams and in the waking world, is, of course, as Sylvia pointed out, a comment on our willingness to be led, I feel it's also a statement on the planet. Sheep roaming the city streets is intended to show the destruction of native habitats and how comfortable we've become as a species with that destruction.

Sylvia: Yes, quite right. The novel is often throwing out these moments of environmental absurdity. Many readers will just pass over, accept them—just as they do in real life—but they're intended to show how far we'll go toward rationalizing the destruction of our planet.

Tess: How do you think this reading fits with the later graphic scene where a wolf devours one of those sheep in the middle of the city?

R: I would say he's using the wolf as a stand-in for industrialization and capitalism and the ways those things have destroyed the Earth.

S: A skilled writer often uses scenes and images to complete more than one purpose. Jack did that here. It's correct to view the wolf as the manifestation of capitalism, as Rose pointed out, but I think there's more to it. I think he's also using the sheep to represent the fragile individuals in our society. The ones in need of protection. He shows the sheep being ignored time and time again. His characters express annoyance with the sheep when they get in their way or follow them places. Then later, in a vivid and beautiful passage, we see a wolf killing and eating a sheep. People stand and watch as this happens. They all know this wolf lives among them. They all know it's a threat to the sheep. But they do nothing. And the reader is left to wonder who is at fault. They are left to consider how we treat the vulnerable and villainous in our society. They are forced to contemplate their responsibility for protecting the helpless from the wolves we all know lurk in our midst.

(Applause.)

T: The novel has a real feminine touch to it. Would you say that an editor can have that type of impact on a work? Do you feel his writing is touched by women?

S: Yes. His most significant immediate influences were the two women sitting here. He, of course, read everything he could get his hands on, but you can't compare that to people who are reading and commenting on your work. Too many writers, men and women, are taught by straight, white, cis men.

That has a massive impact on their writing. Our program is different. We have people of color, we have trans teachers, we have gay and bi teachers and everyone in between. And, of course, he had us.

(The audience cheers, and some even hoot.)

T: Did he ever discuss any of this with you, Rose?

R: All the time. His writing is different. It reads unlike anyone else out there, and I think it's because of that. You have plenty, not enough, but still, many women writers who are taught by men. And their work tends to have a similar read to it. There's often a touch of the man creeping through a woman's prose. The man behind the woman, if you will. Jack is the reverse. He had strong women and other under-represented communities speaking through his male voice. It's powerful to read. It sticks with you. We need more of it. And I think it's why so many of Sylvia's students have had such success. Our writing is different because of who taught us and what and how we were taught. We learned history from people of color. We learned grammar from non-native English speakers. We learned art from LGBTQ-plus teach-ers. We've been crafted outside of the typical hegemonic structure of education, and it shows.

(Rapturous applause.)

T: I know this isn't something we want to talk about, but I feel it needs to be mentioned. Sylvia, one of your former students, Tyson Groff, recently passed away. You have expressed to me in our recent interview and again here tonight that you feel a sense of responsibility for what happened with Jack. Do you feel a similar responsibility with Tyson?

(Sylvia pauses and straightens up, then drops her head in so-lemnity.)

S: I was quite affected by that news. It…it's become clichéd in our society to refer to people as family. People do it at work or in sports or anywhere these days. It's a worn statement, but that's how we are here. There's no other way to put it.

We spend so much time together. People, and you know this, people on campus refer to us as a cult. People outside campus too. In the publishing world and academia, that's how we're referred to. I've always laughed at it, but it's sad when I think about it. Everyone should hope to be a part of a group like ours one day. To have that kind of comradery, that kind of intimacy, to have people who care about you as we care about each other. It's a beautiful thing. Not something to be mocked or derided.

S: So, I was devastated when I heard about Tyson. He was a lovely man. He had his struggles, but we all do. I don't know how much of a role the workshop played in his struggles with addiction. I'm ashamed to say I wasn't close enough to know. Even in a family, there are people you're closer to than others. I wish I'd known him better. That's not to say it doesn't hurt. That's not to say I didn't know him because I did. I will grieve for him for a long time. I wish I could've helped him.

S: I will note that it's another reminder, not that we need one, that our nation is still in the grips of an epidemic with these drugs. And, perhaps of equal importance, we have a severe mental health crisis on our hands. Something needs to be done here to prevent these tragedies.

(Applause.)

S: I suppose this is as good a time as any to mention that we're donating a portion of the proceeds of *The Bewildered and the Guilty* to a few handpicked mental health outreach charities. We're going to earmark some of that money to focus on addiction as well.

(Sustained, rapturous applause.)

T: Rose, you don't have to say anything, I know how hard this year has been on you, but you also knew Tyson...

R: Yes. I, uh, it's been difficult. To lose Jack as we did and then Tyson so close after. It's been hard on all of us. He had a great soul. While I knew him, he didn't struggle with this. Or if he did, he kept it hidden. I wish I'd known. It just shows how fast an addiction can take over and destroy you. I send my love to him and his family and, of course, Lisa Guerrero, his long-time girlfriend, whom I know is still mourning. He'll live in us forever.

(Tepid and then sustained applause. Rose drops her head and covers her face. She appears to be crying. Sylvia puts an arm around her. Tess stands up, walks over, kneels, and takes Rose's hands in hers. This photo, the two women comforting their grief-stricken friend, will be used as the thumbnail for the event. It'll appear in magazines and newspapers and across cable news shows. It'll even become a meme. People across the planet, people who have never heard of any of these women or Jack or Tyson, will use it to express female solidarity, both in jest and otherwise. It'll be captioned with things like "when he leaves (again), and you realize that all you need are your girls," or "when you stub your toe and text your girlfriends, and they don't make fun of you." It will complete the standard life cycle of a meme. Beginning as exciting and funny and traveling from internet community to internet community until it becomes ubiquitous. Being adopted and then discarded. It will even spend some time being used by the far-right to demean and belittle women. Richard Welch himself will use it at one point, seemingly unaware of its origin. The photo will be misattributed for years and never corrected. People will remember it as a show of grief and support as Rose mourned Jack's death, not Tyson's. The world will forget about Tyson. They'll remember Jack. They'll remember Rose and Sylvia and Tess. They'll remember the meme. But not Tyson.)

R: So, I know we're nearing the end, but we would be remiss if we didn't give Tess a moment in the sun.

S: Yes, quite right, Rose.

T: No, no, this isn't about me.

(Applause.)

R: Now, don't be modest. For anyone whose been living under

a rock for the past year, Tess here is one of the most brilliant young journalists in the world. She has even earned the peculiar badge of honor that comes with being a target of the far-right. She's a regular focus of cable news segments, a common message board punching bag, she's been followed, and she's even received death threats. None of this has stopped her from doing her job. She continues to report on the far-right and has even managed to interview some of them. She's written a book that will be published later this year. It's called *While We Slept: The Rise of Fascism on American Campuses*. I've read it and was lucky enough to do some editing on it. It's fantastic and an essential read to understand the world we live in.

S: I've also read it and agree. If you would like my more extensive thoughts, pick up next month's issue of *The New Yorker*, where you will find my review. It's a rare book that's both timely and timeless, and this one qualifies as both.

R: Can I, just for one moment, don a journalist's hat and ask you a question?

T: Rose here is just trying to make me blush.

(Laughter.)

R: I would say I'm succeeding at that.

(More laughter.)

R: Now, my question is simple. In the book, you cite a few anonymous sources close to Richard Welch, the white supremacist who terrorized this campus last year. I would, of course, never ask you to divulge your sources, but what I'm wondering is this: How did you get to them? How did you convince them to talk to you?

(Tess smirks and Rose hides a wink from the audience.)

T: As you can imagine, I can't go into much detail. I always keep my sources confidential. Let's just say they wanted to talk. Sometimes you can find yourself in a situation that you disagree with, surrounded by people doing and saying things you abhor. But it can be hard to extricate yourself from that situation. You come to feel trapped. And I offered these people an outlet. They were able to be part of the solution instead of the problem. And even if they aren't ready or able to come out and join the fight in the open, I thank them for the help they provided.

R: Thank you, she wouldn't tell me anything about it unless I put her on the spot.

(More laughter.)

R: Sorry to do that to you, Tess. It's a brilliant book. The best non-fiction I've read in years.

S: It's exceptional. I can't recommend it highly enough.

T: Thank you both. It means a great deal to me. I couldn't have done it without your support.

(The evening closes with six minutes of unbroken applause.)

ACKNOWLEDGMENTS

Above all, I want to thank Cassie. Without her none of this would be possible. Her tireless support and unwavering confidence in me is the only reason this book exists. For that and for so much more, thank you.

Thank you to my parents. They stood by me through some very dark years, and I will never be able to properly thank them for all they did for me. The same goes for Erin, Kelly, Brian, Maureen, John, Rob, Mary, Courtney, Michael, Deme, Nick, Angie, Grace, and Vinny. There's a long list of other people without who this would not have been possible, but there isn't the space to thank you all properly. You know who you are, and I love you all.

I have to thank my publisher, Regal House Publishing, and its tireless staff, who worked so hard to bring my novel to the world. Jaynie Royal and my brilliant editor, Pam Van Dyk, have been tremendous. This book would not exist without them. Thank you for taking a chance on me.

Thank you to Laura Marie. She is more than a publicist, and I am so happy I found her.

Being a new writer can be terrifying. I want to thank all the writers who I've met since I began this journey. They had no reason to be as kind to me as they were, but I can assure you all it made a world of difference to me, and I'll never forget it. In particular, I want to thank Kerri Schlottman. I was so nervous when we met, and you have been such a wonderful source of advice, support, and friendship. It means more to me than you'll ever know.

Finally, I'd like to thank all my wonderful teachers and professors throughout the years. It's a hard job you do, but it truly changes lives. I would not be a writer if it were not for a handful of educators who helped and encouraged me along the way.